Amanda Hearty is in her twenties and lives in Blackrock, Co. Dublin with her husband Michael and their baby daughter Holly. Amanda works in a busy Dublin publishers, and studied Commerce at UCD and has a Masters in Marketing from the Smurfit School of Business, Dublin. Growing up in a house full of books, writing, dreams and ideas, and with her mother, Marita Conlon-McKenna, being a very successful author, it was inevitable that Amanda would finally put pen to paper and begin to write. *Are You Ready?* is her first novel.

www.rbooks.co.uk

ARE YOU READY?

Amanda Hearty

TRANSWORLD IRELAND

TRANSWORLD IRELAND
an imprint of The Random House Group Limited
20 Vauxhall Bridge Road, London SW1V 2SA

www.rbooks.co.uk

First published in 2008 by Transworld Ireland

A CIP catalogue record for this book
is available from the British Library.

ISBN 9781848270039

Addresses for Random House Group Ltd companies outside the UK
can be found at: www.randomhouse.co.uk
The Random House Group Ltd Reg. No. 954009

The Random House Group Limited supports The Forest Stewardship Council (FSC),
the leading international forest-certification organization. All our titles that are
printed on Greenpeace-approved FSC-certified paper carry the FSC logo.
Our paper procurement policy can be found at
www.rbooks.co.uk/environment

Typeset in 12½/15pt Bembo by
Kestrel Data, Exeter, Devon.
Printed in the UK by
CPI Mackays, Chatham, ME5 8TD.

2 4 6 8 10 9 7 5 3 1

Mixed Sources
Product group from well-managed
forests and other controlled sources
www.fsc.org Cert no. TT-COC-2139
© 1996 Forest Stewardship Council
FSC

For the love of my life,
my husband, Michael

1

'Flip. Flip. Flip, Sarah, flip! The pancakes are burning. Flip them over quickly.'

Sarah stared at the melted butter and pale batter in the frying pan, watching as it turned a golden colour.

'Mum, just because I'm your only single daughter doesn't mean we need to pretend that these pancakes are really important,' she protested.

'Sarah, it's a family tradition on Pancake Tuesday to make plenty of them.'

'Well, as my married sister is busy making pancakes for her husband, I'm just making pancakes for you, me and the cat! It is hardly the massive family gathering it used to be. I don't even think Pumpkin is home, she's probably out with her cat boyfriend.'

'Oh, Sarah, you were always so dramatic. No wonder you're single. I've been looking forward to this day all week, looking forward to whipping up a storm in the kitchen. It's a nice tradition, love, don't ruin it with talk of not being married and cats,' sighed Catherine Doyle, Sarah's mother.

'I'm sorry, Mum. These are perfect. You are great to have made so many pancakes for just the two of us, so let's just get on with it . . . flip.'

★   ★   ★

As Sarah flipped the pancake she wondered how many more Pancake Tuesdays she would be single. As much as she loved her mother and appreciated her excitement at keeping the pancake tradition, it wasn't the same now that she was the only daughter at home. Her elder sister Mel was married, and had left home two years ago. And although she loved Mel's husband and was so happy for them, it was hard to be the singleton, still living in the red-brick family home in Monkstown Park, South Dublin, with her widowed mum and cat. She didn't know how she had got here, how life and men were just passing her by. How had she got to be thirty and single, with all her friends now fiancées, brides or mothers? What was she doing wrong? It had to change. If only she could flip her life over instead of these blasted pancakes.

2

Across town in Heavenly Bakery and Café there was more flipping going on.

'Flip those pancakes, Mum,' Molly Kennedy cried. 'Sterling Bank have ordered two hundred to be delivered by 11 a.m., and O'Keefe's Public Relations want seventy-five by 10 a.m. too. Wow, this is so exciting, I could make these all day long. Life is great, isn't it, Mum?'

'What are you talking about, Molly?' Helen Kennedy argued, flushed with effort. 'We have about four hundred pancakes to make this morning and we are running out of eggs. I can barely see through my glasses for all the batter firmly attached to them, and if I've to cut one more lemon I'll become allergic to them like your cousin.'

'Well, Mum, trust me, this is heaven compared to filing client reports. A few months ago the only thing I made was the odd error in a bloody Excel document, and now I'm making pancakes, buns, cupcakes, salads, quiches. Compared to working in a boring office job, this is a dream come true. Life is great, Mum, I'm telling you.'

'Oh, Love.' Helen softened, staring at her only daughter, whose pretty face, long brown hair and petite frame hadn't changed since she was young. 'I'm happy for you. It's lovely for me to be working alongside you, too, but if we could leave the heart-to-heart chat until after this blasted batter has been peeled off my glasses and every inch of this kitchen it would be better – and I would be a lot calmer. Now, flip!'

Molly just couldn't believe her luck. She was finally working in her dream job. Ever since she was a child she'd loved cooking. Her favourite bedtime reading had been cookbooks and her mum used to joke that she was the only seven-year-old making pavlovas and pudding to go with the Sunday roast each week! But when you are in college it is hard to see how you can make a proper living from baking, and before she knew it she had studied finance and ended up working in the funds department – in a very big impersonal bank in Dublin's Financial Services Centre, which she hated. Moving money from one account to another, and watching it grow by a few euros or dollars a day was hardly fulfilling. She had never been that good at funds and investments, and found it boring – her heart wasn't in it – but still it paid the bills, and so time had ticked on. The older you get the harder it is to make a change, it is nerve-racking to enter the unknown; so if it hadn't been for her boyfriend Luke's support – both emotional and financial – she would never have changed jobs. It had upset him to see her so unhappy and bored with her job and life, and one night when they had drunk too much wine and she had started complaining again, he had told her that if her job was making her miserable she should: 'For God's sake, go and do something you like.' And so she had.

After handing in her notice to the bank, she had gone and signed up for a twelve-week cookery course at Cork's famous Ballymaloe Cookery School. Afterwards she had been delighted when her Aunt Fran had insisted she come and work for her in her small delicatessen and bakery on Mount Street in Dublin's city centre, where Molly's mother often helped out. It was a family-run business, with Molly's cousin Eve and Eve's boyfriend working there, too. It was a small café cum bakery, but they made most of their money from their take-out menu of sandwiches, salads, breads, lasagne, cakes and buns. And they had recently begun to supply the many local offices with daily sandwiches and lunch treats. They hadn't really needed another employee, and hadn't been able to afford to pay much, but Luke had known Molly had to be given a push to go for it, so he had started saving to help her out financially, and she hadn't looked back. She was so grateful to Luke, and because of his generous support she now felt so happy. Sometimes you just needed to make a change.

3

'Mum, I've about 2.3 seconds to talk before that dragon Mary comes back into the office. So be quick and tell me what's new down home on the farm, and remember, if Mary walks back in I'll have to refer to you as Mr Barrington, and ask you about a deposition,' Ali McEvoy whispered, glancing around the high-ceilinged room.

'Oh, Ali! For God's sake, you must be allowed to make a personal phone call every once in a while. It's a solicitor's office not a prison cell. I'm sure your boss makes calls, too.'

'I swear, Mum, she doesn't. She has no friends to call! She even gives me dirty glances if I go to the bathroom. She is a sad old dragon who is taking her single status out on me. She is jealous of me being young and madly in love with Robin, I mean MR BARRINGTON. Yes, Mr Barrington, I'll fax that deposition to you right away. Goodbye.'

Ali grabbed a blank sheet and headed for the fax machine. Once again she was going to have to fax a blank sheet home to cover up a personal call. How had this happened? Ali had worked hard in school in Kilkenny to get enough points to study law at University College Dublin, and even though the move to the 'big smoke' had been hard, she had loved law in college, and hadn't minded all the endless exams, as she had

12

known she could be a great solicitor and make a difference in the world. She had thought she could help the small people fight their cases. But seven years later, and with everyone in Dublin desperate to be a solicitor and become wealthy overnight, it was getting harder and harder to get a job, and she had got stuck working for Hewson & Keane – a very small law firm working out of hard-floored offices in a tall draughty Georgian wreck of a building on Merrion Square. The firm was tight on budgets, salaries, holidays and any kind of fun! They specialized in property law, and all Ali seemed to do was help wealthy clients with the legal side of buying and expanding their property portfolios. Ali spent her whole day checking mortgages, deeds and planning permissions. It was a far cry from protecting the innocent and fighting for justice – the ideals which had made her want to study law in the first place. Her boss, Mary Lynch, was a forty-year-old who was single and seemed to take all her frustration out on Ali. She tried to control everything Ali did. Ali wasn't even allowed to make a work phone call at the same time as Mary, as Mary said it distracted her! With her tall, thin frame, tightly tied-back bun of mousy brown hair, and assortment of black, grey or navy suits teamed with a variety of striped shirts, Mary really did look like an old spinster who had nothing better to do than boss Ali around. It was like working with a strict school teacher or old librarian. Ali was actually waiting for the day when she would be given a detention for speaking! Mary really was awful to work for, but what could Ali do? Law was the only thing she knew, and she needed a job, so unless something exciting happened or changed she was stuck with Mary the dragon.

4

Ben lay half-awake with one eye on the Liverpool match playing on the small flat screen at the end of his bed. He had drunk way too much last night, and even his favourite team playing Man United wasn't going to stir him from his bed, but he supposed that since his best friend was getting married, he had had no option but to get very drunk on the stag night. It had been a great night, and poor Jeremy had been in bits by the time they left the nightclub, but it had reminded Ben how far behind he was on the dating scene. There was a knock on the door.

'Guess who's come to keep you company? Ben, guess who?'

'Oh God, Mum, do not bring Mango in here, do not. Oh, too late! Here he comes.'

'Darling, he loves you, and you adore him. He just wants to keep you company and help you get over your hangover. God, the smell of drink in here is worse than the Guinness brewery back in the eighties,' his mum Maura said, as she stood in her son's room in her pink dressing gown and matching slippers.

'Mum, I do not want Mango the parrot in here with me. Even if we do all love him, I'm thirty and a man, and do not need a child's pet beside me all day long. I've told you that a million times.'

'Ben O'Connor, you will not speak of your childhood best

friend and beloved member of this family like that. Now, I'll ignore what you said and put it down to you being sad that you are the last single man of your group of friends, and instead I will go to the kitchen and make you a BLT. I'll ring the bell when it is ready.'

Ben looked at the slammed bedroom door and then at Mango. Living at home when you were thirty wasn't easy, especially as his mother still treated him like he was ten. Ben had tried to break free, and had left home two years ago, and rented an apartment with a friend. But eventually the friend had bought his own place, and Ben had felt renting was a waste of money, and decided to move back home to his parents and their big home in the leafy suburbs, in Foxrock, so that he could save for a place of his own. He missed the freedom and the parties, but what could he do? He tried to save, but property in South Dublin was very expensive. His dad had offered to help him with a deposit for a place, but it was the monthly repayments Ben knew he couldn't really afford on his own, not with his salary. Of course, as his mum reminded him, if he had a girlfriend they could split the monthly payments, but Ben was a single as his parrot Mango. Of course, at times he wanted a girlfriend, but he just found it hard to meet anyone he liked. There had been plenty of offers, and his last girlfriend Susie had been great, and they had been serious, but the minute she had started using sentences with 'when we have kids' in them he had had to break it off. It had been an awful break-up. He had loved her, but not enough to move in with her, let alone get engaged or start talking about kids.

His mum had been delighted to have him back home to cook for and chat with, but of course with that came the daily question: 'Any girls?' Even if he went to the garage he was greeted with it as he walked in the front door, as if he was going to meet his future wife at Esso.

15

Even Mango seemed to look at him with disappointment nowadays. As if a parrot could tell he was single and thirty! Mango had been his pet since he was thirteen and Ben did love him, but the older you got the more girls and football generally consumed your heart. Yet Ben's mum still looked after Mango for him, and presumed he wanted to have the bird at his side morning, noon and night. Suddenly his mobile rang; he found it under the bed.

'God, what a session last night! Best night ever, I'm hanging.' It was the husband-to-be, Jeremy.

'How come you're awake?' Ben croaked.

'Well, Lisa has it all planned out for us to go looking at wedding cakes today. So I'm up and dressed. Do you want to go swing by Eddie Rocket's before I head off, to get some hangover chips and a burger?'

'I'd love to, Jeremy, but Mum has a BLT waiting for me, it's the pleasure of living at home!'

'What? Ben? Ben, I can't hear you. God, don't say that bird Mango is squawking in the background! BLT or not, for God's sake, man, you need to get out of your parents' place. They are great parents, don't get me wrong, but you are thirty, you know. Anyway I'll talk to you later.'

As Ben put the phone down his mum rang the 'kitchen bell', a cable-car bell from San Francisco that he had brought back with him when he'd spent the summer working in the West Coast of America almost ten years ago. It still worked, and his mum used it to round up everyone for dinner or any meals in the kitchen. As he traipsed down the stairs she shouted up to him not to forget 'your best friend, Mango'.

Oh God, he thought, he didn't want to hurt her feelings but this would have to stop. No more parrots and living at home. He needed to change his job, his living arrangements and his life, as soon as possible.

5

Sarah Doyle pushed back her long blonde wavy hair as she began printing out the catalogue for tonight's opening. The work going on show was from the newest upcoming Dublin artist, Willow McIntyre. Her work was different and strong, yet calming. Sarah really loved her art pieces, and was glad she could enjoy the new ones on her own for a few hours, before they were hung from the art gallery wall and discussed to death by every art critic in Dublin.

Sarah worked in the Stone Studio, a small yet hip gallery in Monkstown village, only a few minutes from where she lived. Having studied art in college, and struggled to become an artist and sell her work for years, she had finally got a job that suited her perfectly. Maggie McCartney's gallery was just the kind of place Sarah used to visit in the hope of one day exhibiting her own work. She had actually shown her portfolio of work to Maggie, but Maggie had kindly explained that it wasn't commercial enough to be sold by her, but that there was some part-time work going in the gallery. Sarah had worked in a variety of awful part-time jobs, from a busy call centre to a grumpy dentist's surgery, where she had answered the phone and dealt with terrified patients, so working in a gallery seemed ideal. And Sarah's artist's eye meant she was very useful to Maggie when it came to hanging pictures, staging shows and choosing paintings. So Sarah worked part-time in the gallery, yet still tried to create her own pieces when she could. But gradually her hours in the gallery grew longer. And months later, when Maggie announced she wanted to spend less time in Dublin, and more in her villa in Marbella, Sarah was offered the job of running the Stone Studio full-time. The day Sarah accepted this job was bitter sweet: yes, she was excited to be offered such an interesting job, but she also knew that her own dream of becoming a full-time artist was now dead. Sarah found this hard to accept, but soon she began to enjoy the job more and more. To be paid to spend time talking to and working with artists, and helping them sell their pieces, was great. She knew how happy and proud they felt when she rang to say she had sold one of their works. Even if she couldn't be an artist herself, at least she could help other creative souls.

Sarah was a people's person, and really enjoyed helping someone find art for their home. She was always interested to discover what kind of home they lived in, what colours they liked, and where they wanted to hang their purchases, and she worked hard to find the right piece for each customer. Finding out how others lived had always fascinated her. One day she hoped to own a house like all her customers did, and have a husband to spend all day Saturday walking around art galleries with, and spend hours debating what artist might be right for their kitchen.

But for now she had her mum, and within another few months hopefully enough money for a deposit on a small place of her own. But no amount of saving would get her enough money for a husband. She found it so hard to meet anyone, and although she loved going out with her friends, she was beginning to settle into a 'spinster' routine easier than she wanted to. Her friends were always trying to set her up on dates, but it never worked out, and more and more she found herself making excuses as to why she couldn't meet the 'perfect man' or 'ideal future husband' for a drink or date. She told her friends how she was too busy working or had to help her mum, and although these excuses were often true, she sometimes simply lied: she preferred to spend the night curled up in front of the TV with her mum, talking about life rather than living it.

Suddenly the door swung open and Clodagh, the final-year art student who worked at the Stone Studio part-time, ran in.

'I'm so sorry, Sarah, the flipping bus broke down, but I'm here now. I'll quickly go and change.'

'OK, and then can you bring up another twenty wine glasses, Clodagh? And we need to count these catalogues to make sure we have enough for tonight. We've Willow McIntyre's new exhibit opening in one hour, there's work to be done.'

6

As Sarah locked up the gallery she felt a sigh of relief that the evening had gone so well. Willow's pieces had been both critically liked and commercially loved by the gallery's customers. She had sold over half of them in two hours. Sarah was delighted by the money the gallery had made and by how happy Willow would be. Even though Willow looked like a hippy who did not have a care in the world, and wouldn't notice whether her art had sold or not, Sarah knew that – like any artist – Willow would care, would be over the moon to see a little red dot beside a piece, and know someone had loved it enough to buy it and display it at home. Sarah had not seen enough of these red dots on her own work to have made it as an artist, but she still knew what it felt like. Helping other artists really did make her happy.

She glanced at her watch and knew she was late. She was meeting her sister Mel and her husband John for drinks in the pub in Monkstown, just up from the gallery. They had been married for two years now, and were a great couple, and Sarah loved hanging out with them. She got on well with John, and he always made her feel comfortable in their house, even when she spent hours discussing her love life, or lack of it. He was always trying to set her up on dates and help her meet Mr Right, though she often joked he just wanted her out of their house. But she knew he did care, and it was this kindness that had attracted Mel to him years before.

As she walked in the bar, she laughed at how she didn't think John or Mel would have any time left for setting her up with men soon, as Mel was eight and a half months pregnant and ready to pop! She was so excited for her older sister, and knew she would be the best mum ever.

'Sarah! Over here!' Mel shouted over the music and loud pub conversations. The two sisters were very alike. They both had long blonde hair, long noses, long legs and long feet – which were the family curse!

'How was the opening?'

'Great, a big success, you should have called in,' Sarah replied.

'We would have, Sarah, but we thought it unfair as "the bump" would have taken over the entire small gallery's space. And when Mel heard you were serving cheese she knew she couldn't make another show of herself like the last gallery opening!' John laughed hard, recalling the last opening, where Mel, who had been craving cheese and crackers like a demon throughout the pregnancy, had lost the complete run of herself and started crying when the artist's mother took the last cracker. It had all been very embarrassing and John had had to run out to Spar to buy more, and then quietly bring Mel home, where he had plenty of emergency stores of cheese and crackers hidden away.

As Sarah sat down she saw John's brother Tom, and another guy she didn't know, sitting at the end of the table. As Tom caught her eye he smiled and stood up to give her a kiss. Tom was really tall, with sandy hair and kind blue eyes, and Sarah had noticed many a girl checking him out every time they were out.

21

'Sarah, this is Ross. He is just back from living in America,' Tom said.

As she shook Ross's hand Sarah could see Tom, Mel and John all look at her excitedly. Oh God, she thought, this is another set-up. What a nightmare! Mel could have at least warned her. Sarah was wrecked from her evening at work, and hadn't even brushed her hair, or put on any make-up. Ross and Tom both started to chat to her, and though she was annoyed by being ambushed, she relaxed when the lads starting telling her funny stories of their days in school, and before she knew it was having a great time, and on her third beer. Then Ross went to the bathroom, and Sarah had a chance to comment on events.

'Mel, as nice as Ross seems, you could have told me what you were planning before inviting me for a "drink". You know I'm getting sick of being set-up. It is embarrassing.'

'I swear I didn't know Ross was coming. Trust me, I just wanted it to be you and Tom,' said her sister. 'Tom brought Ross along unexpectedly. Myself and John wanted to ask you and Tom something, something important.' And with that Mel started crying. She was so emotional nowadays that Sarah just turned to John, who was frantically trying to order cheese, any kind, off the waiter. Once he had, he turned back to the others.

'Myself and Mel wanted you guys here tonight to ask you a big favour. We would like to ask you to be godparents to our soon-to-be-born child – or one large lump of cheese, as I fear! But seriously, what do you say?'

Sarah was in shock. She was so delighted, she jumped up and hugged them both. 'Of course I will. I would be honoured to be your child's godmother. Wow! I don't know what to say!'

Tom looked like he had been hit over the head with a plank of wood; he sat in shock, eventually managing to speak.

'What exactly do I have to do? Oh God, does this involve

making sure they don't drink until they are eighteen or something? Because much as I would love to be a godfather I don't know if I could handle not drinking around the child until then!'

'No, it doesn't involve that,' Mel laughed. 'You will both be great godparents, we are so happy you're taking on the job.'

Sarah was so excited that, before she knew it, she was chatting away to Ross about what kind of godmother she would be. It involved a lot of going to the Lambert Puppet Theatre, and face-painting, and within an hour she was pretty tipsy, but he didn't mind. She was so happy for Mel and John, and about them asking her to be a godmother. Her excitement lasted, and so, when Ross was leaving and asked if he could take her number she didn't do the usual – and back off or give him a fake one – she gave him the right number and a quick peck on the cheek. It was an exciting evening, and Sarah felt life was good. For once she went to bed imagining that her single days might soon be over, and she dreamed about what her children would look like with Ross as a father.

7

'Molly, the orders for Sterling Bank are in, can you start work on them, please?' Fran, Molly's aunt, asked.

Fran was delighted to have Molly working for her. She knew Molly was talented and had a passion for food, but unfortunately for years she had not been able to afford to hire her, so apart from helping out at weekends Molly had been stuck working in her finance job. But since the business had grown and got more and more customers, it had been wonderful to be able to hire her favourite niece.

Fran had worked in various restaurants in Dublin over the years, and then five years ago had made a big jump and bought a nice basement café on Mount Street. It had needed months of work, but eventually she had opened the Heavenly Bakery and Café. They kept their prices reasonable, yet they weren't fools and knew all the young business people in the area could afford to pay extra for homemade delights like speciality breads and outsize filled vol-au-vents. And even though the café had seats for customers, they found more and more offices were asking them to deliver.

Molly's mum, Helen, and Fran had both learnt to love cooking from their own mother, and even though Fran owned the bakery and café, Helen came in to work a few days a week to help with baking. No one could make a chocolate fudge cake like Fran's sister Helen!

Fran's own daughter Eve and her French boyfriend André also worked full-time in Heavenly. Eve was young and very chatty: great with the customers and at making sandwiches. André's tall, dark, handsome looks persuaded many a young single girl to pop in for a sandwich or small salad, only to find out their French dreamboat was very much in love with the waitress.

So with both Eve and André working full-time for her, Fran had never thought she could offer Molly a role in the café, but then when she saw how sad Molly was getting, and how disheartened about everything, she knew she had to try to help. So when Luke had told her he would help Molly out financially if Fran could at least pay her the minimum wage Fran had eagerly agreed. And now she did not know where she would be without her niece. Molly's cooking, enthusiasm and ideas were brilliant! Fran was used to doing the majority of the cooking, and struggling to create new dishes by herself, but with Molly by her side, they now had time to enjoy choosing ingredients, discussing new ideas, even staying late to try out different kinds of salads or quiches. She could not imagine Heavenly without Molly now. Her food – and her passion for it and for life – was irresistible.

'Right, where is my apron, Molly? And let's get going on all these young bankers' lunches.'

8

Molly sat down on the old park bench in Merrion Square. What a day! She must have made ten lasagnes, 120 brownies, twelve salad plates, and God knows how many sandwiches, but she loved it. She still couldn't believe how quickly her life had changed. Her finance job felt like a lifetime ago, and although the gossip and chat with the girls had been good fun in there, and drinks on a Friday had always been wild, she didn't miss the work. Towards the end she had found the constant talk of who got what bonus, and who was on what salary, very cold and materialistic. She had wanted a job that she was passionate about, that made her smile, that stretched her mind, and most of all gave her joy. Salaries and bonuses shouldn't come into it, and although everyone needs to pay the bills, you do have to weigh up what makes you happy and how you want to live your life. And Molly wanted to be surrounded by food, ingredients, tastes, smells, chatter and laughter. Sometimes you needed to take a pay cut to get where you wanted, where your heart wanted to bring you to; and you needed to listen to that heart, and not your bank account.

Of course if it hadn't been for Luke's encouragement and support and her Auntie Fran's belief in her, she would still be stuck working in the bank, earning lots of money but being totally unhappy. But now Molly felt lucky, so blessed. Life was good.

Molly clipped back her long dark hair, and unwrapped her Parma ham and Italian cheese on ciabatta bread. It was hard to get a few minutes to yourself during the day, so she often didn't eat her own meal until well after the lunch crowd had left. That was why, at four thirty, she was finally eating.

As she washed down her lunch with a bottle of the organic apple juice they kept in Heavenly she got a text message from Luke reminding her he was finishing work at five, and not to be late. He had booked to go to the latest James Bond film in the Savoy cinema at half past five, with the intention of grabbing dinner after the film. Luke didn't like her being late, he was always on time. Molly knew she had a few more cakes to finish and deliver to a local firm that wanted to celebrate a birthday after work, and she worried that she might not make it to the Savoy on time; she didn't want to upset Luke, he had been so good to her. Molly had been so unlike herself, so moody and depressed for the last year in her job, and had often taken it out on Luke, and they had fought almost every night. But now that he had helped her move jobs she felt they were getting on better; even though he didn't understand her need to go to work extra early just so she could have the kitchen to herself and invent new recipes. Still, she knew he loved her and wanted things to work out for them. She quickly finished her drink and started to walk back to work. She needed to get her cake icing done ASAP!

9

Ben wolfed down his cornflakes while trying to read the newspaper and iron a shirt for work. He was late as usual, and yet 'the more haste the less speed' was his philosophy, so he was re-reading the *Irish Times* report on that weekend's Liverpool match. He crossed the pristine Shaker-style kitchen and opened the dishwasher to pack his cereal bowl, but saw the dishwasher had just finished and was full of clean dishes and cutlery. Damn, he thought, to pack this one dish I'm going to have to unpack about fifty other ones. No way, he decided, and instead washed his cereal bowl in the sink and replaced it in the press. Mum will never know, he thought!

Ben hopped on the 46a bus and put on his iPod, and as U2 blared away in the background he thought about what lay ahead of him in work that day. He was a sports correspondent on one of the daily free newspapers. He was not an editor, or even a full-time reporter, but he didn't care. He loved sport, especially football, and was having a laugh being able to go to matches and report on them. And although the money wasn't that good, he couldn't expect it to be, either. He hadn't trained as a journalist, he hadn't even studied English in college. He had actually studied commerce at UCD, and specialized in accounting, mainly because his father owned a small accounting firm. His father had taken over O'Connor

& Son from Ben's grandfather, and his dream was that Ben would also work with him and eventually take it over. And although Ben had at one stage wanted that, the older he got the more he had felt pressurized into it, and hadn't wanted the responsibility of running a family company. He liked to feel free and not be tied down, and he knew that the minute he went into the company he would be in it for life, no turning back. And Ben was not that kind of person: he liked freedom and no responsibilities. He liked to feel he could do whatever he wanted, whenever he wanted. But, of course, he did feel guilty quite often. He saw how disappointed his father was with him. His father should have retired a few years ago, but Ben knew he was holding out in the hope that Ben would change his mind and run the business. His father was the perfect gentleman and family man. Always there to help his mother around the house, and then head for a round of golf in Foxrock Golf Club, but making sure he was back in time to get the house ready for the dinner parties they threw almost every second weekend. Both Ben's parents had plenty of friends and were great at having parties, going on holiday and socializing. His father was a fine host, and always made sure everyone felt comfortable in any occasion, and while his mum was always nagging Ben, it was her concern and interest in others that made her so popular. She was always first to visit a friend in hospital, or bake a cake for a family in times of grief.

They were a great couple, and even though seeing them so happy should have made Ben want to settle down and experience what they had had for almost forty years, it didn't. He knew eventually he would settle down, but for now he needed to experience the opposite: live life to the full with whoever he wanted. He wasn't the biggest womanizer or anything, but he just had itchy feet, and liked to work and be with whoever felt right at that time. And at this moment he felt like being an underpaid yet happy and relaxed sports correspondent on his oldest friend Jeremy's latest venture – a free Dublin daily paper. He had only got the job because of Jeremy, and even though he knew that all the sports staff had felt a bit miffed that he had got it without any qualifications, he was able to hold his own and, after a few articles, started receiving praise from the editor and getting on better with the staff. They were a relaxed bunch, really, and usually great for drinks after work on Friday on Dawson Street. Though sometimes, when he ran into his old University College friends, all coming back from work in Dublin's biggest accountancy firms, he did feel a pang of guilt, and regret that he wasn't working alongside them. But then he would always think of O'Connor & Son and tell himself, not yet, or maybe never, and remember he was only thirty, and that was young enough.

10

Maura O'Connor came back from her hour-long walk around leafy Foxrock and Cabinteely. She did it every morning, not only to try and stay fit but also to try and tire out the family dog, Honey. Honey, their golden Labrador retriever, was as mad as a hare, and needed a good long walk every morning to at least tire her out until Joe came home and could take the young dog out again.

As she walked into the kitchen, she noticed Ben must have left in a hurry: the ironing board and iron were still out, as was the milk and a cornflakes box. Tidying them away, she went to put his coffee cup into the dishwasher, and saw it was still clean and full from the wash she had put on earlier. The lazy so and so, she thought. As usual he had hand-washed his bowl to avoid unpacking the dishwasher. He thought she didn't notice his careless ways, but of course she did. Like she noticed how he flung his clothes on his bedroom floor, presuming they would magically walk themselves into the washing machine and then out on to the line to dry. She noticed how he hadn't once helped hoover the house since he had moved back home, even though it was his rugby boots that every Thursday night trailed mud and bits of grass right through the hall and up the stairs. She noticed he never once offered to make dinner, or clean up after it. She loved him deeply, but saw that he was getting more and more lazy each day.

He was never as bad in college, back then he'd been like every regular boy: needed a push when it came to helping around the house, but would do it eventually. But ever since he'd moved back home this second time he'd seen the house as a hotel – somewhere he was temporarily staying and so did not need to help out at all. It saddened her to see him so lost. He had changed job three times since college, and never settled. If only he could see how he was wasting his training and talent as an accountant.

Maura and Joe were heart-broken that he refused to go into the family business. At first, when he left college, Ben had said he didn't immediately want to go into Joe's office, he preferred to experience working for other people and not be tied down to the one job for the whole of his life. So Joe had got him work in a friend's company: it was small but well respected. Ben had only lasted one year and eventually left to do a year's travelling in Australia. It had been embarrassing for Joe, and upset the friendship he had had with the company's owner, but that was nothing to the embarrassment he now felt when people could not understand why his one and only son, a qualified accountant, refused to join him in his company, refused to work side by side with him as a business partner.

Maura did not know what to do, and swung between disappointment and sadness. And even though Joe was heart-broken, he was a perfect gentleman. Not wanting to ever cause a scene, he had welcomed Ben back home when he couldn't afford to buy a place of his own. Ben was great fun, and Maura did love having more company around the house, and fussing over him and hearing all the gossip about his friends, but she knew Ben needed to change, and soon.

11

Ali walked across Merrion Square and up Mount Street into Heavenly, feeling really in the mood for one of their spinach and ricotta tartlets. As she got into the busy queue she could see one of her best friends, Molly, covered in flour and what looked like tomatoes, laughing away with her mother. The two floury, petite, dark-haired women could have been sisters. As Ali approached the till and went to pay Eve for the tartlet, she caught Molly's eye and Molly came out from behind the counter.

'How's work, Ali?'

'A nightmare,' replied Ali. 'Mary has got me checking the legal aspects of planning permissions all morning. It's so boring, I'm dreading going back.'

'But Ali, imagine, in a few weeks' time you will be in South Africa! I'm so jealous, I would love to go there one day with Luke, and visit all the Cape wineries. The food and wines are supposed to be the best in the world. Think of all the treats I could bring home to sell here!'

'Yeah, I know, Molly, I'm lucky to be going away. I can't wait to go on safari, and try whale-watching. I just wish I was going away today.' She laughed. 'Anyway, I can see you are busy, but what are you doing this weekend? Maybe we can go for drinks? I'll ring Sarah and see if she's free.'

'Good idea, I'll talk to you then. I've got to check on some brownies. Good luck with work.'

'Yummy brownies. You're so lucky. I'm going back to an afternoon of total boredom. Anyway, hope to see you on Saturday.'

Ali paid for the sandwich, crossed over the road into Merrion Square, and sat on a park bench. A pity Molly was so busy, as Ali would have loved to have had a laugh and chat with her over lunch hour, anything to get her mind off work. But at least she had the park, and even though it was still a bit cold to be eating outside it was a great place to come and relax during her busy work day. It was here that she had actually met her boyfriend Robin.

It had been August, and Ali had been with some college friends for lunch. It had been roasting and they had all been half-eating half-sunbathing, and one of the guys had brought his work-colleague, Robin, along. Ali had fancied Robin right from the start: he was tall and big, with a massive head of dark hair, and always seemed to have a tan. She was his opposite, being small, with pale skin and short blonde hair. He was popular with the lads as he was very funny, and before long Ali had been praying he would be there for lunch, and wearing her best clothes into work the days when she thought he might be. Soon it was just her and Robin meeting up, and one day when he suggested they didn't go back to work, and instead mitched off for the Friday afternoon, she hadn't needed to think twice about ringing her boss to say she had forgotten a dentist's appointment. She'd jumped in a cab with Robin and they had headed off to Killiney beach for the afternoon, ending with beers and a long overdue kiss. That night, on the way home in a taxi, Robin had rested his hand on Ali's knee and her heart had started flipping – she knew there and then that she was in love and he was the one for her.

That had been five years ago, and she had never looked

back. She was madly in love with Robin, and even though they had become more settled, and spontaneous trips to the beach didn't really happen any more she didn't mind, they were so happy. She knew he was the one. She got her *Lonely Planet* guide to South Africa out of her handbag. Robin and herself had been saving for over a year for this special long-distance holiday. She smiled with excitement as she started reading about lions, wineries and shark-diving.

12

As Ali opened the door of her apartment, the smell of cooking was tantalizing. She was delighted: Robin was a great cook and there was nothing she liked better than one of his meals served up to her after a long day's work. Robin jumped out of the kitchen wearing jeans and his Batman apron and greeted her with a big long sloppy kiss.

'You can't go into the kitchen yet,' he ordered. 'I'm cooking you a surprise dinner, but I've a bath running for you, and you can relax in there.'

Ali grabbed him and hugged him.

'You are the best boyfriend in the world,' she whispered into his ear. 'I love you, but what is the big occasion?'

'No occasion, I'm just getting excited about our trip, and thought we should kick-start the holiday count-down with a special evening. Anyway, I've left all the South African holiday brochures beside the bath so you can re-read them for the millionth time. Relax, I'll call you when the food is ready.' And with that Robin closed the kitchen door.

Ali lay soaking in the bath, reading about the elephants, and the best time of day to go up Table Mountain. As she got out of the bath and started to get dressed she thought: I'm so spoilt, I have a great boyfriend, a beautiful apartment, and lovely friends. If I could just sort out work my life would be perfect.

*   *   *

As she waited to be called in for dinner she looked around and admired the apartment. It was so lovely, so warm, so them. They had bought it two years ago, and even though it had been hard to get enough money together to afford Dublin's crazy property prices, both of their parents had helped them, and with her being a solicitor and getting a 100 per cent mortgage, they had managed to buy a small apartment, part of a new development of eight apartments right in the heart of Dalkey village. It was so handy to be able to walk to the village's fashionable pubs, shops and restaurants. She had gotten so used to being able to walk home that she felt grumpy having to pay for a taxi when she was coming home at night-time!

The apartment had two bedrooms, and even though Robin had had great plans to turn the spare room into a study where he could do some of his architecture work at home, it was now Ali's walk-in wardrobe: full of all her clothes, shoes, bags and books. Her parents kept asking when she was going to get married and have a baby, but she kept thinking if they had a baby they would need to buy it its own apartment, as there was no space here! But she knew she shouldn't complain: she had been so lucky to have met and fallen in love with Robin. For years she had found it hard to connect with the affluent 'South Dublin' boys. She had felt most of them were very materialistic and barely knew where Kilkenny was, let alone Castlecomer, the little country town she had grown up in; but Robin was different and understood how even though she loved Dublin, she still savoured a trip home to her family in Kilkenny, and a weekend spent revisiting the Castle and going out for the day on a small boat in Dunmore East. In college she had at first lived in digs, then in various other apartments with other girls studying law, but there was nothing like living with someone you loved, someone who was 'home' to you.

Living with Robin was like being back living with her family: he was home and love and family all rolled into one.

Finally she was allowed to enter her own kitchen. Robin had turned off most of the lights, and put candles everywhere, with Norah Jones in the CD player. Two bowls of prawns cooked in wine and garlic lay on the table, and Robin was opening a bottle of white wine. She was overwhelmed. She kissed him long and hard.

'What is all this for? Is everything OK?' she asked Robin.

'Of course.' He laughed. 'Like I said, I'm very excited about going away, and want to make sure you are, too. It will be a big trip for us and I wanted to get you in the mood, so I bought some South African wine, and I've got steaks for our main course – I hear they are huge steak-eaters over there.'

'All this to get me in a holiday mood? Wow, we should go away more often. You never fail to surprise me.'

'Well, I was hoping you'd look at those leaflets on shark-diving again. I'd really like you to do it.'

'I should have known there would be an ulterior motive! But to be honest, with enough wine and steak inside me I'd agree to anything.'

And as she washed back the prawns with a beautiful Sauvignon Blanc, she thought, Maybe I will go swimming with the great whites. It couldn't be any scarier than working with Mary every day anyway!

13

As Sarah sat packing envelopes with the art gallery's summer exhibition schedule, to be sent to all their biggest customers, she kept her eye firmly on her mobile phone, willing it to ring. Ever since she had met Ross in the bar with her sister last week, she had been dying for him to ring. She just knew he was different to all the rest of the guys who took her number: he had seemed so friendly and chatty that night, and Tom would hardly have been with him if he wasn't nice. She had actually fancied Tom for a long time. He was good fun, attractive, and unusually tall — which long-legged Sarah needed in a guy. But seeing as he was her sister's brother-in-law there was not much she could do about it, although she often suspected Mel would have loved her and Tom to have gotten together. Then they could have done plenty of couple things in a group. When Mel and John first got engaged everyone used to joke that as best man and bridesmaid they would surely hook up! But even though he used to flirt with her at first, he didn't seem that interested now, and she presumed that like everyone else he felt sorry for Mel's little single over-the-hill sister. But she could forget all about Tom if this Ross guy came up trumps. Ring, ring, please ring. Oh God, she started laughing, most girls want an engagement ring, while I'll settle for even a phone ring!

Just then her mother walked in the door dressed in her cream Karen Millen trouser suit, and Avoca Handweavers long green woollen cardigan. At sixty-two she might be getting older, but she still dressed as stylishly as most twenty-seven-year-olds.

'It's great to see you laughing, Sarah, better than that worried look you've had stuck to your face the last few days, staring at that phone like it held the answer to the Da Vinci Code. Must be a great man to make you want it to ring so badly. I hope he is worth it.'

'I've told you, Mum, it's not a guy. You think I'm obsessed with finding a man, but don't get me confused with what everyone else wants for me. I'm just expecting a very important call from a client.'

'A client! Well, I won't hold the Art World up then. I just came round to tell you I'll not be home for dinner tonight. I'll be late.'

'Why? Where are you going?' Sarah asked, presuming her mum was out on another theatre night with her girl-friends.

'Well, actually, I've a date.'

Sarah dropped the gallery schedules on the ground, sending them flying everywhere. 'What do you mean, a date?' she almost shouted.

Sarah's dad had died almost seven years ago. After a long battle with cancer he had finally slipped away in his sleep one morning, surrounded by his whole family. They had all known he was nearing his end, and persuaded the hospital to let him die at home. It had been so sad, but he had been happy to be back overlooking his green garden full of all the plants and trees he had spent years growing. And even though Sarah knew her mum was still young, and that plenty of men were attracted to her looks and sense of fun, and even though there had been the odd mention of meeting 'a friend' for a drink, she had never thought her mum would be 'dating'.

'Now, Sarah, I know this must be hard for you, seeing as you are still unmarried, unlike your sister, but someone in the house has to date, and if not you, then me. You know I still love your beloved father, but he would want me to be happy. So when Bill Macken from the bridge club asked me out, I thought why not? Anyway, we are going for dinner and drinks in Blackrock, so do not wait up for me. Have a good night, pet, and don't worry: one day your prince will come.' And with that she walked out of the gallery door and left Sarah shocked.

How come her mum was getting dates and Sarah wasn't? It was mortifying. And as happy as she was for her mum, she suddenly had visions of her getting married and leaving home and herself being left all alone with the cat.

Suddenly her mobile started ringing, and even though she would usually have waited a few rings before answering a call from a new guy, she picked it up immediately.

'Sarah, this is Ross, we met the other night with Tom. I'm sorry I didn't ring you sooner. How are you?'

How am I? she thought. I just found out my mum is dating and getting more interest from men than me, and that if something doesn't change soon I'm going to have to marry that creepy old man from the sandwich shop down the road just so I don't turn into Dublin's gloomiest spinster.

'I'm fine, Ross, just busy in work. What's up?'

'Well, I was wondering if you would like to go out some night this weekend for a drink?' As Sarah sat there she thought of her sister Mel, who always told her to play by 'The Rules' and always pretend to be too busy for the first date just to see if the man was keen enough to persist until you agreed to meet him. But times were tough, and desperate times called for desperate measures.

'I know this seems forward, Ross, but what about to-night? I could meet you in the same pub as last week – about 8 p.m.?'

And before Ross knew what had hit him Sarah had the whole night booked and planned. If her mum could go dating mid-week, so could Sarah! Now, what to wear?

14

Ross winked at Sarah from the bar as he ordered drinks and more peanuts. God, she needed more than one pack of peanuts, she needed more soakage. She could feel herself getting more and more drunk. She didn't mean to be like this on a first date, but after agreeing to meet Ross earlier she had spent the whole afternoon thinking of how she was the only one of her friends who was single and always 'on the look-out for a man'. She had had some boyfriends, but none of them that serious, and the relationships had always ended before they reached the 'let's move in' chat. About a year ago she had given up all hope of meeting someone, and slowly begun falling more and more into the single-girl-living-with-her-widowed-mother role. Even though she loved her mum, today had made Sarah realize for the first time that she was not just putting her own life on hold by becoming a young spinster, but putting her mother's life on hold, too. No wonder her mum hadn't been out on dates before: she had probably felt bad about leaving her youngest daughter all alone at home with no man. Well, that had to change, and dating wasn't too bad once you got used to it; and Sarah was well used to it, what with her older sister and her many friends all setting her up. She had got used to knowing what were good and bad signs on a first date, and the way Ross was laughing so much meant he was having a good time, and she hoped he would ask her out again. Having a few extra drinks on her had made her louder, more confident, and if she said so herself, funnier. This date was going great.

Ross arrived back from the bar with their two pints of beer.

'So let's get the whole single dating chat and stories out of the way, Sarah. We are both in our thirties and—'

'Our early thirties,' Sarah interrupted.

'OK, we are both still clinging to our twenties,' he laughed, 'and dating is hard, and we have been out there and got our dating stories, so what are your best and worst?'

Sarah did not know where to begin. She had been on dates with everyone from guys who pretended they were younger, to boys who pretended they were older, richer, and even foreign! But a fake French accent hadn't been as bad as her last boyfriend.

'Well, the last guy I dated was tall, blond, and an avid soccer player. He was very attractive and knew it, but was fun and a great laugh, too. He was great at planning unusual dates – as long as they were not on Saturdays, when his football team played. But suddenly our meetings started to become shorter and less interesting – a coffee here and a DVD there – and I knew something was up. And then one night, after soccer training, he said we were not suited. I was pretty shocked as we had grown quite close, and I was starting to plan a weekend away. He told me that we had to break up, that he did not see a future with me. When I managed to gather myself together I asked why, and he said we didn't have the, and I quote, "the X-Factor"! I almost choked on my drink. I started laughing, thinking he was doing a Simon Cowell impression, but then he said he wasn't, and that although he was a fan of the TV show, he was being serious. He was surprised that I hadn't suspected we were going to break up. Had I not guessed something was wrong when he had not asked me to come and watch him play football at the weekends?'

'Why? Was he a professional player?' asked Ross.

'Professional? He played for the third team of a fifth-division local club. He was so full of himself, expecting me to be upset that I hadn't had the honour of watching him kick a ball around for hours.'

'OK, well that guy does sound like a creep.' Ross laughed. 'I have tons of dating stories from America. As you know, New York is the dating capital of the world! I've been on dates with girls on every diet possible, girls who will eat but not swallow their food; others who will swallow but then excuse themselves to the bathroom for half an hour after; girls who won't eat but just want to go to oxygen restaurants; and girls who will eat but just not stop! I'm telling you, dating and eating is a nightmare for me.'

'Well, trust me,' Sarah started to slur, 'I love food, big time.'

After a few more drinks, and more bad dating stories, Sarah knew she had to go home, but first there was the walk there, which was full of slow and long kisses, and a plan to meet for dinner on Friday night. And as she walked up the stairs and noticed her mother's coat in the hall, she thought: Well, at least I'm still able to stay out later than Mum!

15

Molly was just taking a tray of spring rolls from the oven when Luke arrived back from the gym.

'They smell yum, I can't wait to eat them all.' He laughed, hugging Molly, while attempting to grab them from the hot tray.

'They are not for you, silly, they are for Ali and Sarah, and they will be here soon enough.'

'What do you mean? Why are they coming over?' Luke asked, the look on his face growing cold.

'Luke, I told you during the week that on Saturday night the girls were coming over to the house for a bottle of wine and some light food, and that we were going to go into town later.'

'You never did. Why are you doing this? I barely see you any more, what with all your cooking and baking and stuff. And every weekend you are either working or trailing around the country for ingredients and ideas. I mean, I thought at least tonight we could hang out.'

Molly put the hot tray down and closed the oven door. 'Luke, I'm so sorry, but I thought I had told you. The girls are arriving soon, so it is too late to cancel. I really am sorry. Why don't we do something exciting for the whole day tomorrow? Like a picnic to Malahide or Glendalough?'

Luke was silent, before finally nodding. And as he turned to leave the kitchen Molly swung him around and kissed him, and before he could say anything else rammed a spring roll into his mouth.

'I'm sorry, Luke. I know how supportive you have been, but tomorrow I'll make it up to you, I promise. Now, no more feeling sorry for yourself! Go meet the lads for a drink, I'll text you later and maybe we can meet up in Leeson Street or something.'

As Molly uncorked some New Zealand wine and got out some of the fancy Vera Wang china plates she kept for 'good use', she worried about the small fight with Luke. She knew it had been tough for him. At the moment she was work-ing crazy hours – early morning in the bakery, and often late nights as she tried to cram cooking lessons into her day also – but she just needed to do it at the moment, to get her career and life back on track. It was so hard to explain this to Luke, as he worked regular hours, and was not that passionate about his career in insurance. He made good money and that was enough to satisfy him. Also, as Luke was helping her pay her share of the apartment rent, and supporting them most, she found it difficult not to just go along with whatever he wanted to do. Anyway, he was great and did love her, he just needed time to adjust. She couldn't think about it any more tonight though, as she had heard a car pull up outside their house and knew the girls had arrived.

16

'So, Sarah, tell us what this Ross guy is like. How was the dinner date?' squealed Molly, as she opened another bottle of wine and cranked up Beyoncé on the stereo.

'It was great, very relaxed and casual, and just so funny. We went to ITSA4 for dinner – it is so yum there – and we finished with drinks in Sandymount Village before sharing a taxi home.'

'Whose home did you go to?' Molly laughed.

'We both went home separately, actually, Molly. I might have been drunk the last two dates, but not that drunk. It's too soon for that. But I must admit I think I'm really falling for him. It's early days, but I like him.'

Molly was so glad for Sarah; she had always been with losers, or guys who just broke her heart, so it would be nice to see her happy and madly in love.

'It would be great to finally meet someone and get out of that crazy dating scene.' Sarah laughed. 'I mean, when I look back on all the dates I've been on! Like your friend from college, Molly, who came across as the biggest player when we met, and spent half our dates listing off the best-looking girls he had kissed, until me and Mum bumped into him at a Barry Manilow concert one night! I should have known he was gay, he was always asking me to swap seats with him, so he could be "in a better light"!'

The girls laughed for hours about men, dating, old college stories and the latest celebrity gossip. Molly and Sarah knew each other from school, and while they hadn't met Ali until college, they were all firm friends. They might have very different careers and personalities, but they had great fun together and cared for each other as much as sisters. After two more bottles of wine, and trays of spring rolls and chicken satay, they went on to Renards nightclub, where they met other friends. When Luke and his mates finally arrived about 1 a.m., Molly was relieved to see him make a beeline for her, and as she put her arms around him, he apologized for being so short-tempered earlier. After hours of reliving their school days by dancing to Take That, herself and Luke decided to head off home. In the taxi she fell asleep leaning against him, and thought that as much as she was happy that Sarah and her new man were getting on well, she herself was so lucky to have found her soulmate, and to be out of that awful dating scene.

17

Ben was hooking up his PlayStation 2 and inserting Pro Evolution Soccer 7 game into the living room TV, when he saw his mum carrying groceries through the front door.

'Mum, why are you grocery shopping? I thought that you and Dad were heading off to Wexford for the weekend?'

'No, darling, we cancelled that last week. Your dad and a few of his friends are taking part in some big charity golf competition in the club. So instead we're having supper and drinks here for everyone after it later on tonight.'

Ben put down the game. 'But, Mum, I was having a few of the lads over tonight, we were going to get a take-away and some beers before heading out to town later.'

Maura kept on walking to the kitchen, and started unpacking the Superquinn bags piled high with breads, pâté, steaks, wines and beers.

'Well, Ben, you will have to go to one of their own houses tonight, as we've plans for here.'

Ben started helping her unpack, mainly as he was starving and dying for a sandwich, but he was annoyed his evening was ruined. Living at home really wasn't all it was cracked up to be.

'You know, Ben, if you had more money you could afford to buy your own apartment. A bigger salary, like what your father would pay you for working for him, would cover what you would need for monthly repayments.'

Ben put the bread down.

'Mum, I'm not a child, I know that I'd earn more working for Dad, but I don't want to. Why can't you understand that? I'm going to Eddie Rocket's for a sandwich, at least I can enjoy myself there.'

Mango squawked and screeched at Ben as he slammed the kitchen door, which rocked his cage.

'Oh, Mango, why can't you speak in complete sentences and talk some sense into your side-kick?' Maura asked the bird.

Later that night, as Ben grabbed his coat and started to head towards the front door and a night out with his friends, he noticed his dad in the kitchen trying to open a bottle of wine. It looked like he was struggling with the cork. Though Ben was annoyed with him and his mother for kicking him out on Saturday night, he thought his dad looked tired and suddenly old in the early-evening light.

'Dad, let me help. Are you OK?'

'Oh, Ben, I must be tired from all that golf, I just can't seem to get this stubborn cork out.'

Ben took the bottle and managed to open it easily enough. 'You need to relax. Slow down, Dad, you do too much.'

It took patience for Joe O'Connor not to say, 'and you do too little' to his one and only son, but it was Saturday night and he didn't want to upset Ben as he left the house.

'Don't worry about me, Ben. You go out and meet a nice girl. That would make your mother so happy. Imagine her planning a wedding!'

The two O'Connor men laughed at the idea of Maura planning food, music and a guest list.

'No doubt Mango would be the ring bearer,' Ben joked, and Joe roared with laughter.

It was fun to just relax and enjoy time with his son. Joe often felt that Ben could no longer do that as he was so aware of a talk about the accounting firm looming in the background if they had more than a two-minute conversation.

'I have to go, Dad, and I do promise to look for girls later. But let me open some more wine before I do.'

'OK, son, and as you do let me tell you about the night I met your mother. It was fate . . .'

18

'OK, who ordered the Americano pizza with extra pepperoni?' the waitress shouted over the loud table. Milanos restaurant was packed, and Ben and his group of friends had been lucky to get a table for ten at such short notice.

'Me, I ordered it,' said Ben and a girl with brown eyes and long dark brown curly hair at the same time.

'What? You did?' they both said again at the same time.

'OK, your comedy duo routine is great, but I've four plates in my hand. So which one of you ordered the pizza?' the waitress asked again.

'We both did, but let the lady go first,' Ben finally managed to say, after thinking how weird it was that the only girl he didn't know at the table had ordered the exact same pizza as him. Could it be fate, like what his dad had talked about earlier?

Laura was an old college friend of Ali's. Like Ali, she had studied law, but now worked in the human rights area. Laura was obsessed with justice, and she'd spent some of her time volunteering to work with the big Irish aid charities abroad. She wasn't stunning-looking, but she had great energy, a good figure, and opinions about everything. As Robin was going out that night with the lads, Ali had dragged Laura along to meet some of Robin's friends. Laura didn't know many of them, but Ben and herself seemed to hit it off. Hours and many pubs later, Laura and Ali decided to leave the guys to it, and grab a taxi home together. Before they left, Ben asked Laura for her number, and she gave it, even though Ali told her to be cautious.

'We all love Ben, Laura. It is just that he is a bit immature. He is gorgeous – those tall, dark, handsome looks – and he's fun, and full of life, but be careful. You should have seen him last weekend in Renards, he was all over the girls!' But Laura gave her number to Ben anyway, who knew what could happen? They had chatted all night and he had seemed gentle, not at all like the tough guy Ali had described.

As Ben and Robin started walking down Leeson Street later, trying to get a taxi, Robin asked Ben what he thought about marriage.

'Marriage? Well, my parents are very happy, but that's all I think about it for now. I'm too young to be thinking of rings and all that crap.'

'Crap? Crap?' shouted Robin, annoyed. 'You're a lousy friend, you know that?' And he started to walk off.

'What the hell's going on?' Ben asked. 'Why are you freaking out? This is crazy!' Ben actually started laughing.

Robin turned to Ben as he got into a cab. 'You need to wise-up, Ben.'

Ben was shocked and almost shouted at Robin, 'OK, I guess if it's the right person marriage is great. I really don't know what's got into you, Rob, but I hope you and Ali have a great time in South Africa. Talk to you when you get back.'

Robin shrugged and closed the taxi door.

What is wrong with him? Ben wondered. He must be more locked than I thought.

★　　★　　★

As Ben walked up the stairs he could hear his parents laughing in their bedroom.

'Hi, you guys are up late!' he joked.

His mum looked like she had had a good few glasses of wine. 'Well, the party only ended an hour ago, and then we were tidying away, and now we are just chatting. You know how we like to chat in bed,' she replied.

Joe winked at Ben. Joe was a big sleeper, but as Maura loved to chat in bed he ended up only sleeping half the amount he would have liked. But it kept her happy, and he napped in the afternoon instead.

'So, the Andersons and the Whites are both going to be grandparents soon. Isn't that great, Ben? One of these days might we be grandparents, too? I can't wait until you have children of your own.'

Ben didn't bother replying, and just wished them goodnight and headed for his own bedroom. His mum had gone mad. Far too much wine! Why did everyone want him to grow up so soon? As soon as his head hit the pillow his last thoughts were not of babies, but of Laura, lovely Laura.

19

'I need those four reports written up and on my desk by tomorrow morning,' Mary, Ali's boss, announced to her at 5 p.m. 'Owen wants to see them before we meet with the clients tomorrow.'

Ali had been swamped with work all week, and it just kept on building up. Mary had given her lots extra to do, obviously in the hope that Ali would have to cancel her holiday, but no way was that happening, Ali thought. Just because Mary was an old sad bossy spinster who never went anywhere, that did not mean Ali had to be the same. Hell would freeze over before she would cancel any time off. She didn't mind the extra work, but giving her so much at once, when she was getting ready to go on her holidays, just wasn't fair.

Ali had always been interested in law at college. She thought wistfully about the dreams she'd once had of being a barrister and standing up in court. But the training had been too expensive and, besides, you needed connections, and as her dad was a farmer and her mum a local primary-school teacher, they were not any help. So instead she chose to work as a solicitor. And even though connections still helped you in the solicitor business, she was a good worker and had managed to get a job in a firm, and even though her boss rarely spoke to her, apart from barking work orders, it was fine. She still dreamt of fighting for the poor man's rights, but for now she had to settle for at least having a job in the legal world, even if she was just dealing with wealthy South Dublin fat cats and their boring property issues all day long.

She was trying to print a document and type an email at the same time when her computer froze for the tenth time that day.

'God, why can't this stupid computer handle doing more than one thing at a time? It's like a man.'

She hadn't meant to say it out loud, but she had, and before she knew it she heard Mary laugh. But as she turned around to join in she saw Mary become poker-faced again, and grab her shapeless tweed coat to go home for the evening, leaving Ali to work late. Ali couldn't believe she had seen Mary's stern headmistressy face smile for once. She couldn't ever recall seeing her laugh or smile before. Mary was always too busy looking cross, fixing her hair back into a bun, or just making Ali feel unwelcome. Well, at least I know she is not a complete robot, Ali laughed to herself.

20

Days later, Ali was literally sitting on her suitcase trying to make it close.

'What is the story with all your luggage, Ali?' Robin asked in amazement, looking at the bikinis, skirts, T-shirts and sun-dresses thrown around their spare room.

'I don't know what to say. I can't stop packing things. Help!'

Robin picked up a pair of cream beaded flip-flops. 'Well, I've never seen you wearing these, so don't bring them.'

'No. You don't understand.' Ali almost shouted as she grabbed the shoes back. 'They go with the cream Zara dress I'm bringing. I need those shoes.'

'OK, what about this handbag? It's just taking up space in your suitcase.'

'No way, that's the only one that goes with the green linen sundress I got last year in Greece.'

'Ali, for God's sake! No wonder you have too much. You can't be bringing items that you will only wear once. We are going on holiday to relax and enjoy ourselves, not to have a fashion parade.' And with that he went back to watching foot-ball on TV.

Fashion parade? He doesn't understand, Ali thought, as she repacked the flip-flops and handbag. How did guys take so little on holiday? All Robin was bringing was one small suitcase and his Quiksilver backpack. Ali was so stressed. She had lots to do before flying to Cape Town tomorrow. She had intended to pack during the week, but what with all the extra work she hadn't had a chance to, and now was tired and anxious. Bring on the sun and cocktails, she thought, as she started packing make-up and sunscreens and trying to ram in her hairdryer. She opened Robin's backpack to sneakily stuff in the new Jodi Picoult book she had bought for the flight, as her bag was filled with the camcorder, camera, spare camera and more make-up, when suddenly Robin saw her and went mental.

'Leave my bag alone! Why can't I have any privacy? You have your own bags! God, you are impossible to travel with.' He grabbed the bag back and stuffed it under their bed.

Wow, what was wrong with him? Ali thought. It was only one book. His football team must be losing; they always lost. She laughed to herself as she reopened her flight bag and debated if her short blonde hair really could handle three weeks without a hair straightener.

21

Sarah was on a day off from the gallery, so herself and her mum had a visit to her father's grave in Shanganagh, followed by a lovely lunch of salad and apple tart in a café in Greystones, County Wicklow. Sarah loved Greystones, mainly because her mum had grown up there, so it made her feel even closer to her mum to spend time in the place she loved the most. Years ago people went to Greystones for their summer holidays, to enjoy the beach and quaint seaside village. Sarah couldn't imagine going on holiday to it now, as with the new roads it was only a twenty-minute drive or DART rail ride away, but it had still never lost that seaside-village feel, and had great galleries, shops and pubs. Her mum had only moved to Monkstown in Dublin when she married Sarah's dad, and even then she had only chosen Monkstown because it, too, was right on the water. Her mum always said she could not live far from the sight and sound of the water. But Monkstown had been the perfect place to raise a family: close to the sea and nature, yet near all the best schools and the city for working. Sarah looked back fondly on her childhood, and could only wish her future children would grow up in as loving and happy a family as she had. Her mum was a 'stay-at-home artist', as she always joked, and their house was full of paintings and sketches, and it was this that had inspired Sarah to be an artist herself. And even though she now worked more at selling art than painting it, she still had the passion for it, and her mum still encouraged her to draw as much as she could.

Her parents used to bring them all down to Greystones for a day at the beach. Her mother would bring her paints, and while Sarah's dad played with the children in the water she would sit on the beach looking so creative and exciting, as she drew and painted.

As they walked along the beach now, Sarah could see in her mum's eyes that she, too, was thinking back to those happy days.

'You miss Dad, don't you, Mum?'

'Of course I do, Sarah, but I'm lucky I've years of wonderful memories to relive over and over in my mind. I just wish you would find your soulmate soon, too, to create your own memories and dreams with.'

Sarah nodded, and for once knew her mum didn't mean to nag her about being single, but simply wanted the best for her. As they walked along the beach and talked about Sarah's date with Ross, her mum's dinner with Mr Macken, and Mel's last few weeks of pregnancy Sarah realized that sometimes the best days were the days you just relaxed, slowed down, and listened to the water, the memories and your mum.

22

Today was Molly's thirtieth birthday. She could not believe she had reached the big 3-0! Where had time gone? It only seemed like yesterday herself and Sarah were sixteen and having to get fake IDs to get into the local rugby club discos on a Friday night.

When she looked back now on all the years she had spent studying business and numbers she felt it was such a waste; it annoyed her that she hadn't started working as a cook earlier. But then, as her mum said, everything happened for a reason, and if she hadn't studied business first, she would never have met Luke, so fate had worked out. She had put up with boring balance sheets in order to meet the man of her dreams. It was worth it, she laughed, as Luke walked into their bedroom with a cake and candles alight, singing 'Happy Birthday' while trying to take a photo of her at the same time.

Luke got her a beautiful Dior watch and a Fendi handbag. So much money, she thought, and they were impractical for any average day for her – she could never wear them to work, as they would end up covered in batter and flour! She did appreciate the expensive treats though, and was glad they were not more cookbooks; she had received a lot of those recently!

★　　★　　★

Herself and Luke spent the day in Howth, walking, chatting and just being happy. He was in great form, and even though he had wanted to go away for the weekend to celebrate, Molly was happiest at home and with her family and friends. Like anyone else, she loved nights out, but her heart was with being close to people, making them happy, making them smile, and making them full! She loved nothing better than a night in making dinner for her friends; it gave her the greatest satisfaction. And though she would happily have made dinner at home for her whole family tonight, Luke had put his foot down, and instead they were all going to Peploes on St Stephen's Green for dinner, and then to meet some friends for drinks after.

As they walked the pier in Howth, and Luke chatted about possible summer holidays, Molly watched the fishermen come back to port with their day's fishing, and thought of all the great fish dishes she could make with just a few simple ingredients. God, she laughed to herself, when she had worked in a bank she never thought about funds and investments over a weekend, and yet here she was calculating how much fish there was and how much she could buy it for. How life had changed.

The rest of the day flew by, and before she knew it she was at home drying her long dark hair and trying to decide what to wear for her big birthday dinner, but what did a thirty-year-old wear, anyway?

23

Peploes was the perfect place for a birthday dinner: it was lively, loud and there was a great buzz. They had been lucky to have gotten a reservation for a Saturday night, the restaurant was full of businessmen and wealthy tourists, due to its proximity to the best hotels and offices in Dublin.

Molly had a starter of crab claws, and a main of salmon and asparagus; the food and atmosphere were both great. She looked around the table at Luke, her mum, dad, brother Patrick and his girlfriend, all happy and chatting. It was a great night. After the main course she suddenly noticed a look of glee on Luke's face as he saw the birthday cake being brought out; it was way bigger than he or anyone else had thought! Molly's aunt had actually made it and sent it to the restaurant that morning. It was chocolate and praline, Molly's favourite! After having 'Happy Birthday' sung to her by the whole restaurant and staff, Molly was finally able to taste the cake and wash it down with a glass of champagne.

Her dad said a few words about how they were all so proud she was following her dream, and how at thirty, she was still their little girl and that they all loved her so much. Molly welled up, she was lucky to have such a great family, but the tears stopped when her older brother started to remind everyone of the funny and embarrassing things Molly had done when she was younger.

'Well, we all knew Molly was destined to be a great cook, but she got off to a rocky start that would have shut any restaurant down in a minute!'

Oh no, thought Molly, here comes the 'garlic bread' story. Her brother began.

'You see Mum and Dad loved having dinner parties, it was all very eighties, and along with baked Alaska and After Eights it was perfectly acceptable to just serve garlic bread for starters! Anyway, Molly was dying to help, so Mum gave me and her the job of mixing the crushed garlic into the softened butter and then spreading it on the fresh baguettes. So we did all this, and were chuffed with our chunky garlic and butter paste. After cooking the breads we served them out to cries of how great we were from all the guests. It wasn't until we had served the last batch that Molly announced to me and Mum that her loose baby tooth had fallen out. Now that wasn't too bad until she said she hadn't seen it come out, and thought it might have fallen into the garlic bread! Well, as you can imagine, it was anyone's dinner party worst nightmare, and we spent ages looking at everyone's bread trying to spot a baby tooth, but we never did, so God only knows which one of the guests ate your tooth, Molly, but as long as it wasn't me I don't mind.'

Everyone cracked up laughing, even Molly. After dinner they met Molly's friends in The Shelbourne Bar for sparkling wine and more funny stories, but by 2 a.m. Molly was home in bed, exhausted but very happy. It had been a perfect birthday.

24

Ben was furiously typing up a review of the previous night's Bohemians versus Shamrock Rovers football match, while keeping his eye on the clock. He played rugby every Thursday in Blackrock Rugby Club, and did not want to be late. As he tried to concentrate on the report and remember who had made what pass and to whom, his mind kept thinking ahead to tonight's friendly against the first team. Ben had been a bit of a 'rugby jock' in school. His parents had actually sent him to the private Blackrock College, as his dad had gone there; it was well known for its great academic results, and it was the best rugby school in Ireland. And even though he had played rugby all through college too, he hadn't made it any further than club rugby. And after he spent a year away in Australia, his fitness had fallen and he never quite got good enough again. So now he played for the second team, but he was still very very keen, and enjoyed the tough game and after-match banter with the lads. He had known many of them since he was little, and loved it that everyone knew his name when he walked into the club. It was like living on the set of the hit TV show *Cheers!*

It was great to have a social and healthy interest and hobby, and he knew his dad loved to watch him play, as he was a very keen rugby supporter also. Joe O'Connor had come to every match Ben had played in from Under Eights right through to his match against Clontarf last weekend. Ben just loved the fresh air against his face, the rush of getting a 'try' and the joy of winning; it was tough and fun at the same time, but worth it. If he just got through this report now he could get on to that pitch and get into a good scrum.

'I can't believe we've beaten the first team,' laughed all the lads, as they headed to the bar for after-match pints.

It had only been a friendly and a practice match, but it was a great win, and Ben was thrilled. He had won them the match in the last minute, so was delighted to be accepting some winning pints. What with getting praise for his last-minute football-match article and now this, the day had been a lucky one. Maybe I should send that girl Laura a text, he thought. He hadn't seen her since they'd met, but had been in contact once or twice. Today's been a lucky day, he thought. If I get in touch with her, you never know, I might score another winning try!

25

Wow! Ali actually felt her breath being taken away as they stood at the top of Table Mountain, Cape Town. It was one of the most beautiful sights she'd ever seen. Here with Robin beside her, she felt like she was on top of the world looking down. She could see the beautiful white sandy beaches of Camps Bay, Bantry Bay and beyond, she could also see the Cape Town city, and the crowded V&A Waterfront – with its restaurants, bars and shops. It was so busy and loud down there, she thought, a hive of activity, but up here it was peaceful and still, with nothing but the blue blue sky and sun to distract her. They'd taken the revolving cable car right up to the top of South Africa's most famous mountain. Some people had walked, or even jogged, up to the top, but they were happy to watch those crazy energetic people as herself and Robin soared by them in the glass lift. It still astounded her how flat, like a real table, the mountain top was, it was no hassle to walk around in her Old Navy pink and blue flip-flops, unlike most other mountains in Ireland, where you needed at least a good pair of runners.

They had only been in South Africa for twenty-four hours but already Ali was madly in love with the place. It was all so beautiful. They got a taxi from the airport to their hotel in Camps Bay. Camps Bay had a very long white sandy beach, and was overlooked by Table Mountain, giving it a from-the-movies feel, as it had the beach and the mountains all in one picture-frame! Everywhere was busy with throngs of tourists and wealthy locals, and the funky local African music playing gave the place an atmosphere of its own.

They had arrived at the hotel and been welcomed by 'sun-downers' – early evening drinks. And even though they were tired after the twelve-hour flight, they had quickly changed and sat in the outside bar watching the world go by. Ali had almost cried, it was all so beautiful. A far cry from the rainy Dublin they had left behind.

'People just won't believe how stunning it all is, so relaxed and beautiful and out of this world. Even the colours of the sky and sea are different. I want to live here for ever.'

'Ali we've only been here three hours, how could you know you want to live here already?' Robin laughed.

'I know, Robin, with you here I could.'

Robin smiled, kissed her and ordered more drinks.

Being in South Africa was a far cry from any holiday Ali or Robin had been on before. Each summer the couple normally headed for a package holiday in Spain or Portugal. Relaxing on a beach and staying in an apartment had always been nice, nothing exciting or wild, but nice. But last year after two weeks in an Irish holiday resort in Greece, Robin had said he had had enough. He hated the all-day-long sunbathing, and found going for dinner every night in the same strip of restaurants boring; he wanted to try something else, go somewhere exciting. And so they had decided to do exactly that – save money and go to a different place. And as Ali looked around Cape Town, and they discussed the different activities and sights this country held, she knew they could both agree this was certainly a different kind of holiday for them, or anyone!

They managed to drink another two cocktails each, before

heading to the waterfront for dinner. They stumbled upon a steak restaurant. Ali ordered prawn cocktail to start, Robin had barbecue grilled prawns with a wine and garlic sauce. The food and wine were great, and by the time their fillet steaks and potato gratins were finished they were very full, happy and tipsy. Ali kept grabbing Robin's hand and squeezing it, just to make sure they were both not dreaming. This has to be a dream, she thought, to be on a different continent with the man I love, away from it all.

The harbour was overrun with boats, both private ones and tourist charters, and then there were the boats that went to Robben Island —where Nelson Mandela had been in jail. The waterfront was teeming with conversations – all in different languages – with children, musicians, street performers, locals, tourists, and Ali and Robin. It was perfect.

Ali had wanted to look in the shops after the meal, as they all opened late, but after the flight, cocktails, wine and excitement, she was too tired, and just managed to make it back to their African-themed hotel room, before falling asleep dreaming of lions and tigers and bears. (Oh my!)

The next morning Ali dragged Robin out of bed so they could get to the buffet-style breakfast as soon as possible. As they walked into the restaurant Ali gasped: the view was amazing, overlooking the sparkling Atlantic Ocean. Robin ordered a fry, while Ali chose French toast, with bacon and maple syrup, as well as helping herself to muesli, fresh fruit, toast and chocolate muffins. The food was endless! As they ate they planned their next few days. They were driving up to Franschhoek, one of the famous winery towns, in two days, and from there down following the Garden Route to other cape towns, but for now all Ali wanted to do was sit by the pool and sunbathe with a cocktail in her hand!

As the afternoon wore on Robin began getting all anxious,

Ali presumed it was the sunbathing, as even though he could
tan easily it bored him, so when he suggested that they go
to Table Mountain that evening rather than tomorrow as
planned she decided to go along with the change in plan. He
seemed strangely attached to his backpack as they bought their
tickets for the trip to the top of the mountain, and didn't let it
go all afternoon; but when they were on top of the mountain
he seemed to relax and for once let Ali take plenty of photos
of him to show all their friends at home.

As the sun began to set on the mountain, the clouds suddenly started rolling around the tourists.

'The mountain looks on fire, it's amazing!' Ali said, totally
overwhelmed by the sight. 'And look, Robin, I can't believe
there's a cocktail bar here, too! So we can have some sun-
downers!'

'I knew they had this bar,' said Robin gently. 'I have known
about it for months,' he added, as he brought Ali and their
Strawberry Daiquiris over to the edge of the rocks overlooking Camps Bay.

Ali was impressed. She was usually the one sneaking a look
at holiday websites online during work. She thought Robin
only researched football online.

Robin cuddled in beside her as he lifted something out of
his backpack. 'Ali, you know me better than anyone ever has
and will, but there are some surprises that you do not know,
but not for long. Ali, I love you more than anyone or anything.
You are my soulmate and best friend,' he said softly. And as he
knelt on to the ground and opened a small blue jewellery box,
his eyes fixed on hers, he asked: 'Ali, will you marry me?'

26

Stunned, Ali stared at the perfect white-gold and diamond engagement ring, and at Robin's happy smiling face looking at her bursting with pride and excitement. Ali was in shock, she had not expected Robin to propose at all. And for a brief moment she worried that she was not ready for marriage, to become a wife, but then, as she looked at Robin, the love of her life, she knew she was ready – ready to spend her life with him.

'Yes, yes, a million times yes,' she shouted out loud. She grabbed him and knocked them both to the ground. 'Robin, I love you so much, I would be honoured to be your wife.'

And as he slid the huge ring on to her finger, with the diamonds glistening in the last of the day's sun, they kissed.

Suddenly the tourists around them starting clapping, laughing, and offering them more sundowners. Robin had proposed and it was the best day of Ali's life.

27

Sarah Doyle had tears streaming down her face as she talked to Ali on the phone, she was so happy for her friend. As Ali brought Sarah up to date on the proposal, the romantic dinner afterwards, the ring and her plans for bridesmaids' dresses, Sarah just smiled and smiled, picturing Ali talking at a hundred miles an hour while poor Robin sat there in awe of her. Eventually Ali had to get off the phone, as she still had most of her friends and some family members to ring. She quickly put Robin on, and Sarah congratulated him for being so romantic and brave to ask a girl to marry him with a ring already bought. He let her know that they were still on their celebration dinner, and if he could get Ali off the phone then they could actually talk about the engagement to themselves and not to everyone in Ireland!

'Never get engaged abroad, Sarah, unless you want to end up with a phone bill that costs as much as the engagement ring,' he joked as he hung up.

Engaged? Some chance, thought Sarah. Things with Ross were going well, but very slowly. He always seemed to have other plans, and even though it had only been a few weeks she wondered if it was going anywhere. He was great fun, but very very laid-back and casual, maybe a bit too casual. She went to text him and let him know about Ali's news, when a customer walked into the gallery. They had actually closed, but Sarah had forgotten to lock the door due to Ali's call. She was about to explain that she was closed when she saw it was Hugh Hyland. He was one of the gallery's biggest clients. He was quiet enough, but a real gentleman and seemed to love spending hours walking around the building soaking up the new works and the art-world atmosphere.

'Sarah, sorry to bother you but I wanted to collect those Willow McIntyre pieces. I'm a huge fan of hers.'

Hugh had been away for Willow's show, but being such a big client of the gallery, he had been invited to preview her work a few days earlier, and had bought three pieces to be put aside for him for when he got back to Ireland. Sarah took Hugh to the loft upstairs, where she had Willow's pieces wrapped ready for him. He chose the frames he wanted to complement the pieces, and then paid her; and after she had checked what day the framer would have the pieces back, he arranged a day to collect them. He paused, as if he was about to ask her something else, when Ross suddenly burst through the door singing, and with a big bunch of roses in his hand.

'I will leave you to it, Sarah, and see you in two weeks.' And with that the fair-headed Galway man walked out the door.

'Wait until you hear about Ali,' Sarah exclaimed to Ross. She locked up the Stone Studio and they walked down the road.

28

Ben was out bringing Honey for a walk after work, anything
to tire the Labrador out before the Liverpool match came on
TV later, when he spotted Laura coming out of a local newsagent.

'Hi!' she shouted across the road.

Great, he thought, why is it always when you are out in
public in your oldest rugby shorts and gym T-shirt that you
meet someone you fancy? He crossed the road and introduced
her to Honey, who was slobbering all over him. He and Laura
had talked on the phone once or twice but hadn't met for a
date yet, so it was a bit awkward to meet like this, especially
when he was looking so scruffy.

'So, what are you doing in Foxrock village?' he asked her.

'Just dropping a friend home from work. I thought I would
stop in the shop and buy some dinner, although it is hard buying for one. Everything nowadays is in family packs or for
two people. It's like the food industry forgets there are single
people around who might like the odd pizza!'

Ben liked her. She seemed so relaxed and full of life, and
better looking than he remembered. And suddenly, before he
knew it, he was asking her to grab dinner and drinks with him
now in his local pub, where he also knew the Liverpool match
would be on in the background.

'OK, sure, beats staying in! Why don't we drop your dog home first?'

As they drove up Ben's driveway in Laura's cream and black Mini Cooper, she gasped. 'Wow! How can you afford a house like this?'

Oh God, he thought, how was he to explain that he still lived at home? But he needn't have worried, because his mum suddenly opened the door. She started asking him whether it was bow- or curly-shaped pasta he liked best? She could never remember. Ben stared in horror, and quickly looked at Laura to gauge her reaction, but she just laughed as she took Honey's lead and handed it to Maura O'Connor. Ben introduced the two women, and headed upstairs for a quick shower and change of clothes, praying that Mango, Honey or his mum wouldn't make Laura run a mile. Although he had to laugh, thinking of all the times his mum had asked him 'Any girls?' when he came home. And here he was, returning with one after taking the dog for a walk.

Maura O'Connor was thinking the exact same thing, and laughing inwardly at how Honey deserved some extra treats this evening for bringing home such a lovely girl!

Laura was very impressed by the O'Connors' big house. It was an old, cream gabled building, with a huge porch, large heavy wooden front door and a half-acre of gardens. With the evening sun shining down on the lawn, and tasteful furniture and paintings everywhere, it was like something from a magazine. The Shaker-style kitchen with its Aga was big, yet inviting and warm, and she and Mrs O'Connor sat and had a cup of tea while Maura introduced her to Mango and tried to explain how devastated Ben had been when he'd moved from home and been unable to see his beloved parrot every day. Laura just relaxed and listened to the warm heartbeat of the house and Ben's family.

Ben got dressed as quickly as he could, and before Laura knew it they were in the pub. They ordered tapas and beers, and relaxed, starting to get to know each other. It was about an hour later when Ben's mobile rang. It was an international number calling, and he was surprised to hear Robin's voice all the way from Cape Town.

'Guess what?' Robin shouted.

And as Robin filled Ben in on the engagement, Laura received a text message from Ali. It was great news.

'So now you know, Ben, why I was so annoyed that night when I started asking you about marriage and all that. I was going to tell you about it,' Robin told Ben.

'Sorry, Robin. I'm a fool, but forget me, get back to your fiancée and give her a big hug and kiss from me. Talk to you when you get back.' And with that Ben hung up. He was delighted for his friends.

'Imagine being engaged!' Laura exclaimed.

Oh God, abort mission, thought Ben, we haven't even finished one date yet and she is talking about engagements. Laura saw the look on his face.

'No, I didn't mean us. I meant, you know, in general?'

'Oh yeah, great,' Ben answered.

'Anyway, let me get some more beers to celebrate.' And with that Laura headed for the bar.

She is lovely, thought Ben, but let's just take things easy. His eyes returned to the big screen and to the football match.

29

Molly and her aunt were on their way to cater a twenty-fifth wedding anniversary party in Stillorgan when she got the news that Ali was engaged. She was delighted for her. Ali was a very good-hearted person and deserved only the best. Molly secretly wondered when she and Luke might get engaged and married!

Molly was small, and so struggled to help her aunt carry the big, heavy trays of food in to the 'happy couple's' house. It was large and red-bricked, and their children had decorated it with old photos of the couple.

'How sweet,' her aunt said. 'But Molly, we need to get cracking on getting things cooked and served, so let's find the kitchen.'

Even though the Searsons had booked in their anniversary party weeks ago, Molly was still nervous. It was the first big party that she was mainly responsible for, and she had spent all week working late, selecting, tasting and cooking the proposed dishes. Her aunt said she had confidence in her, and even though she had come along to help today, she was merely 'overseeing things' and not the 'head chef'. As there were eighty people coming, Molly had decided on a selection of tasty vol-au-vents, followed by chicken with broccoli, wine and cream. And for dessert she had made chocolate roulades and a large celebratory cake. Mrs Searson had kept the plastic bride and groom from her wedding cake twenty-five years earlier, so Molly was using that and candles on the Gateau Diane.

As the cooks began melting cheese and chopping mushrooms for the vol-au-vents, Mr and Mrs Searson stormed into the room.

'How could you?' Mrs Searson shouted at her husband. 'You know I hate that woman, why did you invite her?'

'What could I do? I met her in the golf club yesterday and she practically invited herself,' he replied.

'You are so stupid, after all these years you still have no cop on. She just wanted to snoop around our house, you stupid man.'

And with that she stormed out. Mr Searson shrugged, and let the women get back to chopping, peeling and baking. It was the first of many squabbles Molly witnessed all evening between the couple. They fought over the garden not looking right, over 'his relations', over that 'awful speech', and shouted 'you're drunk' at each other. So that by the time Molly carried the cake into the living room – where the guests had all gathered to wish the couple 'another twenty-five years of marriage!' – she was almost sick to her stomach. She thought: If this is what marriage is like after so many years then I'm glad Luke has not knelt down on one knee with a ring yet. And more important: What had Ali let herself in for?

30

Sarah had just spent a wonderful afternoon walking around Powerscourt Gardens in County Wicklow with Ross. He had wanted to go and look at their garden centre, as he'd just returned from five years in America, and his house, which he'd let out, was in need of repair and the garden needed a good overhaul. Sarah was always happy to have lunch in Avoca and a wander around the shops and gardens. The pet cemetery was her favourite, and herself and Ross had spent ages laughing at the tombstones for Betty the cow, and Ruby the dog.

Over vegetarian lasagne Ross had filled her in on how different life in Dublin had become compared to when he'd left to work in Merrill Lynch in New York half a decade ago. He had loved the thrill of being in the biggest, most exciting city in the world, but he had gradually realized that all his best friends and family were still in Ireland, and that he really wanted to settle back in Dublin. He'd begun to feel that thirty-one was too old to be still living a young man's dream in NY. So he was back home now, and getting settled. He told Sarah funny stories of the people he had hung out with in America: from Wall Street bankers to firemen and models. He told the stories fondly, but said that once he had stepped on that Aer Lingus plane he had known he wouldn't miss the huge and at times lonely New York. He had known he wanted Irish tea, Clonakilty pudding, and people who understood Gaelic football and watched *The Late Late Show* on a Friday night!

'You must miss Abercrombie & Fitch and all the shopping, though,' said Sarah, who could easily have spent all her wages in Victoria's Secret and Macy's.

'Yeah, the shopping was cheap, and they do have every store possible, but you can get sick of all that "have a nice day" crap. There is one shop I guess I'll miss, although it almost ruined my career. Do you know Payless shoes?'

Sarah didn't.

'Well, they are a huge American chain that sell discount shoes. They also specialize in big sizes, and as I'm a thirteen I always find it hard to find anything large enough. So on the day I arrived in New York I went clothes shopping for my first week at work. I knew I needed work shoes, as up until then I'd been happy wearing Converses and whatever other runners I could fit my feet into. So when I stumbled on Payless I thought I had died and gone to heaven. Not only were the shoes big, but they were cheap. So I decided to stock up. Then, on my second day at work I was sitting at my desk, still being introduced to all my new colleagues, when this fat annoying guy from accounts walked by, took one look at my feet and said: "You know, Buddy, I'm not sure how the business world works in Ireland, but over here we are serious about our appearance and wear matching shoes to work." I looked down and almost died. I was wearing one brown shoe and one black one! I had seen one type of "work shoe" and bought it in two colours, thinking I was clever buying them in bulk. But I hadn't realized I had put one of each on. What a nightmare it was for the rest of the day! I never lived it down, and my going-away gift from the staff was a pair of mismatching shoes!'

Sarah had snorted the can of Coke she had just bought out of her nose and all over her new Coast cardigan. It was the funniest story she had ever heard, and the tales had continued for the rest of the day. It really had been a perfect afternoon.

31

That night as Sarah and Molly sat down for dinner in Tribeca to discuss Ali's engagement, Molly asked her what Ross was up to later, and to be honest Sarah didn't know. She'd been disappointed when, after spending most of the day with Ross, he had not wanted to see her in the evening, too. She knew they had only been dating for over three weeks, but they still talked every day, so it felt like longer. Instead she had arranged to meet Molly, and now the two of them were getting the chance to chat about Ali's wedding. The girls discussed what kind of bride or bridezilla Ali might be! And swooned over how sweet Robin was, and how they couldn't wait to see the ring.

Sarah was on her way to the bathroom when she suddenly spotted Ross. As she walked over she noticed he was eating with a girl, a young gorgeous girl. Ross looked surprised to see Sarah, but introduced her to 'Michelle'. Sarah didn't know what to say. Was it his sister, cousin, or just plain and simple his girlfriend? Could she have been that stupid, to have dated someone who was already taken? What a creep. Ross could see she was flustered, and followed her to the bathroom.

'Who was that?' Sarah tried to ask calmly.

'Sarah, this is going to seem weird to you, but that is my date, Michelle.'

Sarah began to feel sick. 'What do you mean, date? I was your "date" all day today, in case you have forgotten.'

'I'm sorry, Sarah, it is just that the New York dating scene is all about dating lots of people until you both agree to go exclusive. And I thought we were both happy just keeping it light and casual for the moment. I've had a great time with you, and thought from the start you were just like me: laid-back.'

Sarah thought back to her forwardness in asking him out for a date sooner than he had planned, and her drunkenness on their first few dates. Maybe he had seen that as her keeping things casual, but still, this was Dublin, not the Big Apple.

'I was going to tell you, but I didn't want to upset you un-necessarily, and seeing as I didn't know how things would go with Michelle I thought I would wait. I'm sorry, Sarah, it's just that New York has rubbed off on me!'

Well *Sex and the City* this, she thought, as she stormed off, deleting his number from her mobile phone as she walked back to tell Molly. She turned and half-screamed across the restaurant at him: 'By the way, just so you know some other New York things that don't fly with us here in Ireland . . . it's "rubbish", not "trash" and "sweets", not "candy", and for God's sake, "chips" not "fries", although I think the word for someone like you is the same on both sides of the Atlantic – it's "player".'

And with that she grabbed Molly and headed off for as many cocktails as she could drink.

32

The last few days in South Africa had been a whirlwind of romance, excitement and pure happiness for Ali. After Robin's proposal, they'd had dinner overlooking the beach in Camps Bay. There, after a beautiful meal and plenty of staring at the ring, she had called all her friends and family. Her parents were so proud, and especially happy that Robin had been a real gentleman and travelled to Kilkenny a few weeks ago to ask them for their daughter's hand in marriage.

'How come I didn't suspect?' she gasped.

'Well, I thought you definitely had, when I was being so over-protective of my backpack,' Robin laughed.

'That explains it.' She laughed. 'Well, no wonder you didn't want me rooting around in it for spare room for all my junk!'

'I actually bought the ring three months ago, Ali, but I just wanted to wait until we were here in Cape Town before I proposed. I hadn't decided when in the holiday I was going to do it, but, after trying to hide the ring from you for the last few months, and especially since we arrived here, the stress of it all was too much for one man to take. I was terrified I was going to have to propose to you in Dublin airport! I didn't know if jewellery beeped when you went through security and got so nervous that my romantic proposal plans would be ruined by an electronic scanner!'

Ali laughed again but his story made her realize how lucky she was to have Robin.

'You really are the most romantic and thoughtful person in the world.'

'I'm the lucky one, Ali. I've loved you since I met you. Not only are you gorgeous with your blonde hair and blue eyes, but you were always so grounded, so normal, and perfect. My nice country girl!'

'I'm not so country now, am I? I can hold my own in any conversation about schools rugby, the best Dublin hotspots or why Cavistons is really the *only* place to buy fish in South Dublin!'

Robin laughed and ordered more champagne for his fiancée.

When they arrived back at the hotel, it was clear Robin had informed the staff of his 'proposal plan' as not only did they greet them with flowers and champagne, but showed Robin and Ali into their room, where they had not only covered the bed and room with fresh rose petals, but had run Ali a bubble bath with the petals just everywhere! And as Robin drifted off to sleep with a rose petal stuck to his forehead Ali had to pinch herself that this was all real, that she was about to get married.

33

A few days later they drove up to the Cape winelands. They checked into an old-world hotel in Franschhoek. Along with many wineries, the town was famous for its art galleries, shops, restaurants and quaint feel. They drove their rented car straight to La Petite Ferme, one of the most famous restaurants, wineries and hotels in the winelands. Ali and Robin sat down on the terrace and opened a bottle of wine that had been grown and harvested right in front of where they were sitting. As they ordered their food, Robin started laughing.

'Ali, here we are surrounded by a valley full of vineyards, fields of lavender, and mouth-watering food, and yet you are like a magpie and can only stare at the engagement ring!'

'I can't help it! I'm in love with it. I just can't wait to show my sisters and all the girls. You have great taste.'

'I know, sure, didn't I choose you?' And with that their food was served and they settled back to watch the world go by.

South Africa was so laid-back, Ali didn't know how she was ever going to return home to her boring work, get the bus every day in the wet weather and put up with the stress of living in a big city again. As if Robin could read her mind, he tried to reassure her.

'Don't worry, Ali, we'll come back here again, I promise.

87

We are not even halfway through the holiday, but already I know that this will be our place! It's our paradise; we'll be back.' Reassured, Ali smiled at him, and then started her vegetarian tartlet.

34

I must be mad, thought Ali, trying to control her fear as she looked down at the deep dark water. How had she let Robin persuade her to join him on a shark-dive?

'Just trust me, Ali, you can do this. I know you can,' Robin whispered to her, as she zipped up her wetsuit.

After the winelands they had travelled across the mountains to stay in a seaside town called Hermanus, and it was from there that they were now going shark-diving . . . great white shark-diving! Robin had been dying to do it for years, ever since he had seen a documentary about people doing it on the Discovery Channel. It seemed like madness to Ali, to willingly lower yourself into shark-infested water, all for the pleasure of saying you had done it. Robin had been trying to persuade her for days that it was safe and a great achievement. No wonder he proposed before this, she thought. He was just trying to butter me up! But as the day approached Ali swung between not wishing to go near the sharks, and wanting to be able to say she was not afraid and was able to do it. She just couldn't decide what to do. So here she was now, in her wetsuit, with Robin and two American guys trying to persuade her to get in a cage. Each cage took four people, and was lowered down from the side of the boat into the bloodied water below.

'You will be fine, darling. I've been married and divorced

four times, and nothing could be scarier than a divorced woman,' laughed the large Texan man.

Oh, that's it, I'll have to do it now, just to prove I'm not as ridiculous as this man, Ali thought, as she tied back her short blonde hair and began to lower herself into the water.

'Just don't drop the ring,' shouted Robin as she felt the water hit her toes.

Oh no, too late, she thought, why didn't I take it off?

At first there was nothing to see, just the blood and dead fish that had been thrown into the water to encourage the great whites; but then out of nowhere they came, three of them all circling in front of her. Ali was actually in the water with sharks. They came close to the cage, and suddenly one of them head-butted the cage right in front of her. I'm going to die, just like in *Jaws*, except I was stupid enough to pay two hundred euros for it, Ali screamed in her head, but then the shark disappeared as quickly as it had come. After that the sharks kept trying to head-butt their way into the cage, and ran their fins up against the bars, but Ali was braver and kept her nerve. She was with Robin and that was what mattered, nothing could harm her. She had been rattled in a cage by a shark, and survived! And as she was pulled out of the water by the boat-owner she grabbed Robin, and high from the adrenaline rush gushed that their shark encounter would be a good story to tell their future kids.

35

Ben was on the 46a bus on the way to work. My God, he thought as he sat down, why did the bus always smell of a brewery every Friday morning? It was from all the people going for drinks on Thursday night, he knew, but one day someone would light a match and some poor bus would explode. Ben chuckled to himself. He was on good form, work was going well, and things with Laura were progressing slowly but nicely. He had been in a serious relationship before, and didn't want to just slip right back into one that wasn't going to work again.

He had a few match reports to be written up, and an interview with a young Limerick Gaelic football player to do that day in work, and then he was hoping he could finish a bit early, to try and meet Laura for a bite to eat, before heading off to see *Rocky Balboa* in the cinema with the lads. They were all dying to see how their eighties hero now looked in the boxing ring.

Jeremy was in Ben's office when he walked in. His friend's stag do felt ages ago, but Ben knew the wedding was soon, he had the invite somewhere.

'How are you getting on, buddy? Still avoiding accounts and balance sheets by hiding out here?' Jeremy joked.

'I love the work here. I really do, and I have some good stuff to hand in today. Thanks for all your support.'

'No problem, just make sure you keep up with the work and all. I still have to answer to the sports editor, who isn't quite sure why we hired someone with no journalism qualifications! Anyway, I also wanted to ask, should we be setting an extra place for this Laura girl at our wedding in four weeks' time?'

Ben dropped his file. 'No way, not yet. That might look too serious. Thanks, Jeremy, but definitely not yet.'

'You'll never change,' laughed Jeremy as he walked across the newsroom.

Laura looked lovely as she walked into Pasta Fresca in jeans, a tight fitted polo-neck and knee-high black suede boots. After a meal and bottle of red wine Ben had to dash to meet the lads. Laura seemed miffed that their Friday-night date was over by eight thirty, but Ben had already booked the cinema tickets. As they kissed goodbye Laura worried if he was too immature for her. He might be tall, dark and handsome, but she was too old to be messing about.

Over a full Irish breakfast the next morning, Ben told his parents about the film, and filled them in on all the gossip from his friends. He was so sweet sometimes, Maura thought, so gentle and calm. As he fed the parrot and dog, Maura could still picture him as a two-year-old playing in the sandpit in their back garden. When he offered to drop his dad off at golf Maura thought his new love-interest Laura might be having a good influence on him. But then, when she asked him to unpack the dishwasher later on that day and he cried off saying he was late for a rugby match, she felt annoyed. She had always wondered if being an only child had made him a little bit more selfish and immature, and if he valued his friends more than anyone else because they were the closest he got to siblings. Would he still be refusing to pack dishwashers and living at home if he had a sister or brother?

36

Sarah had just received a text from Ali saying they would be home next week and to keep the following Saturday free for their engagement party. It was exciting, but Sarah couldn't help feeling a little jealous too. Ali was so lucky, while Sarah seemed to go from disaster to disaster – Ross being the latest. Even though they had only been on a few dates, she had been so hurt by his behaviour, and though Ross tried to ring her a few times she just ignored him until the calls stopped. Of course, he was entitled to have whatever kind of dating lifestyle he wanted, but even so, she couldn't help feeling used and embarrassed – and now she was back to square one. She hadn't been out since that night, and had been happy to stay home with her mum. She was taking this afternoon off work to go and visit her sister Mel. Mel was overdue and ready to pop, so Sarah thought an afternoon of chick flicks and chocolate might help her relax. But before that she had the delivery from the gallery's picture-framer to open. In it were all the pieces that had been sent to be framed, or reframed as people's tastes changed. It still amazed Sarah how a frame could totally change a picture, making it seem bigger, smaller, brighter or more expensive. She unwrapped the three pieces that Hugh Hyland had ordered. He had good taste and not only an excellent eye for art, but for the right frame, too. He seemed to buy an awful lot of art, but he had explained once that not only was he an avid collector, but the firm he worked for also liked to have plenty of expensive-looking art around their offices, so he took it upon himself to pick out the pieces because, as he often joked: 'The rest of them wouldn't know Monet from Mozart!' She rang his mobile to remind him his new purchases were ready. He said he was coming down to Monkstown for lunch, so would pop in before she left. Clodagh, who worked part-time, was covering for her this afternoon, and would handle any other orders.

Sarah was surfing the internet for the other galleries that had exhibitions on at the moment, to see what artists they were handling, when Hugh Hyland came in. It was hard to know what age he was but Sarah guessed late thirties. He was well-dressed, and very polite, and, as usual, asked if any new pieces had come in that he hadn't seen yet. So Sarah showed him some, and checked that his three new frames were OK. Clodagh arrived as they were finishing up.

'You work so hard here, Sarah, how do you make enough time to go out with that boyfriend of yours?' Hugh enquired.

'Boyfriend?'

'The man I met in here a few weeks ago.'

'Oh him! He isn't my boyfriend,' she politely replied.

'I'm sorry to hear that, but I'm sure there are plenty of guys queuing up for a date with you. I mean I would . . .' But before Hugh could finish Sarah's mum ran into the gallery. She was in her slippers and hair-curlers. Oh my God, Sarah thought, is she drunk? What was going on? And how could she explain it to Mr Hyland?

'Sarah! Mel has gone into labour. John has brought her to Holles Street, but I'm too nervous to get behind the wheel.

95

You'll have to drive me in right now. I mean, my first grand-child is on the way! Come on.'

Sarah was too stunned to say anything, but Clodagh grabbed her and pushed her out of the door, telling her not to worry, she would look after everything, It wasn't until Sarah was walking in the doors of Holles Street hospital that she realized she hadn't even said goodbye to Hugh Hyland.

After four hours in the waiting room, Sarah and her mum had drunk the soft-drinks machine in the hospital dry of Lucozade. In times of crisis, stress, sickness and excitement it was all their family drank. They had rung Tom to bring more in. As he walked in the door with a crate of the 'sweet nectar' as Sarah called it, Tom tried to ask: 'Am I an uncle yet?' It was not until the Lucozade was cracked open that Sarah explained that Mel and John were still in the delivery room.

'My nerves are shot,' her mum almost cried. As this was to be her first grandchild, she was up to ninety, and she was excited and nervous at the same time. But it was another two long hours before John calmly walked out to say that he was a dad.

Mel had given birth to a little girl.

As they rushed in to see Mel, Sarah noticed her mum was weeping.

'I just wish your father was here to see this.'

Sarah was thinking the same thing, family had been so im-portant to her father. He would have done anything to have been there.

'Mum, I'm sure he *is* here, looking after Mel and us all. He wouldn't miss it for the world.'

And as they caught a first glimpse of new, beautiful little 'Fiona', Sarah could see her father in the baby's eyes and knew he was still with them all. Everyone stared at this stunning little new creature. It was such a happy occasion, it made Sarah crave for a husband and baby herself, and she was only distracted from this fantasy by Mel shouting: 'If I don't get some Lucozade quick . . .'

37

Ali gasped as she felt the tough skin of an elephant trunk in one hand, while trying to take a photo with the other. Robin and herself were in an elephant sanctuary near Plettenberg Bay. It was their second-last day in South Africa, and before they flew back to Cape Town they had come to this well-recommended sanctuary. The only other time she had ever seen one of these animals up so close before was in Dublin Zoo, where there was a big old elephant. But being surrounded by elephants in the wild was a totally different experience. Ali had spent the last few hours helping wash and walk these beautiful creatures. They were so calm and relaxed. Most of them had been saved and were now living in the sanctuary, which had acres and acres of land and muddy puddles for them to play in. Now as she and Robin walked trunk-in-hand with the elephants back to the camp Ali almost had a tear in her eye thinking that these amazing experiences were nearly over. In two days' time she would be home in Dublin. The last three weeks seemed to have flown by. With wine-tasting, shark-diving, tours of game reserves and washing elephants, it had all been like a dream. Robin had almost crashed their rental car the other day, when an actual real-life monkey had run across the road in front of them. Ali hadn't been quick enough with her camera, but she was ready when, a few miles later, they saw springboks feeding metres from their car. The food had been great, too, and Ali had never had so much fish. And the massive steaks, all chargrilled, were turning her into a real carnivore!

Later that night, in the famous beach-side shack restaurant, Robin discussed what he thought they should do on their last day, but Ali knew exactly what she wanted, she needed a new dress for their engagement party, and wouldn't it be great to buy something that no one else in Dublin would have: a dress from Cape Town!

So after a short internal flight the next day Ali and Robin were back down in the V&A Waterfront. Within minutes of shopping Ali had seen it, the perfect I-have-just-got-engaged dress! A strapless pink to-the-knee dress, with a large black ribbon and bow, it was perfect for her petite frame and fair hair. As she paid she thought how great it would be to get her bridesmaids' dresses here, but then changed her mind as her two younger sisters back in Kilkenny would kill her if she didn't let them decide what they wanted to wear. They were picky enough and it wasn't worth crossing their paths.

After a last dinner of outrageously huge steaks Robin led Ali to a moonlight cruise he had booked for them. It was the perfect end to the perfect holiday. She would miss South Africa and all the memories it had created for them, but the closer she got to home the more excited she was about showing people the ring and making wedding plans. On the long flight home they started to discuss churches, the best man and the honeymoon.

'It is not all about the big day; marriage is a lifetime commitment, not just one day of fuss,' Robin joked. Ali knew that, and felt the same, but it was exciting to plan the wedding venues and what kind of music they needed.

'Mum and Dad are so happy,' Robin said. 'They're so excited to be finally having a daughter. They can't wait for you to be having Christmases with us in Dublin!'

What? Ali thought. Christmas away from Kilkenny? Oh my God, she had never imagined anything beyond the honeymoon. Married life wasn't just about changing your surname, it was going to be all about change. Changing things for ever. I just hope I'm ready, Ali thought to herself, as the flight left sunny Africa and headed home.

38

Molly carried Heavenly's large wicker basket into the offices of Sterling Bank. Every day the bank faxed through a list of the sandwiches, wraps, salads and quiches their staff wanted. It was time-consuming delivering them, but as Molly's aunt reminded her, they paid very well and were loyal customers. As she made her way to the funds department she got the sandwich list ready. She laughed at how each department could be identified by their order. Marketing was always full of surprises – salmon, cream cheese, olives and capers – while the funds department seemed to be all men, and men who loved ham and cheese and not much more! She approached Mr Williams and Mr Shortall. Mr Shortall did the odd time throw in a tuna salad as a surprise, but Mr Williams had ham, cheddar cheese and mustard every day. How boring, Molly thought.

'Thanks so much, Molly. I don't know how I'd get through my afternoon meetings without you.'

'No problem, Mr Williams,' Molly replied, turning to leave, and get back to the busy café.

'It's Scott, you know. Calling me Mr Williams makes me sound like my father.'

Well, maybe your father would be a bit more adventurous,

Molly thought, but then felt mean as Scott was only trying to make small chat.

'Glad to help,' she cried as she headed back, unaware her arms and dark hair were covered in melted chocolate from making brownies earlier. Scott Williams smiled to himself, watching her, before getting back to his computer.

39

Molly was chuffed. She had just received a call from Ali, who had rung her the instant she had arrived back from her holiday to see if Molly could make 'niblets and finger food' for the engagement party.

'You will be paid like a proper caterer, Molly,' Ali had explained.

It was going to be in Ali and Robin's apartment, and even though the kitchen was small and it was last-minute, Molly was thrilled. It was the first proper job that she was doing alone, where no aunt or café was involved.

Molly had borrowed some of her aunt's recipe folders, and as she waited for the bus on her way home, she found it hard to concentrate, she was so excited. It would mean hard work for the next few days, experimenting and testing out food to see if it was right for all their gang of friends – who would be hungry and probably drunk on Saturday. But she didn't mind the long hours, it was worth it. A man waved to her as she took her seat. Who the hell was he? she wondered. She tried to keep her head low.

'I had another successful meeting, thanks to your sandwiches, Molly.'

My God, who was this? she thought. Then she remembered it was Mr Boring-Sandwich Williams.

'Great, thanks.' And with that she delved into a page of recipes for mini-quiches. Mr Williams was nice enough, but still she didn't want to have to chat to all her customers every night on the way home. He seemed to take the hint, and as she waved him politely goodbye when she got off in Donnybrook, he was engrossed in some business magazine.

Luke was happy for Molly and her engagement party job, but less pleased that their theatre date the next night would have to be cancelled.

'I just can't make it, Luke, I've so little time before the party, and it's only fair to Ali that I practise making a few things for the next few nights.'

'Well, she is hardly being fair herself, giving you only a week's notice,' Luke argued back.

'Luke, how can you say that! She's one of my best friends, and she's giving me a chance to prove myself as a cook.'

'Fine, I'll rearrange the theatre if I can, but remember to ask your friends to give you more notice next time. We can't let your cooking obsession take over our lives.'

'It's my job – my career,' she reminded him, trying not to feel angry. 'Luke, you know I'm trying to build up my reputation, build up the business – I thought that's what we both wanted.'

Luke at least had the grace to look a bit apologetic. 'Molly, I didn't realize that catering and cooking was going to take up so much of your time; if it's not recipes, it's testing menus or cooking trays of bloody stuff.'

'Cooking is hard work,' she said firmly. 'I always knew that . . .' she added, as Luke grabbed his coat and went out to meet the lads for a game of pool. 'And so did you,' she continued out loud to herself, gutted at Luke's behaviour. How can he not understand? she wondered, as she had more and more recently.

40

The next day Ali and Robin were in the car on the way down to visit Ali's family in Kilkenny. She hadn't seen them yet, and couldn't wait. She was dying to ask her two sisters to be bridesmaids and to show them the engagement ring and photos of South Africa and Table Mountain, where it had all happened. Robin and Ali were both the first in their families to get married, so it was both exciting and bit daunting for them.

Ali was so tired with all the engagement excitement that she soon nodded off, much to Robin's relief, as he couldn't have stuck one more minute of discussion over what colour the bridesmaids should wear.

Ali awoke as the car rolled over the cattle-grid entrance at the end of her family's long driveway. The sound of that always made her feel right at home, and she could barely contain her excitement at the thought of seeing her family. As they drove up the long path her family house came into view. Riverhouse was a large cream and ivy-covered family home. It was set right in the middle of a large courtyard, in front of where the cows were kept, and you could see the family fields for miles in each direction. As Robin was a city boy, he still found it hard to get used to the farmyard smell and occasionally walking in cowpats, but he looked forward to his visits and the warm welcome he always received.

Ali's mum ran out to hug her daughter, all emotional at the thought of Ali soon becoming a married woman. She gave Robin a big warm hug, too, and welcomed him officially into the family, and with that ushered them both into the kitchen where she had dinner ready and a bottle of champagne open.

Robin's head was in a spin with all the screaming, hugging and crying that came once Ali's two younger sisters and dad came into the house. The family were all very alike: all small, and pale-skinned. But while Ali and her sister Kate had short blonde hair, her other sister Jill was slightly taller and very dark. Before Robin knew it they were taking pictures of the newly engaged couple, and then discussing which priest would be the best to marry them. He knew he and Ali were lucky both to have families who were so happy for them, and so excited by the wedding details and discussions, but still – could he last months of this wedding talk?

The rest of the weekend went well, with Ali being reminded how much she did miss the farm and long walks around the river and herds of cows. It was so peaceful here, unlike the busy city buzz. Her mum had written down a list of things Ali had to start researching and booking, and had said that she would talk to the local church and priest for them. After many home-cooked meals and wine, and plenty of late-night chats, Ali and Robin eventually got back in to the car on Sunday night and headed back to Dublin.

41

On Saturday night at the engagement party, Molly was serving crab spring rolls, homemade fresh sushi, layered focaccia with cheese and rocket, chicken satay, prawns with chilli, parsley, ginger and garlic on toast, followed by profiteroles. The food was a hit, and Molly felt like she was floating as she was congratulated time and time again as the night went on. Luke had been in a bad mood all week, but by Saturday afternoon had come around and helped her deliver the dishes to the party. After a few beers he relaxed and praised her culinary skills.

Ali looked stunning in her new dress, and surrounded by herself and Robin's families and all their friends she felt herself glowing. Although her head was also in a spin from all the questions everyone wanted answered. Which church? Which band? What colour for the bridesmaids' dresses? Which flowers? What menu? What invite? It was like her guests were running an engagement quiz show with herself and Robin as the only contestants. Ali didn't have many of the answers, and after being asked about how her hair would be styled, for about the fortieth time, had to pull Robin aside and laugh.

'No one cares that we are madly in love, and happy to commit to each other, they just want to know if I'm going on the Atkins diet or not, or some other ridiculous question like that. Help!'

'Don't worry, fiancée, they are just excited, and maybe even a little jealous, but it will be fine. Just say that you intend to put on plenty of weight for the big day, and that you are getting your hair permed, that should shake them all off!' Robin laughed as he hugged and kissed her.

Wow, Sarah thought, how happy and in love Robin and Ali looked! They were so tanned, healthy and perfect; it was great to see her friends like that. She had not had time to hear all about the holiday from Ali yet as Sarah herself had been busy, very busy with her new niece, baby Fiona. She was a dote and had everyone fighting for a chance to hold her. But as god-mother Sarah got special privileges, and holding was one of them! As she turned to tell Molly what Fiona had done today, Robin was by her side introducing her to Ben. She had met him once or twice over the years with Robin, but she could see from the way Robin was pushing Ben practically on top of her, that not only was Robin a little too drunk on beer and wedding love-talk, but that he thought Sarah might fancy Ben. Did she look that desperate? Sarah worried. The minute Robin left, Ben apologized.

'Sorry about that, Robin obviously wants us all married now! But I'm actually kind of seeing someone. It has all kind of happened since Robin's been away, so I had better let you go back to Robin's match-making.'

And with that he was gone, and Sarah returned to telling anyone who would listen how important godmothers were.

Ben and Laura were having a perfect night, too. They hadn't seen much of each other that week, so it was good fun to relax and unwind with some wine and fine food. It was a great party, and the apartment was packed with friends and family.

After a few drunken dances Ben knew Laura needed to go home. As he helped her into a taxi, she told him she had to go away with work for a week, but that she hoped when she got back they might start seeing each other more.

'I hope so, too,' he whispered to her, as they kissed the whole way home. And this time he actually meant it. Laura had looked gorgeous that night, and Ben had started to realize that if he didn't cop on he could lose her. It wouldn't be long before she was snapped up. Ben thought back to when he had first met Laura and wondered how he could have missed her beauty.

The engagement party had been a success, and afterwards, as Ali tidied up some of the glasses before heading to bed, she realized how great her friends were. They'd all been so happy and pleased for her. The air was electric with people hugging, kissing, and congratulating herself and Robin. Such positive energy. If the engagement was like this, she thought, what would a full-blown wedding be like!

42

Ben and Joe O'Connor were out playing a round of golf. Ben hadn't played in a while, but there was an office competition coming up soon, and there was no better person to ask for tips than his dad. Joe had been president of their local golf club for years, and still spent almost every day there, meeting friends, having drinks with Mum, and getting in as many rounds as he could. It was a great social scene to be involved in, and Joe would have been lost without it. Walking through the clubhouse, Ben was constantly reminded how popular his dad was. Everyone wanted to stop and chat, find out how Maura was, ask Joe's advice on a club, or competition, or just say hi. I wonder if I'll be this loved when I get to his age? Ben thought.

'Nothing makes me happier than playing a round of golf, surrounded by nature and crisp air – followed by a drink in the bar. It's a great sport, Ben, you shouldn't have given up on it so easily. You're a good player.'

'Thanks, Dad, I must play more. It's just rugby takes most of my time now, and I had forgotten how good it feels to walk around and get some fresh air, unlike rugby where you are being attacked every five minutes!'

As the afternoon rolled on Joe started asking Ben about

work, and as usual attempted to broach the subject of Ben coming to work for him.

'You would have your own business, son. How can you say no?'

'Dad, can we not just enjoy today and talk about work another time?'

Joe O'Connor never said another word about it, but as they approached the eighth hole he dropped his club, and started to bend over.

'Dad, are you OK?' Ben was shocked to see the colour drain from his dad's face.

'I'm fine, I just got that pain again in my arm, and I'm a little short of breath, but I'm fine. Pass me some of your water.'

'Let's go back inside, Dad, take it easy.'

Ben expected his dad to argue, but he didn't, so they walked back inside the club. By the time their lunch of fish and chips had arrived, Joe was feeling and looking better, and chatting about the new club president. Ben was relieved, but still a little worried. Then, as they left the club, Joe turned and said: 'Ben, let's not tell your mother, you know how she worries, and I'm fine, never felt better. I probably just overdid it this week, too much golf and gardening.'

'OK, Dad.' And with that Ben felt reassured, and started worrying about his work golf outing.

Ben was at home trying to clean Mango's birdcage out when Laura rang.

'Hi, bad news, I can't meet you this weekend, the project in London is taking longer than I thought. I'm going to stay here this weekend with friends, and carry on all next week, but what about the following weekend? If you can still remember what I look like by then!'

'Oh, I won't forget that smile and those tight jeans,' Ben

joked. And after catching up for a few more minutes, he promised to take her out for dinner the following Saturday night.

When he'd put the phone down he turned to his parrot. 'So we are free and single this weekend Mango, both bird-less.'

43

Sarah had just arrived home from work and was sitting watching Sky News when her mum came in and handed her a piece of paper. Sarah looked at it and saw it was a shopping list.

'What's this, Mum? I thought you only went grocery shopping yesterday?'

'I did, but we are short a few things and I was thinking you could head to Superquinn in Blackrock and pick up what we need.'

'Oh Mum, I'm wrecked from work. Can we not just survive with what we have in the fridge for tonight, and I promise I'll go shopping tomorrow evening?'

Her mum looked put out.

'Sarah, please go. You never know what could happen there. It could be fun!'

'Fun?' Sarah said, suddenly sitting up and looking suspiciously at her mum. 'Since when has grocery shopping been fun? What's this really about, Mum?'

Catherine Doyle sat down and turned off the TV.

'Sarah, I was having lunch with a few of the girls today and Joyce was telling me about these Superquinn Singles Shopping Nights. Apparently, her niece went once and met a man by the frozen pizza section! I think it could be perfect for you. You don't seem to meet the right men when you are out with your friends, and then after the Ross fiasco, meeting a nice man at one of these Superquinn nights could be just what you need.'

Sarah looked in shock at her mum and felt herself getting flushed and annoyed.

'Have you gone mad, Mum? I am not going to a singles shopping night. No way. My God, what do you take me for?'

Sarah looked at the shopping list that included food she'd never seen her mum eat.

'I mean, do we even need these random groceries, or are they just a ploy to get me running after some man and his trolley? Like when was the last time we ate Vienetta or ice-cream wafers? My eighth birthday party, probably. God, you are so obvious, Mum.'

Catherine looked taken aback and after a few minutes took the shopping list from her daughter and crossed out the majority of it, leaving only wine, crackers, cheese and grapes.

'OK, Sarah, maybe I was being too pushy, but I do really need a few things as it's my turn to bring snacks to bridge later tonight, so while I make dinner for the two of us can you please go and get these for me? Thanks, love.'

Sarah was about to complain but thought it better not to fight with her mum or raise her own blood pressure even more, and so instead grabbed her coat and made her way to the door. Just as she did so she heard her mum shout at her from the kitchen.

'And don't forget, Sarah, not only would it be great to meet a nice man tonight, but you know that any man who can do his own grocery shopping must be domesticated and that's a great quality in a husband!'

She didn't answer back but just slammed the door and made her way to Superquinn.

★ ★ ★

Sarah vowed to be as quick as she could in the supermarket, she didn't want anyone thinking she was desperate enough to attend a dating event at her local shopping centre. Just as she'd made her way to the cheese counter she ran right into two old school friends, Val and Jessica.

'Hi, Sarah! God, we haven't seen you in ages. How are you? You look well, although I didn't know you were still single,' Jessica said to a stunned Sarah.

'Single? What makes you think I'm unattached?' Sarah replied.

'Oh, Sarah, don't play innocent with us,' Val laughed. 'We single girls know all the tricks, and these Superquinn Singles Shopping Nights are something we'd heard about, too. Jess and I have come the last three weeks and although we have yet to meet Mr Right, we have seen some cuties! I mean, it's easy to spot who's here for a potential partner rather than a box of cereal and some milk!'

'Yes,' Jessica agreed, 'when you see someone at the last aisle with an empty trolley you know they are here to check all the singletons out!'

Sarah looked at the girls in horror. 'You two honestly believe you can meet a husband here alongside potatoes, orange juice and mince?'

'Well, Sarah, we can only hope. Of course we don't want to close off other options in case these shopping trips don't work out, so at the moment we are doing a blitz on speed dating, blind dating and, of course, online dating,' Val said matter-of-factly.

'Dating is a serious game, Sarah,' Jessica added.

Sarah looked at her two old friends, girls who were intelligent and very popular in school. What had happened to the world, she wondered, that made girls like them have to resort to fake shopping trips in the name of meeting a partner?

Sarah wished the girls luck, bought the goods she needed and drove home as quickly as she could. As she watched TV alone that night, with not even her mum for company, she wondered would she become as desperate as Val and Jessica? Would she soon be resorting to looking in a shopping aisle or online for a man?

44

The Stone Studio had been quiet enough all day, so Sarah was on the phone with her sister Mel, filling her in on the previous night's awful experience in Superquinn, when Hugh Hyland walked in.

'I have to go, Mel, but don't even tell Mum about Val and Jessica's ideas of meeting men online, or she'll have me signed up to those websites by the time I get home.'

'Mr Hyland, I'm sorry for rushing off the last time you were in,' Sarah apologized.

'No problem, Sarah. I was actually in Monkstown for a meeting today, so I thought I would drop by to find out how your sister got on.'

He is so kind, remembering about Mel, Sarah thought. Although he must think me and my mum are mental cases, and that I'm not the sophisticated gallery manager I'd hoped he'd think I was.

'Well, I'm now the proud aunt and godmother to baby Fiona!'

'You will be a great aunt, very funky.'

And as they chatted away Sarah realized for the first time how nice he was. She had always just seen him as a client of the gallery's, and treated him as that, but now she saw that he

117

was interesting and relaxed, and with his good taste in art and kind eyes was actually becoming more and more attractive to her. Almost an hour had passed when Sarah realized it was time to close up the gallery.

'I'm sorry, but we need to close. Was there anything else I could help you with, Hugh?'

Hugh Hyland cleared his throat, suddenly looking rather awkward.

'I know I'm a client of the gallery, Sarah, but do you know why I've been calling in quite so often?' He looked at her. 'It's because I'd love to ask you out, just for a drink or something. I've tried to ask you before, but other men, and babies being born, kept getting in the way!'

Sarah didn't know what to say. She'd never been asked out at work before, and it was a little daunting that an important client was the one doing it. But then she remembered that her mum was out tonight for salsa lessons with Mr Macken, and that she didn't want another night in fretting about not having a boyfriend or a baby like her sister, so she grabbed the keys, locked the gallery and headed for the pub, with a very happy Hugh Hyland beside her.

The drinks went well. Sarah was careful not to drink too much, and give Hugh the wrong impression, the way she had with Ross. She was not easy or casual or whatever that American wannabe had thought she was. She and Hugh talked about art and exhibitions, and Sarah was fascinated by how much he knew. She told him about her failed attempts at becoming a full-time artist, and how the gallery had become her saviour. Hugh now worked in Dublin, and loved the social life in the big city, but he did crave to one day move back to Galway, and be closer to his family and friends there. As the night wore on, Sarah got to know him more, and liked what she heard, and was almost sad when the barman started flicking the lights off and pulling the shutters down.

As Sarah walked into her house that evening, her mum started demonstrating the different steps and moves involved in salsa, and as she dragged Sarah up for a spin around the kitchen table she could see a glint in Sarah's eye that hadn't been there for quite some time.

45

The next afternoon when Sarah arrived back at work after lunch, there was a package on the step, with her name on it. She opened the large, yet very light box. Inside was a blank stretched canvas, with a note.

Sarah, I had a great time last night. Whether we go for drinks again or not, I hope one day I'll see your work on a wall in the gallery. I know with your spirit you could be a great artist. Take care, Hugh

His business card was attached. Sarah didn't even have to think twice about grabbing the phone and ringing him. Men like this don't come along often, she thought, and I'm not going to be the fool who lets him get away. And within minutes they had a cinema date booked for that evening. Sarah looked at the canvas. Maybe sometimes you just needed a blank canvas to start something new, something exciting!

46

Molly was happily making her mum's version of gingerbread men, called 'honeymen'. Her mum used to make them for her and her brother when she was younger, and since they didn't like ginger she'd used honey instead. And as Molly had some spare time, she'd thought before the lunch rush began she would make some new treats for the customers to try out. She made some big ones to sell and a few mini-men as samplers for the counter. Heavenly was doing well, and each day Molly worked here it felt more and more like home. The smell of baking, coffee brewing and apple pies all made her feel calm, safe and so happy. There was always a great buzz about the place, it was full of people chatting, laughing and enjoying their food. The atmosphere was so different from Molly's last job where everything was serious and competitive; and it seemed like years ago that she wore a suit to work. Nowadays jeans, a T-shirt and her apron were all she needed, with her suits being banished to the back of her wardrobe, hopefully never to appear again. It was amazing how much your life can change in such a short time, she thought, giving her little honeymen marzipan buttons and eyes.

After another busy day at the café, Molly was meeting Ali in Merrion Square after work. Ali had said in her text message that she had 'something very important' to tell her. I wonder what it is? Molly thought, as she found a free park bench. She began reading a magazine while she waited. Ali arrived in a flurry from work.

'Sorry I'm late, I've been so busy since I got back from my holidays, it is like I never had a break I'm so stressed. Anyway, it is great to see you.'

As they hugged, Ali pulled out her wallet and handed a cheque to Molly.

'What is that?' Molly asked in surprise.

'It is for the engagement party, of course. You were a huge hit, Robin is still talking about those profiteroles! Thank you so much.'

'Ali, are you mad? I can't accept this. I did it for you as a friend, and I was delighted that you trusted me, but I don't want your money.'

'Too late, Molly, we are paying you, you are our first "wedding expense"!'

So Molly took the cheque, and was secretly delighted, and knew straight away she would take Luke out for dinner tonight to celebrate. Somewhere nice, as he was always treating her to the finest restaurants in Dublin.

'But Molly, that isn't the big news I had. Well, I wanted to ask you something else, in relation to cooking. Will you cater our wedding?'

Molly was speechless. A wedding was a huge deal, a massive event, it would blow the niblets and finger food engagement-party job out of the water. But would it be too much for her to handle? she wondered.

'And before you say you won't be able to: I know you can. We would love you to do it, you are so talented and I would trust you completely. I would rather give you the business than some other random old caterer. Molly – I know you can do it.'

Molly didn't know what to say. A job like this could really get her going on the catering scene and would also be extra money for her, a lot of extra money. And she was sure she could get her cousin and aunt to help her.

'OK,' she said impulsively. 'I'll do it. Thanks so much, and I promise the food will be to die for!'

The girls spent the next few hours chatting about the wedding, food ideas and the all-important wedding cake!

47

Ali was busy at work, but so happy that Molly had agreed to cater her wedding, or as Robin kept correcting her, 'their wedding'! Molly was a great cook, and Ali trusted she would know what was best for the day, and she liked to help a friend out. It was weird to be back at work, and back to real life after the excitement of being on holiday on a different continent, and then the engagement. Now she was back to hundreds of files, emails and meetings.

It had been a bit of an anti-climax arriving at work the first morning. The receptionist and the girls in accounts had seemed very excited, and asked her a million questions, and had kept trying the ring on. But Mary, her boss, had congratulated her, had a quick look at the ring, and then, after a few awkward questions about how it had happened, turned back to her computer and begun working as usual. She must be jealous, Ali had thought, but even so, her reaction had put a dampener on the whole thing. Although that didn't stop Ali checking wedding websites and forums every time Mary turned her back or left the office. It was amazing how obsessed some people became with themselves and their own wedding. There were people on those forums that had minute-by-minute countdowns to their weddings, even though they were years away! Ali and Robin did not want a long engagement. They had waited long enough, and just wanted to walk up that aisle and say I do. As exciting as a wedding is, it was being married that was the important thing for them, so they were going to do it as soon as they could.

48

Sarah and Tom were discussing what godparents should buy a newborn baby, over a cup of coffee. Sarah wanted to do something different, like buying a star in her name or adopting an animal on her behalf, while Tom preferred something more practical, like a year's supply of diapers. 'Because that's all she seems to want and need,' he joked. They were both very proud godparents, and were for ever taking out their camera phones to show everyone the latest picture of baby Fiona. Sarah was convinced Fiona was going to be tall like herself, and kept checking the baby's hair to see if she would be blonde, too!

Mel said having a baby was a real shock to the system and she hadn't slept one wink yet, and that, as everyone kept reminding her, she wasn't going to sleep properly until the baby was eighteen! Sarah loved calling in and holding Fiona, there was nothing like the smell of a newborn baby. Her mum had practically moved in and spent every minute advising Mel what to do and not do, in-between ringing her friends to give them every possible update on Fiona. They were all very excited and couldn't wait to be grandparents themselves, she informed Sarah.

It was so cute to see Tom so excited also. He was madly in love with his new niece, had helped his brother John erect the baby crib, and didn't bat an eyelid when Mel had to breastfeed in front of everyone. It was lovely to see men so excited about babies, and Sarah just wished her dad had still been alive to help them all celebrate.

While she was discussing baby gifts with Tom, Sarah received a phone call from Hugh. In just over a week, they had seen each other three times. He was very interesting, and more grown-up than any of her previous dates: a real man, who rang when he said he would, and was not at all scared of making plans a few weeks down the line.

'Sarah, I'm running into a meeting, but wanted to see whether you were free on Saturday afternoon. My local rugby club from home, Galwegians, are coming to play in Dublin this weekend against Blackrock. Anyway, my two brothers are coming up to see the match, and they would love to meet you, and it would be great if you came. What do you say?'

Sarah wasn't so sure, meeting someone's family was way down the line in dating – it wasn't supposed to happen so soon – but then Hugh was so nice, and she didn't want to disappoint him, so she agreed. As she hung up the phone, Tom looked at her with his big blue eyes.

'So you have got another boyfriend? That was quick!'

Sarah knew he was referring to his friend Ross.

'Tom, I really don't want to talk to you about this and get into a he-said, she-said thing, but Ross was not who I thought he was, and he was hardly my boyfriend. So, yes, I'm entitled to date someone else, someone who is just perfect.' After that Tom shut up and just stirred his cappuccino.

Later that night Sarah was meeting Ali to go and see the latest Leonardo DiCaprio film. Sarah filled Ali in on Hugh Hyland and the impending rugby match date.

'Rugby matches are a nightmare for girls,' she said. 'You

need to wrap up warm to go to the match, so you go along in your hat, gloves, and plenty of warm sensible clothes, but then when you go for drinks after, you don't want to be standing there all night in your fleece and sensible flat shoes. And you can't go to the match in stilettos and a string top just to look good later, as you then look like you've tried too hard – and freeze to death. It's a nightmare!'

'You will be fine. Sure, guys don't notice anything – you could run into the bathroom and come out in your deb's dress and they wouldn't notice you'd changed!' Ali laughed.

'You are probably right, Ali. It is just that I'm nervous about seeing his two brothers. Meeting family for the first time is always hard, everyone is scrutinizing you, and you don't know what to expect.'

Ali paid for their popcorn and drinks and they started walking up the cinema escalators still continuing the conversation. Ali said: 'You think that rugby match will be hard? The first time I met Robin's parents it was a real nightmare. We were all going to Cork for the night for his granny's eightieth birthday. So first of all I had to sit facing his parents for three hours, and that is a long time face-to-face with your boyfriend's parents who you have just met. And then when we got to the hotel I didn't know what to expect, as his dad had booked three hotel rooms. One was obviously for the parents, but then there was me, Robin and his brother and sister, and as this was my first time meeting them, I didn't know if they would let me stay with Robin or if I would have to share with his sister. So you should have seen my bag: one side had all my Victoria's Secret best lingerie, while the other had my Penney's granny-style fleece pyjamas and dressing gown! It was so funny, but such a relief when his dad handed me and Robin the keys to our own room.'

Sarah was relieved to hear that really everyone was nervous about meeting their partner's family, and decided to relax and enjoy the movie, and not worry about what to wear until Saturday came.

49

Luke was walking into his apartment when he froze: all over the kitchen table were wedding magazines, and little bride and groom ornament cake-tops. There were also candles everywhere and wine open. Oh my God, was Molly going to propose? Had she lost her mind? He didn't even hear Molly approach from behind to give him a big hug and kiss. She stopped when she realized he was stiff with shock – literally frozen.

'What's wrong?' she asked.

'Molly, what are you doing? What's with all the wedding stuff?' Molly looked at the magazines and wedding-cake toppings and started laughing.

'Luke, did you think I was trying to give you engagement hints? As if I would be that obvious! No, I just want to start getting ideas for Ali's wedding, so I bought some magazines today, and I got a bit carried away when I saw some lovely Mr and Mrs cake toppings. Relax, they are for them, not us!' But Luke didn't laugh.

'It's obvious you are thinking about it, why else would you leave this stuff here for me to trip over? Well, if you think we are going to get married when every night our house is full of your work projects, and all we talk about is other people's parties and what you will make for them to eat, then you can forget it. I don't bring my work home and I don't see why you have to, either.'

And with that Luke walked back out of the door. What was wrong with him? Molly worried. She looked down and saw one of the little marzipan bride and grooms had fallen off the table and smashed in half, totally broken.

50

On Saturday morning Ben booked a restaurant for that night with Laura. He hadn't seen her for a few weeks, and was eager to make a good impression. He didn't quite know her taste yet, but thought Baan Thai in Ballsbridge would be a safe bet. Thai was his favourite and that restaurant was always busy and had a great atmosphere. It would be perfect. He was looking forward to meeting her later, and was trying to iron a shirt when he saw his mum out in the garden pruning bushes and planting new flowers.

Maura O'Connor was having a dinner party that night and was trying to get the garden looking just right. She still had the shopping to do, but would run out to Donnybrook Fair for fish and a nice dessert for later. Joe was taking Honey for a walk while he went to get the newspaper, in the hope of tiring the over-energetic dog out. Maura did not want a night of dog-barking and whingeing to ruin her dinner party. Maura dragged the lawnmower out of the garage and dumped it in the middle of the lawn. The grass was in desperate need of a cut, and she wanted it looking well tonight. Her gardener was away, but since Ben was home she would get him to do it. As Ben made himself a BLT and watched *Soccer AM* his mum came into the kitchen.

'Ben, I need that lawn cut this afternoon, before our guests arrive later.'

'What? Mum, I can't. I'm running late for meeting the lads, we are all going to watch the Blackrock versus Galwegians rugby match at two p.m.'

'Well then, you can race home from the rugby club and do it after the match, it needs to be done.'

'I can't, I'm meeting Laura for dinner right after. Sorry, Mum. I'll do it next time, I promise.'

And with that Ben headed out the door, but as he did Maura shouted after him. 'Ben, you will have that grass cut by tonight or I'll let Mango out of his cage to fly away, I really will.'

But Ben did not hear his mum, and jumped in his car and headed for the rugby club. Maura followed him out shortly, herself, to buy food for the dinner party, all the while complaining to herself that Ben was so lazy – and how would any girl ever marry him?

Joe O'Connor came home from his walk, and after making sure himself and the dog had plenty of water to help them cool down, he put the kettle on for a cup of tea. Then he saw the lawnmower out on the lawn. Maura must want the grass mowed. As he couldn't see Ben anywhere he decided he would give it a go himself; he hadn't cut the grass in a while, but he knew how important it was to Maura that the place looked good for their guests. He was an avid gardener himself, and it was a passion they both shared, but cutting the grass held no passion for him! Even so, he changed into a T-shirt and his old gardening shorts, and started up the engine.

Within ten minutes the mower started feeling heavier and a shooting pain ran up and down Joe's right arm, but it wasn't until his chest felt like it was about to burst, and he couldn't breathe that he thought something more serious than being unfit might be wrong. But by that stage he was lying on the lawn, and as he fell unconscious all he could worry about was that Maura wouldn't be able to cope with seeing him like this, and he prayed that Ben might find him first. And then everything went dark.

Ben had just congratulated the Blackrock captain over their mighty win over the Galway team when his mobile rang. It was home. He ignored it at first as he thought it would be his mum asking him to come back and mow the lawn. But when it rang for the fifth time he answered and heard not his mum or dad's voice but their neighbour Breda.

'Ben, it's Breda, I'm so sorry to tell you this, but your father has had a heart-attack. He is in a bad way. Your mum found him right in the middle of the lawn, but we've no idea how long he was there for, he was trying to cut the grass. Your mum has gone to the hospital in the ambulance, but asked me to ring you. You need to go there straight away, Ben. It is serious.'

Ben didn't even reply. As she talked he just started walking, and then running out of the clubhouse. His dad was dying, and he needed to get there as soon as he could.

51

Sarah was having a great Saturday at the rugby match. After hours of stress about her clothes she had decided to wear a v-neck cream top from River Island, but with a black Roxy polo neck and a warm puffa jacket over it to keep her warm, and now she was relaxing and enjoying a few beers with Hugh and his two brothers. They looked very like him, but older. Both were enjoying the day, even if their team had lost. But, as they said, they had really come to see Hugh anyway, so they weren't too upset. She was very nervous at the start, and felt like she had to crack lots of jokes, but they were kind, and laughed, and seemed to enjoy her company. It was still all very new with Hugh, and when he rested his hand on her lower back as she chatted to people she felt tingles go up her spine. It felt nice, right.

She had spotted Robin's friend Ben earlier, and he had waved over at her. Wanting to say hi properly, she had made her way over to him, but he had literally run past her while on his mobile phone and hadn't even said hello. How rude, she thought. Thank God Robin never succeeded in setting me up with him. And with that she had headed back to Hugh.

Hugh's brothers loved telling embarrassing stories about Hugh when he was a kid, and joking about how he was now a city boy and not a true Galway man any more. Hugh took great offence at this and insisted he was going to go back one day to live there. All four of them enjoyed the live music that the rugby club had arranged and settled in for a few more beers, before deciding to go for dinner to a local Italian.

'You are doing great, Sarah, they love you. Thanks so much for coming,' Hugh whispered to her as they walked in the door of Toscana's Italian restaurant overlooking Dun Laoghaire harbour.

Sarah was delighted at how it was all going, and as they ordered bruschetta and big bowls of pasta she felt herself relax and enjoy just being there with Hugh.

52

Laura was on her second glass of white wine when the waiter asked her for the fifth time if she wanted to order any food. Food? Laura thought. I just want to cry. She had never been more embarrassed in her whole life. Ben had said he would be here by 9 p.m., and it was now after 10 p.m. She had tried his mobile but it was turned off. How immature to stand me up like this! He was old enough to just say he didn't see them going anywhere, instead of arranging a dinner date and then not turning up, leaving her mortified and the talk of the whole restaurant. It was obvious she was waiting for someone, but she'd waited long enough, so as she signalled for the bill she rang Ali to see if she was still out for drinks with the girls, and if they could meet up. She wasn't going to waste this new dress and the fact that she had gotten her long curly hair straightened in the hairdresser that afternoon. She might as well go out and have a good night, and as she jumped into a taxi she vowed never to talk to Ben O'Connor ever again.

Ali was having drinks with some of her friends in the Clarence Bar. They had ordered bottles of sparkling wine, and it was going down a treat. She was having a great night, retelling the Table Mountain story again and again. It was a great feeling to have everyone wish you well and offer congratulations.

The barman had even been persuaded to give them a bottle of wine on the house to help celebrate the engagement ring!

It was funny, though, Ali thought for the millionth time since she had come back from South Africa, how people didn't seem to feel happy you were committing yourself to someone you adored, and they didn't congratulate you on finding your soulmate. Instead, once they saw the ring all anyone was interested in was how you would be doing your hair on the big day. It did get to her, sometimes.

One of the girls was asking which church she was booking. 'I presume Donnybrook, or maybe Booterstown? I mean, that would be the closest if you are going to book the Four Seasons in Ballsbridge or something for after.'

'Donnybrook? Ballsbridge? Are you girls mad?' Ali asked. 'I'm from Kilkenny, in case you have forgotten. Myself and Robin have decided that we are going to have the reception at my family home, on the farm, in Kilkenny.'

'Kilkenny? But where will I get my hair done that morning? And what about your fake tan and all? Will they be as good as Blue Eriu on South William Street? I only ever get my beauty stuff done there. I wouldn't trust anyone else,' one of the girls informed Ali.

Ali was in shock as the girls all started asking a million questions about how a 'Kilkenny farm wedding' would work. It was at times like these that she did feel isolated from her slightly spoilt South Dublin friends, and wonder if she should move home and sink back into her country girl routine. She was very glad when Laura suddenly arrived, and with a cocktail in each hand began a rant about Ben, men, and Thai restaurants. It was good to get the focus off weddings and Kilkenny, thought Ali, as she ordered more wine.

53

Ben had gotten a huge shock when he had arrived at the hospital earlier. His mum, normally so loud, chatty and full of life, was totally still, stunned. She looked like she had aged ten years. She appeared frail as she talked to the doctor, but when she saw Ben walk through the doors of the emergency room, she just crumpled. Ben had to run to catch her. She broke down in sobs.

'I can't live without him, Ben. If he does not survive I'll not survive. I'm devoted to him, I'll not be able to live.'

Ben didn't know what to say, he felt the same. He took his dad for granted, but the sudden thought of not seeing his cheerful face ever again made Ben almost throw up.

'Where is he?' is all Ben could finally say.

The nurse showed him through to his dad's room. Joe was still unconscious and hooked up to monitors, drips and machines. That is not my dad, Ben thought, it can't be. My dad is strong and tall like me, plays golf almost every day, and has a permanent tan from the wind on the golf course. This man was so frail-looking he barely took up any space on the bed. His face was white as a ghost, his lips almost blue.

'How can this be? Why did it happen?' Ben cried out.

His mum choked up. 'I came in the door from grocery shopping and saw him lying right in the middle of the lawn, with the lawnmower still on beside him. He was totally still. I thought he was dead. The silly old fool was trying to cut the grass for our party. I don't care if we never cut the grass again, if it means even one more day with him. He should never have gone near that blasted lawnmower.'

Ben felt sick. He knew what his mum was not saying, what she was trying not to say as she looked at him. It was all his fault. She had asked him to cut the grass. It's all my fault, my stupid lazy fault, he thought. And with that tears rolled down Ben's face.

54

Ben and Maura never left Joe's side all through that night. His vital signs never changed, but it did not matter, they held his hand and hoped and prayed that God would save him.

'He means too much to people here to go anywhere yet,' Maura whispered, as if to God himself.

'Ben, what will I do if anything happens?' Maura asked the same question over and over again. Ben had no answer. What could he say?

The nurses and doctors came in to check on Joe regularly. Eventually, when the cardiologist came back in, Ben took him aside.

'What can I do? I'll do anything for him, doctor. Anything to help save my dad.'

'I'm sorry, but there is nothing you can do for now. He has suffered a major heart-attack and we need to do more tests to see if we need to operate. We'll know more in the morning,' and with that the doctor was gone.

Ben felt like everything was moving in slow motion. Nurses walked by him chatting, going about their daily lives, but Ben felt as though he was walking in quicksand, nothing was working. He couldn't get his brain to think, he was in too much shock. Everything had been turned upside down.

Maura O'Connor was in total shock, too. Her husband lay

totally still in a metal hospital bed, in a crammed room, in a cold hospital. This was not right. This can't be happening, she kept telling herself. How can it be that one minute your life is perfect, you have a great husband, great house, great friends, a comfortable life, and next minute everything is wrong? Joe was her life, he was her soulmate and best friend. He knew her better than she knew herself. She had known from the day she met him that she would marry him. He was always so kind, caring, and gentle, and she had known he was the one for her. All those years of marriage and happy times seemed to have flown by, and now was this how it ended?

By Sunday evening Ben knew his mum needed to sleep and take a break.

'Why don't you go home for a few hours, Mum, and I'll keep vigil here? I'll ring you if anything happens.'

'No way. I'm not leaving your dad. Over my dead body. I would not forgive myself if anything happened while I was gone.'

Ben knew one of them needed to go home to get some clothes for them both, and some of Joe's things in case he woke up, so he decided to rush home himself. He promised to bring back clothes, food and his dad's favourite slippers.

After a quick talk to the nurse, asking her to ring him if anything happened, he jumped into a taxi and headed home. The house was cold, and felt so empty when he walked in. How could they live here if anything happened to Joe? His dad made this house a home. Honey was asleep in the kitchen, but jumped up with great excitement to see him.

'You just want food, isn't it?' Ben almost laughed.

Their neighbour had left food out for Honey but it was long gone now. Ben let the Labrador out into the garden as he opened a fresh can of dog food. Mango awoke as well, and Ben cleaned out his cage and left more seeds in it for him.

The kitchen table was covered in groceries from when his mum had been shopping the day before. Their neighbour had kindly put anything that could spoil away in the fridge, but the breads, pastas, and his dad's favourite biscuits lay out. Ben took out a bag, and placed the biscuits into it. He started to make some sandwiches, too – his mum could do with them, as the hospital food was like plastic. He packed up a mini-picnic, and set it down by the front door, while he went upstairs to shower quickly and change his clothes. His ticket stub to the rugby match fell out of his pocket. The match seemed like months ago, Ben thought, a lifetime ago.

After changing, he went into his parents' room to get some clothes. His mum had asked for her tracksuit and some warm jumpers. He also packed her perfume and some make-up: he knew she liked to look nice, even under stress. He grabbed a book that was by her bedside and flung that in too. You never know how long we'll be in the hospital, he thought. He approached his dad's wardrobe with apprehension: he was nervous, it felt wrong going through his things while he lay almost dead miles away. The smell hit him, it was his dad's smell. It reminded him of hugging his dad when he was younger, of running into his arms when he had fallen or was upset. When was the last time I hugged him properly? he wondered. The last time I told him I loved him? As he packed up Joe's clothes and slippers, an old photo frame caught his eye. Ben was about seven years old, and his team had just won their mini-rugby cup, and Ben was sitting on Joe's shoulders, raised high with the cup swinging around, but he had one arm wrapped tightly around his dad's neck, as he still needed his dad for protection and security. His dad's arms were clasped firmly on Ben's legs, and Joe's smile was bigger than anyone's, he was so proud. Ben choked up.

'Have I ever made you proud since then?' Ben said out

loud to an empty house. 'Ever let you know I still need your protection?'

'It is my turn to protect you now,' Ben said to the photo, as Joe's face smiled back at him.

As he called Honey back into the kitchen, he saw the lawnmower lying sideways on the grass. Ben ran up to it and kicked it with the anger that had built up since his dad's heart-attack.

'You bastard,' he shouted at the machine. Honey joined in, and barked at the machine, and before he knew it Mango was squawking, too. The three of them stayed like that for quite some time, howling at whoever would listen.

55

Molly tried to go home every weekend for a Sunday roast with her family. Tonight her mum was making a rhubarb crumble for dessert and Molly was helping her. Her mum was still the best cook she knew.

'Now, if you want to make this gluten-free I can show you. It's handy to know how to do it.'

Molly loved it that her mum knew so much about cooking, yet took it all in her stride. It was like she had been born with the gift. Molly never remembered them ever being given a bad meal or a burnt cake or biscuit. Their food was always perfect and yum!

As Molly stewed the rhubarb she mentioned to her mum that she was thinking of taking up a new baking class that was taking place in Temple Bar every Monday for the next eight weeks.

'The only problem is that myself and Luke had said we might take up scuba-diving lessons, so we would be prepared for our summer holiday in Greece. Luke has great plans for many scuba holidays. I don't mind once we work our way up to somewhere like the Caribbean! But I'm worried he might be upset if I cancel that course to do the baking one.'

Molly's mum put down her baking dish.

'Molly, you are only young once, and have to do what

makes you happy, and not regret anything. Cooking is your passion, and your job now, and I think the course would not only give you more confidence but would be very helpful for the café, and for yourself, what with the wedding job coming up and all. I'm sure Luke will understand if you explain it properly.'

Molly didn't know that he would, but she didn't want to upset her mum, so she just nodded and patted the crumble.

Dinner at home was so relaxing, and Molly always felt so warm and safe with the Aga cooker in the background and her mum preparing food. Their kitchen was like an old country kitchen, with not only the Aga, but a large dresser, filled with a collection of painted delft. Cookery books fell out of every shelf, and there was a permanent smell of baking no matter what time of the day you walked into this heart of their home. Molly loved the old picture on the dresser, too, showing her at about six years old, covered in flour as she helped her mum make a Christmas cake. She was standing on a chair, leaning up against their island unit in order to reach the mixing bowl, her mum smiling into the camera, proud of her budding chef daughter.

Molly's brother was home also, and it was good to catch up with him.

'Getting that wedding job is great news, little sister. Maybe you will be able to set up your own business soon. Don't forget, you can hire me as your business director, and get me out of my boring job!'

Molly promised she would, but told him not to hold his breath, that was a few years off yet. As her mum dropped her home that night, she kissed Molly.

'Don't let your holiday plans ruin your cooking dreams and your job. We all love you, Luke loves you, he will understand. I love you, Molly, thanks for your help tonight.' And with that her mum was gone and Molly walked back to her very modern apartment, and into a kitchen that could have been a million miles from the one she had just left.

56

Luke was not a bit happy when Molly told him she was cancelling her scuba-diving course. They'd been fighting so much recently that she sensed he didn't want to make a big deal out of it; he just sulked around for the evening, and didn't mention it again. The next day at work, Molly's aunt was delighted to hear she was doing the baking course.

'It will help inspire you, pet, and we could do with a few new recipes here.'

Molly was in great form, thrilled about starting her new training. Her excitement lasted all day, and when she went to take her usual sandwich delivery to Sterling Bank, she decided to throw in some of her honeymen biscuits for free, anything to spice up those men's taste buds! Scott Williams was deep in conversation on the phone when she walked through the door, but he stopped abruptly as she approached. He smiled when she handed him his sandwich.

'And as a treat, I've one of these for you,' she said, giving him the little honeyman. 'Compliments of Heavenly.'

Scott looked at the biscuit man. 'Isn't he the lucky man to be spending time with such a lovely cook!' And with that he turned back to his phone and started to unwrap his sandwich.

Weirdo, thought Molly, as she walked through the office

handing out the rest of the sandwiches. But when she got back to the café her aunt said there was a message from Sterling Bank saying they would like to order a hundred honeymen for a staff-training exercise the next day. Maybe Scott Williams wasn't so bad, after all.

57

Sarah's mum had been driving her mad with questions about Hugh Hyland. Ever since he had dropped her home on Sunday morning, after she had stayed at his place the night before, Sarah's mum had been saying how polite and nice he was, and wasn't Galway a fabulous city! And when she had heard that he was a big art collector, Sarah had thought her mum would faint.

'He is perfect, Sarah, and it is such a romantic story that you met in the gallery,' her mum exclaimed. Sarah knew it was a great story, but didn't want to jinx the relationship yet by predicting what might happen in the future.

'Let's just take it slow, Mum. People don't just rush into things nowadays.'

'I know, isn't that the problem, though? You all have too many options, and think there will be something better around the corner, when really you are missing out on what is in front of you. Don't let that happen to you, pet,' her mum said, as they got in the car to go and visit Mel and the new baby.

It was at times like these that Sarah wished she had enough money to buy her own place, just to have more privacy. She loved her mother, but made a mental note to go some time soon to see a mortgage broker that worked near her. It might be worth finding out what property she could afford.

*　　*　　*

When Sarah and her mum arrived at Mel's place it was bedlam. There were dirty and wet clothes everywhere, dirty dishes piled high in the sink, and Mel looked like she hadn't washed her hair in weeks.

'Mum!' Mel cried, as she saw them come through the door. She handed Sarah Fiona and fell into her mum's arms. 'I'm so exhausted, I don't know how I'm going to cope. The place is a mess, Fiona goes through more clothes than a catwalk show, and if I don't bring the bins down soon the health authority will shut this place down for all the smell of dirty nappies.'

Sarah's mum guided Mel into her bedroom. 'Why don't you lie down for a little while, and I'll run you a bath? Sarah will look after Fiona and we'll help get this place shipshape.'

Mel was too worn out to protest, and after only a few minutes Sarah could hear heavy snores coming from her sister's bedroom. She started to change Fiona's nappy. It was at times like these that being a godmother seemed a lot more attractive than being an actual mother.

As if her mum could read her mind she said: 'All mums get a little panicked at the start, Sarah, but Mel will be fine. And so will you, one day.'

Once Mel and Fiona were settled Sarah headed off to meet Hugh at the cinema. He was an avid film fan, and Sarah laughed at the way he got excited about every 'coming soon' movie poster on the way up the escalator. He was sweet, and fussed about, making sure she had a good seat and plenty of food. As the film played, Sarah relaxed her head against his shoulder, and it felt right. She was at the cinema with her boyfriend. It might be a mundane activity for most people, but it made her feel excited and yet calm at the same time. Things were going right for her. This time she could make a relationship last, she could feel it.

Her mum thought she could feel it, too, and when Sarah came back from the cinema that night she was surprised to see her mum looking through Mel and John's wedding photo album.

'What are you doing?' Sarah asked hesitantly.

'Well, I just wanted to look at photos from that day at the golf club. If you and Hugh were to get married we would need to book it soon, as it has gotten so popular, and when I look at these old photos I am reminded why. It really is a beautiful venue and so close to home. I know you might think I'm looking too far ahead, but you are no spring chicken, pet, so you might want to rush this relationship on quicker. It would be fabulous to be planning another wedding!'

Sarah didn't know what to do, except head for bed. But as she got changed into her pyjamas she took out the mortgage broker's number and decided to go and see him first thing in the morning. She had to move out! It was urgent, she needed a change.

58

Ali had just got off the phone with the priest, Father Patrick Conway. He was an old family friend from back home, and only too happy to agree to marry her and Robin. After a long discussion the night before with Robin, and an even longer one on the phone with her parents, they had all decided that a marquee on one of the fields on the farm down home would be the best wedding venue ever. They would have no restriction on numbers, or available dates, or decor; they could get married when they wanted, and have the marquee looking however they felt. Her father had said, though, that it would be better to get married in drier warm weather, so the marquee wouldn't sink, and none of the girls would ruin their fancy shoes or dresses getting muddy walking in and out of it. So even though it was only four months away, they decided on the August Bank Holiday weekend.

It was much sooner than they'd thought they would tie the knot, and Ali knew everyone would think it was a shot-gun wedding, but it wasn't. She just wanted to be married to Robin as soon as possible. She knew it would be more hard work, trying to organize dresses, the church ceremony, the reception music, honeymoon and God knows what else in four months, but she knew she could do it. And once Father Conway confirmed he was free that weekend Ali was relieved and excited that they could now plough ahead with all the other plans. She rang Molly to say the date and venue had been confirmed. Molly was only too happy that it was a marquee and that she would not be stepping on the toes of another chef in a hotel.

Ali's mum had given her a gift of a 'wedding planner' diary and she took off the wrapper and stated filling in the date, making lists of things to do. It was going to be a long list!

She rang her mum to see if she and Ali's two sisters Jill and Kate could come to Dublin the following weekend, to start looking for 'the dress'. She had no idea what she wanted yet, but knew she had to get cracking on finding it.

Ali had tilted her computer screen, so her boss couldn't see she was surfing bridal-dress websites, and the second she was on her own printed off any dresses that caught her eye. Two-piece strapless simple ones grabbed her the most. As she filled an empty folder with the pictures she started to get excited. I'll be wearing one of these soon! Just then the silent but deadly Mary came in to leave a file on her desk, Ali managed to minimize the Kathy de Stafford bridal-dress website just in time. Thank God for the minimize button and whoever invented it, Ali thought, as her screen now showed a boring word document.

59

Ali and Robin had met for lunch and sandwiches in Merrion Square.

'Can you ring your cousin to see who she used for photographs? Wedding photographers are so expensive, but all the websites say you do need them as you want to have the best photographs to keep for ever. And can you also ask your parents to start making up their guest lists? Dad needs to know what size marquee to book.'

Robin opened his chicken tikka wrap and sighed. The wedding was all they talked about, all Ali seemed to think about. And she used her mum like a hotline twenty-four hours a day. Of course he was dying for the big day, but guys just didn't care as much about all the fuss and little details as girls did. Ali didn't seem to understand this. And yet, she read his mind.

'Robin, I know I'm driving you mad, but if we don't book things like a photographer, florist, caterer, priest, musicians, et cetera, no one else will, and the wedding will be a disaster. We just have to discuss and book them now, so we can have the most perfect day ever.'

Robin smiled, and was trying to talk about the latest TV episode of *Lost*, when Ali interrupted.

'Father Conway says we've to do a marriage preparation course, and soon.'

'What? Why would we need to do one of them? We've been together for years, we own a place together, and know each other inside out. I mean, those courses sound old-fashioned, and are probably just priests trying to tell you not to sleep together until marriage. Well, too late!' He laughed.

'Robin, I know it sounds weird, but it isn't just about sex or religion. It's about building a future together, talking about kids, family issues and more. And anyway it makes no difference if you want to do it or not, Father Conway says we've to do one, and show him the course certificate when we've finished.'

They never show you this in Hollywood wedding films, Robin thought: being locked up on some stupid weekend course talking about God and children.

'Now, Robin, I rang ACCORD, the organization that holds these courses, and there is a huge wait for all the Dublin ones, but when I mentioned I was from Kilkenny they said we would be allowed to do one there. So they have a place for us in two weekends' time, and we can stay with my parents, too! It will be great. What do you think?'

Robin didn't know what to say. A weekend talking to strangers about marriage, and staying with Ali's parents, who would be talking non-stop about florists and marquees, didn't sound appealing. But when he saw the look in Ali's eyes, he knew he had to say yes.

'That's great, I'll ring them to confirm when I get back to the office.' And she opened her wedding planner to write more notes. That planner was like her holy grail, Robin laughed to himself. I should have proposed with one of them, instead of a ring that took years to save for, it would have been cheaper and a lot more useful.

60

Ben sat watching as the nurse took his dad's pulse and checked him over.

'We will bring him to theatre first thing in the morning. Mr Daly, the surgeon, will take good care of him there. Try not to worry,' the lovely staff nurse told Ben and Maura.

The doctor had told them the day before that Joe was now ready for surgery. He had been in and out of consciousness, but Ben didn't know if Joe even knew where he was. I hope he doesn't, though, Ben thought. His dad would hate to know what had become of him: that days had passed, drips been attached and disconnected, blood tests taken, scans and ultrasounds done, and yet Joe had felt nothing, his body betraying him.

The last few days had all blurred into one. Ben had sat with his mother, and side by side they had silently worried about Joe. Ben felt angry: his father was a good man, he didn't smoke, or drink much, he played golf and exercised, he was a great husband and tried to be the best father. Even if I refused his help over and over, Ben thought. Ben didn't understand why this was happening. When he looked at his father, images and memories flashed before him, from Joe bringing him to school for the first time, to Joe teaching him how to play golf, and helping him study for college. His father had always been

157

there for Ben, and Ben intended to be there for him now. In the past Ben had let his father down, he knew that, but he promised God he would change if only He would let his father pull through. Ben would change and be there for his mum and dad from now on.

The day after the accident he had rung his friend Jeremy to say that he needed to take all his holiday entitlement, he had to be here with his mum and dad. Jeremy had understood, and said to keep in touch. Jeremy had briefly informed him what was happening at work, but it felt weird to Ben to think that normal life was going on, while his life was on hold, waiting and watching to see what would happen to his dad.

Life within a hospital was like being inside a bubble, with everyone only thinking of charts, test results, drips, doctors' rounds and medication. It wasn't until Robin rang, under pressure from Ali, to ask him why he had stood Laura up the previous Saturday, that he even remembered they'd had a date. Once he told Robin what had happened Robin had felt awful, and said not to worry, he would tell Laura. Ben knew he should have rung her himself, but he barely even knew her. How could he explain how he felt: that if anything happened to his dad not only would his mum die, but Ben wouldn't be able to live with the guilt of causing his dad to have a heart-attack. Ben's brain wasn't working, and he felt that speaking to Laura could only make things worse. She was better off without him.

The O'Connors' neighbours and friends had been marvellous, with someone looking after the house and pets, while others dropped in home-cooked meals – which was a godsend as the hospital food was stereotypically awful. It all made Ben realize how loved and respected his father was, how many friends his parents had. Ben felt he would be lucky to have people care for him as much.

When his mum wasn't crying she was telling Ben old stories: of how she and Joe had met, how Joe had proposed, how he was so romantic, how he was so proud the day Ben was born, and how he had worked late all those years to build up the business and pay for Ben's school fees and their comfortable lifestyle.

'I am blessed to be with a man like your father, Ben. I hope one day some girl can say the same about you.'

The next morning, when Joe was wheeled down to surgery, Ben followed his mum into the small hospital chapel. She clasped her hands around her wedding ring, and prayed that her husband would survive. Ben prayed that God would save his mum the pain of becoming a widow, and promised that no matter what the outcome was he, as the only child, would provide for her, would become the man of the house. And even though he knew he could not fill his father's boots, he was determined to try his best.

61

Molly sat on the DART. She was going out to visit Sarah for dinner. She had been dying to see Mel and the new baby, and when Sarah invited her to dinner with them she had jumped at the chance. She'd known Sarah and her family her whole life, and was so excited that someone she knew actually had a small baby!

She had gone to Next at the weekend and picked some beautiful babygros for Fiona: they had dog paw-prints on them and little hoods with dog ears. She had also brought a basket of cheeses and homemade brown bread for Mel. Molly didn't know if Mel was still craving cheese, but thought it better to err on the side of caution, after all the cheese-related incidents she had heard from Sarah!

When she arrived at the house, Sarah's mum greeted her with a great big hug and kiss.

'I know my cooking won't compare to the fabulous delights you normally make, but I hope my chicken wrapped in bacon will be all right.'

Molly assured her that she was no masterchef and was just delighted to see them all again, and finally meet Fiona. The baby was so cute: she was fair-headed and very long, just like her mum and aunt. As Sarah and Molly opened a bottle of wine and gloated over her, Mel talked about the christening.

'John's mum is very keen to have her christened very soon, I think she is afraid that the Antichrist will snatch her or something while we are out grocery shopping! And since John's uncle Kevin is a priest and home from America on holiday in a few weeks' time, she wants to have it then. I think it is way too early, but what can I do, Mum?'

'Mel, just do it. There's no harm in christening a baby early, is there? And I would love to help with the party. Myself and Sarah could decorate the place and Molly, you could do the food, couldn't you? You are the food expert, and we would pay you, of course.'

Molly was delighted, she was chuffed to be getting asked to do another event on her own, it would be a great experience for her. As Mel delved in to the cheese, herself and Molly discussed what food you should serve at a christening.

On the train back home that night Molly couldn't help wondering how she was so lucky: why she was getting asked to do so much work, and above all, why so many people trusted and believed in her. She texted Luke the good news, and literally skipped into the apartment with excitement, but stopped short when she saw he wasn't home. She was surprised two hours later when he still hadn't returned. Where was he? she thought, as she fell asleep alone.

62

The next morning, Molly awoke early, as she did every week-day to open up the café and get the ovens on. Luke was not beside her. She immediately ran to the phone. Maybe he was hurt and in hospital. But when she went into the kitchen she saw him lying asleep on the couch. She would have woken him, but could smell alcohol on his breath, and thought it better to have any conversation or fight later.

The whole morning she couldn't concentrate, and burnt two loaves of walnut bread. Aunt Fran looked at her petite niece, who seemed smaller than usual. 'You look wrecked, honey,' she said, taking in Molly's pale face, with its tight, fearful expression. 'Why don't you finish up the sandwich orders early and head off home? Maybe you are coming down with something.'

Molly was too embarrassed to tell her the truth, that her boyfriend was the problem, so she just finished a vegetarian quiche off, then took the sandwich order to Sterling Bank. How could she concentrate when her boyfriend had not only stayed out all night, but chosen not to sleep in the same bed as her, and then chosen not to ring her and apologize? She was both furious and scared.

'Are you OK, Molly?' Scott Williams asked, as she handed him his usual sandwich.

'Oh, I'm fine, Mr Williams. I'm just tired, so after this I'm heading home.'

'Well, I hate to see our favourite chef unwell. I've a meeting in Killiney in half an hour, and that must be near you as we seem to get the same bus. I've my car with me today, so why don't I drop you home on my way?'

Molly was about to refuse: she hardly knew a thing about this man, except that he loved ham, cheddar cheese and mustard on white bread. But the thought of facing the long bus ride home when she felt this sad and tired made her agree to his kind offer.

'If it is not too much trouble, Mr Williams. I mean, Scott.'

'Of course it isn't. I'll see you outside in twenty minutes.'

Molly tried to make small chat with Scott, but he sensed she was distracted and put some music on. They flew out of town, and before long Molly was getting out of the car.

'Molly, I hope you feel better soon,' Scott said. 'And that whatever is bothering you doesn't make you too sad. You don't realize how much your visits brighten up our office.' And with that he drove off in his black BMW.

'Who was that?' Luke shouted as Molly walked in the door.

'What are you doing at home?' Molly asked, surprised to see him standing in the hall.

'I was too hungover to go in, so I rang in sick, but don't try to change the subject. Who was that man? Let me guess. I'm helping you pay your bills, and subsidizing your crappy job, and you're busy having an affair, and turning me into a sucker.'

Molly almost fell back against the door.

'Luke, how can you talk to me like that? I love you, I've always loved you, and only you. That man was just a client, helping me out, giving me a lift because I've been feeling

163

worried sick all day because you didn't come home last night until God knows when, and preferred the couch to me. What's wrong with you?'

Luke sat on the couch.

'I don't know what to believe, Molly. About that man or where we're going. I went out last night for a few drinks, as you seemed as usual too busy, taking on even more work. Since you changed jobs, I thought you'd be happier, we'd be happier, but you seem more interested in pots, pans, cookers and recipes than in me. I never see you any more. We've to keep cancelling dates and nights out because of your work, and then last week to hear you didn't want to do the scuba-diving course . . . I mean, what the hell are you trying to tell me? And then when I go out for a few drinks you text me to say you have taken on more work. Where do I fit in, Molly? I seem only to be there to pay the bills.'

Molly was speechless. She couldn't believe it, Luke getting so upset and angry with her.

'You don't know where you fit in?' she shouted. 'I'll tell you where! It's beside me. You're my soulmate. I love you, Luke. If it wasn't for you and Auntie Fran I would probably still be stuck back in that miserable job in funds. I'm sorry you are not as happy about my new job, but I am. This is my life now. I adore cooking and baking, and am lucky people are paying me to do it, paying me to be happy. Why can't you see that?'

'Molly, to me, work is just work,' Luke explained. 'I don't understand why you want to spend extra hours and weekends baking and engrossed in cookery books. I'm glad you love your job, but I didn't think it would become an obsession.'

Molly was about to reply when her mobile started ringing, and she saw it was Sarah's sister Mel. Mel had said she would ring today to confirm numbers and menu for the christening.

'Take the call, Molly, it probably means more to you than I do, anyway.' And with that Luke walked out the door, and Molly had no choice but to answer the call: a client was a client.

63

Sarah was sitting outside, having her lunch overlooking Dun Laoghaire pier. She had walked down from the gallery in Monkstown and bought a chicken caesar bagel in Itsabagel, and was now watching boats coming in and out of the harbour, mothers walking buggies and babies, people strolling up and down the pier to lose weight, and people like herself getting some fresh sea air and escaping work for an hour. The bagel was very filling, and Sarah washed it down with a bottle of pink lemonade. It was a beautiful day, summer had finally arrived.

Sarah had always loved the pier, it was so refreshing to be able to spend time watching the waves, birds and boats. It was very popular with all Dublin southsiders, and you could never walk there without bumping into someone you knew. Her mum and dad had always walked her and her sister down here from their house in Monkstown when they were younger, and if it was hot enough Sarah and Mel used to walk on to Sandycove beach to play in the sand and paddle in the water. Mel was a brilliant swimmer, and when she was old enough swam in the famous Forty Foot before school each morning. Sarah was never that fond of leaving her bed early, but still always enjoyed spending weekends near the water, sand and boats – it was like being on a permanent holiday!

Sarah knew how lucky she was to live close to work, and within walking distance of the pier, beach, great shops and restaurants. It would be hard to leave this beautiful affluent area, and even though she didn't want to, the likelihood was she would be forced to if she wanted to buy her own place.

She had gone to see the mortgage broker, and after calculating the maximum mortgage she would possibly qualify for, and the largest repayments she could manage, he had told her that really it would be better if she bought a property with someone else. But who? she had asked. Her sister was married, and all her friends were in relationships.

The apartments and townhouses she could even consider buying were miles out of Dublin, or else the size of a garden shed: little matchboxes! The alternative was moving out and renting, but she always felt that was a waste, as you were just paying off someone else's mortgage. It wasn't that she hated living at home, but it was simply time that she moved out. Secretly she had always hoped she could avoid all that flat-sharing and renting with strangers, and just move from her family home to a house with her fiancé or husband, but so far that had not happened. There was such pressure to own the perfect apartment or house now, and so many people who could afford to buy something the minute they got a job. But working in a gallery was not the biggest money-earner, and being single was also a big black cross against buying anywhere. She wasn't sure what she was going to do, but for now she had to get back to work and back to earning money that one day would help her decide.

64

After days of scanning newspapers and the web for houses and apartments, Sarah was happy to forget about it for one night. So when Ali asked her if she was free to meet after work for a bite to eat and a catch-up, she said yes at once.

'That new restaurant Real Gourmet Burger has opened up in Dun Laoghaire, why don't we go there for a burger, and maybe a walk on the pier after?' Sarah suggested.

Ali had agreed and at 7 p.m. they headed into the restaurant. As it was new and had gotten rave reviews for its organic burgers with every possible topping, there was a huge queue.

'Why don't I take your name and number, girls?' the waitress said. 'I'll ring you when your table is ready, it will be about forty-five minutes.'

Sarah and Ali decided to walk the pier while they waited.

'This will help us work up an appetite for one of those big burgers,' Ali joked.

'And for me to hear all about the wedding,' Sarah said. 'I can't believe it is so soon, I can't wait.'

Ali eagerly brought her up to date on all the plans.

'My mum and sisters came up to Dublin last weekend, so we headed into Grafton Street, but it was a disaster! Every shop we went to asked what time our appointment was. Appointment? We had none, and we realized after about the sixth snotty stuck-up sales girl that you have to make appointments with all the bridal shops. And they all have waiting lists, it's awful. After all the years of waiting for a guy to ask you to marry him, you then have to wait again for a dress!'

'Yes, Ali, I should have warned you. My sister went through the same nightmare. So what did you do?'

'Well, we all had lunch in Café Bar Deli, then we went looking for bridesmaids' dresses, but that was a nightmare too. Once again you had to make an appointment, and the shops that you could walk straight into were mostly awful. Their dresses were long and heavy, completely wrong for a summer wedding. Jill and Kate are young, they want to look pretty and kind of sexy, not like some over-the-top American debutante!'

'Ali, we found a few nice places. I'll write down their names for you. But it is amazing how many bitter and twisted sales girls there are. We couldn't believe it, but I suppose they must be jealous of beautiful brides and their husbands, as most of them are over-the-hill spinsters!'

'That is exactly what we thought the other day. But Sarah, it is going to be hard, my sisters are complete opposites in every way. And they fight like cats. I can't imagine them agreeing on anything. They are so difficult. But they are coming up to Dublin again this weekend, so we'll see.'

Sarah knew the stress of picking out bridesmaid dresses, because she had been a bridesmaid along with Mel's best friend Julie. Julie was tiny and had only wanted short dresses, while Sarah, being so tall, had wanted something long. It had taken months of discussions and alterations before they had both agreed.

'Don't worry, weddings always turn out right in the end. You will find perfect dresses for everyone, and it will be fab!'

★   ★   ★

Sarah's mobile rang and it was the restaurant saying their table was ready. As the girls walked back up the pier, Ali turned to Sarah.

'Sarah, there was another reason I wanted to meet you to-night. You know I've asked Molly to do the catering?'

'Yes, Ali, she is chuffed, you are so sweet,' Sarah said.

'Well, I've got another friend who is very talented and could help me out . . . you!'

'What could I do to help you?' Sarah asked, thinking she couldn't cook or sing or perform a marriage ceremony.

'Well, you are a great artist, and you are always doodling and sketching when we are out, and your work in college was always fabulous, so I would love it if you could design me a wedding invitation.'

Sarah was stunned. She had never done anything like this before; she hadn't even shown her work in public for years.

'Sarah, I would adore it if you could do it,' encouraged Ali, her face serious. 'Imagine having my own personalized one-off invites! Please consider it.'

As they walked into the restaurant and were shown to their table a million thoughts ran through Sarah's head: could she do it, would she like to do it, what if her work was awful? But then her overriding feeling was that she loved art and painting, always had, and that she would love to do something creative to help her friend. Ever since Hugh had bought her that canvas she had been doing a lot of painting in the evenings, in her back garden, and bringing canvases down to the beach to paint surfers, boats and waves. That act of kindness and encouragement from Hugh had inspired her, so before she knew it, she had agreed to design Ali and Robin a fabulous wedding invite. And as the girls cracked open a bottle of wine, they discussed ideas, colours, paper and envelopes.

65

After meeting Sarah during the week, Ali had a large list of shops that stocked bridesmaids' dresses. Ali's mum and sisters were arriving from Kilkenny on Friday evening, so that they could head to Dublin city centre early on Saturday morning. Ali was in the middle of making them all salmon and noodles when she heard them arrive. Ali opened the door and was almost bowled over by Jill and Kate, as they both screamed how they were bursting to go to the bathroom, as their 'mean' mother hadn't stopped the whole way up. As they ran to the bathrooms, Ali gave her mum a big hug and kiss.

'They are driving me nuts, Ali. You would swear they were both getting married with their carry-on. All week they had me up and down to the city looking at other dresses, and all night looking at dresses online, and then on Wednesday after I had made a big lasagne for dinner they both announced they were on diets for the big day! Diets for bridesmaids, did you ever hear the like? Well, I was furious, so your poor father and the dogs had to eat the whole dish. So I haven't cooked them anything all week; they can cook their own bird food for all I care. And they drove me crazy all the way up here, asking how much was the budget, as they would like to get dresses tailor-made. So I just ignored them, and their cries for the bathroom, and drove as quick as I could to come see you, my little pet.'

Ali opened a bottle of red wine and handed her mum a glass. She obviously needed it.

'I know they are difficult, Mum, but they are my sisters and I want them as bridesmaids. Sarah gave me the names of places to check out, so tomorrow we'll try to find them – and me – something good.'

'Oh, don't worry about them, love, we'll look for you first, it's your big day. Did you get any appointments?' her mum asked as she sank into Ali's oversized couch.

'Yes, I did, we've the first in The Wedding Boutique at 10 a.m., then Ciara Bridal, followed by Bridal Wraptures and Pronuptia. It will be a busy day, but they have all warned me that appointments can only last a maximum of half an hour. No fairytale bridal bliss day out, then. It's all very businesslike, in and out. So we should have plenty of time to look for the girls also. Even if they are acting like Cinderella's two selfish ugly sisters!'

66

Ali spent hours fighting with her sisters over dress colours – she wanted baby pink and they wanted anything but. They kept explaining to Ali how their different hair colours and slightly different heights meant they could never wear matching dresses; but eventually they all put their differences aside and enjoyed a nice evening of food, wine and TV. The next morning, though, that wine must have gone to their heads, as Ali couldn't get Jill or Kate up.

'Five more minutes,' Jill kept on whispering.

'Jill, if we don't make this appointment by 10 a.m. then I'll have to wait two weeks for another one. That's not fair, get up.'

Kate was the same, and Ali got upset, as the day she had looked forward to all week was about to turn into a disaster.

Eventually her mum went in and shouted at the girls. 'If you two lazy lumps do not get up, then not only will Ali make me the bridesmaid but you won't be allowed to go on the hen night, or mingle with any of the groomsmen on the day. I'll make sure you are kept so busy you won't even know there are any men at the wedding.'

The fear of not meeting men must have scared Ali's two single sisters, as suddenly the girls were flinging on their tracksuits and running to the car. They were still late for their appointment, but only by ten minutes.

173

They arrived in the renowned Wedding Boutique bridal shop and saw the queues of girls and their mothers.

'You see, people are not only here early for their appointments, but others who don't even have appointments are hopeful that someone might not show at their allotted time, because then they could get to try on our fabulous dresses,' the sales assistant said.

'I was about to cancel yours, but I suppose you have made it just in time,' she added snootily, looking Ali up and down. Ali wished she had put on make-up and not worn her runners, but she had wanted to be comfortable, and ready for a day of walking all around town.

As she walked into the bridal chamber, she was stunned by the range of dresses. They were beautiful, like masterpieces. Each could paint a different picture, tell a different story. They were made of lace, silk, chiffon; they were sparkly, simple, over-the-top, short, long, and in more shades of cream and white than Ali knew existed. The range here suited the range of different girls that would walk through the door, Ali thought. No two girls are the same, so I guess no two dresses should be, either.

The dresses were surrounded by beautiful veils, tiaras, bags, shoes and wraps. 'There's everything you could possibly need,' Jill gasped. The last time they had tried to go bridal-dress shopping they had not even been allowed to look at the clothes, so they were amazed to see these once-in-a-lifetime dresses up close and personal. Ali's head spun, how could she choose the right one for her? Which type should it be?

A different sales assistant steered Ali into the extra-large changing room. 'It's to fit in all the layers, trains and veils,' the assistant laughed. She explained that it looked like there were hundreds of dresses, but really there were only about five styles.

'So, what style do you like: fishtail, A-line, column, empire or ball gown?' She showed Ali some and Ali's mum thought the two-piece A-line was the nicest. The girl then brought them all to a rail with this style of dress.

'Pick out four, and I'll be back in two minutes,' she said.

'Two minutes to pick your wedding dress? Is she mad?' Jill laughed. 'This is the most important thing you will ever wear, we need more than two minutes.'

But they did do it, and then Ali and the assistant went back into the changing room.

'You need help getting a wedding dress on. There are so many layers, and they are all so fragile, so never try one on when you are alone.' The girl nattered on. Ali was too much in shock, starting at her reflection. She couldn't believe she was seeing herself in a wedding dress.

'I'm really getting married,' she said out loud, by accident.

The assistant laughed. 'Most girls say that. It is a bit of a shock, you never believe it until you are in the dress. But wait until you have the veil, shoes, jewellery and your hair done. You will float down that aisle with excitement.'

As the assistant laced up the back of the two-piece, Ali felt like ringing Robin to thank him for asking her to marry him. She wanted to tell him what she was up to, but knew it was bad luck to even discuss the dress, let alone show it to your fiancé.

As she walked out of the dressing room, her mum started crying. 'My beautiful baby girl is getting married. I don't believe it.'

Kate held her mum's hand, while Jill went to take a photo. 'So we can look back later and see what ones we want.'

'Oh no! No cameras. You are not allowed to take pictures of these designs. I'm sorry, but please take that camera out of your hand,' the assistant almost shouted.

Blushing, Jill put the banned camera down.

'You look gorgeous,' Kate congratulated Ali. 'Robin will die when he sees you walking up the aisle!'

Ali tried the four dresses on, all variations on the first. They all looked amazing, so pretty, but none of them compared to the first, so Ali tried it on again. The sales assistant passed her shoes and a bracelet, and attached a small veil to her hair.

'No one ever forgets the first dress they try on. Some people could try on hundreds of dresses, but will come back to the first one. Something about seeing yourself in a wedding dress for the first time makes you love that moment – and that dress – for ever.'

As Ali sized up how she looked, she could really see the wedding happening: she could imagine walking up the aisle; her father passing her to Robin, and all the love, fun and excitement that would follow. She could not wait for the big day.

As she showed the dress to her mum and sisters again, she could see Jill pretending to text someone on her phone while really trying to take a photo with her camera phone.

'You look like an angel, honey, so beautiful. But sure, you would be beautiful in a sack.'

'I would love to see you walking up the aisle in a sack,' laughed Kate. 'Let's go and get some Coca-Cola, it's roasting in here and you are taking ages.'

Ages? Ali thought. She had only tried on four wedding dresses, and had maybe hundreds more to try on. She knew her sisters were not going to have the stamina and patience for this.

'We will meet you two useless lumps outside, leave myself and Ali alone,' her mother said, as she shooed the girls out the door. 'Ali, is this the one you like? We could get it. It is perfect, wait until your father and Robin see you in it.'

Ali looked at the price tag. 'Oh my God, it is five thousand euros! Is that normal? This is crazy. It is far too much,' she said as she started to take the dress off.

'Ali, your dad and I've the money for this wedding, and want you to have whatever makes you happy, so if you want the dress we could get it. Forget the rest of those places and appointments.'

Ali looked at the two-piece corset and skirt. 'No, let's just take the dress details, and go check some others out. Anyway, I'm too hot to decide. These dresses are all so heavy. I'll need a mini-fan built into one of them on the wedding day, or else I'll collapse before the altar.'

As Ali walked out of the shop, she took one last look around at all the dresses and eager fiancées, and saw the dress she loved being hung back on the rail, ready for someone else to squeeze into. Hopefully no one else will like it, she thought, as she headed to the car and on to the next shop.

67

It had been a week since Joe O'Connor had had his heart-attack. Ben felt like his whole life had been on hold. He had barely left the hospital. He had had to bring his laptop in once or twice and email some older reports to work, from the hospital canteen, as you were not allowed computers on the wards, and apart from running home every night to sleep and eat, himself and his mother had mainly stayed right at Joe's bed.

Joe's operation had been successful, they thought, and he had awoken briefly, but then, after complications he had had to be operated on again. Now he was just back out of theatre, and sleeping.

Maura looked like a shadow of herself: she had not only managed to age in one week, but to lose weight – and her spirit, it seemed. Maura went through phases of telling Ben every story possible about Joe: wonderful ones about when they first married, as well as funny holiday anecdotes. But then, other times, she barely spoke for hours, seeming to focus on just looking at Joe, wishing him to awaken and be better.

Ben thought his dad's heart-attack had maybe made his mum aware of her own mortality, made her realize none of them would live for ever, that the older you got, the less time you had. The experience had made Ben feel like that, too.

Made him realize he had no one apart from his parents to sit beside his own hospital bed if he got sick; no one to will him better. He needed to change that: his young single days were wasting time that should be spent with someone he could love and care for, and who would love him back.

Ben had gone down to the canteen to buy some sandwiches for lunch, and after negotiating a long queue made his way back to his father's room, with lunch for himself and his mum. When he got back he saw his mum had made a big list of things on an A4 page.

'What is that, Mum?'

'It is all the things your father does and organizes that I don't have a clue about. A list I don't know how to cope with. How will I manage if he never recovers? I don't even know which health policy I'm on, or when the golf club membership's renewal date is, or how much they cost, or who we've our house insurance with, or when my car tax is due. I'm lost, Ben.'

Ben didn't know what to say, but started looking through the long list. It reminded Ben how much his dad took care of everything in their house, from mortgage payments to plumbers, from paying the car insurance to credit card bills. Ben himself didn't know the answer to half the questions. What have I been doing? he thought. Living in a bubble, oblivious to real life and grown-up responsibilities, while his dad had carried all the stress. Ben felt guiltier than ever.

68

Ben was talking to his mum about when he would have to go back to work, when suddenly he heard his dad whisper.

'Maura, Maura?'

'Joe, oh my God, Joe, are you OK?' Ben's mother cried.

'I don't know what is happening, I feel like I've been dreaming. Am I really in the hospital? I remember trying to talk before, but it seems like years ago,' Joe replied.

'No, Dad,' Ben answered, 'that was a few days ago, you had a heart-attack a week ago, and have been into surgery twice. We were so worried. Mum has been here all this time, and so have I.' Ben hugged his dad, tears of joy and relief in his eyes.

Maura filled Joe in on what had been happening, and explained how she had found him. 'You scared me half to death. Joe, you know I can't live without you, don't ever let anything like that happen again.' And she started crying.

Joe looked at Ben, and Ben felt guilt burning inside him.

'I am so sorry, Dad, it's all my fault. I should have mowed the lawn, and should have told Mum about that day on the golf course when you felt ill. I'm so sorry. I'll never forgive myself.'

Joe took Ben's hand.

'You are my own son, my only child, I love you, and am not

upset with you. I'm a foolish old man who should have known better. Thank you for looking after your mother for me.'

They talked for a few more minutes before Joe fell back asleep; they knew he was in for a long recovery and they were not out of the woods yet. As his mum chatted to the nurse, Ben walked into the corridor to answer his mobile phone.

'Ben, it's Jeremy. How's your dad?' Ben filled him in on the good news.

'That's great, I'm delighted. And I hate to ask you this now, but I need to know when you will be back for work.'

Ben knew he had to go back, and if his father was improving he had no excuse.

'I will be back tomorrow morning. I still might need to take a few holiday days, but tomorrow I'll be in first thing, I promise.'

'That is great, Ben, thanks. And another thing, are you still coming to the wedding? Have you booked your flights?'

Jeremy was getting married in Spain, and Ben had completely forgotten it was next week. He had booked his flights ages ago, and even though it would be great fun, a holiday, he knew his mother would not be able to cope without him yet.

'Jeremy, I'm so sorry to do this, but I'm going to have to cancel. I really am. I'll make it up to you, I promise.'

Jeremy went quiet, but then said he understood, and said they could discuss it more in the morning, and with that was gone. Ben felt a pang of annoyance that he was going to miss the wedding of the year in Marbella. All his friends would be going, but then when he saw his father still asleep and hooked up to machines he knew he had made the right decision. It was time he stepped up and became the person his father knew he could be.

69

Molly was so distracted: at work, at home with her family, or out with her friends. Herself and Luke were not getting on, and her mind was preoccupied the whole time with thoughts about them and whether they had a future. She was in a daze, and even though what she cooked, baked and made was good and perfectly edible, she knew she could do better. Her mother, who was working in Heavenly for just one day that week, noticed straight away that Molly was troubled.

'Molly, you have barely spoken all day today. What is wrong, pet?' she asked.

Molly didn't know where to start. She didn't really know why Luke was so cross and unhappy with her and she was also embarrassed about telling her mum that everything was not going swimmingly with him. She sniffled, trying not to cry.

'Mum, I think Luke might not want to be with me any more.' And with that all the worry and tension that had been building up inside her came rolling out, and tears streamed down her face.

'Oh Molly, I'm so sorry. Tell me what is wrong,' her mum said. She poured Molly a cup of tea, and started slicing the chocolate fudge cake that she had made earlier. Molly explained about the arguments and about how, even though

Luke had been supportive at the start, he now seemed to resent her new job and passion for cooking.

'You know, Mum, one of the hardest things I ever did was quitting my funds job. I was leaving a job I'd trained and studied for for years. I was frightened of change, but I told myself I had to cope with it. And after I started work here I thought everything was settled at last. But now it seems I've got to adjust to even more change: my relationship with Luke may not last otherwise. I do love him, Mum, but I'm so worried about what's going on between us at the moment.'

'I know you love him, pet. Luke is a lovely guy. He's been so good and patient – he's a saint – but now he has to understand that you are at an exciting time in your career. It is a busy time, but it is fulfilling, too. I'm so proud of you. But now that things are beginning to settle and you are finding your own niche, maybe Luke is the one finding it hard.'

'Do you think so?' Molly considered.

'You just need to talk to him calmly and quietly, love.' And with that Molly's mum went back to making fresh salads for the café, as it had started to fill up for the lunchtime rush. Molly spent all day thinking about what her mum had said, and didn't even look at Scott Williams or any of the café's sandwich order clients as she did her deliveries. All she wanted to do was get home, and talk to Luke.

70

Molly had left work early, so she and Luke could have the whole evening to talk. They needed to sort through this mess. She decided to prepare Luke his favourite meal: fillet steak, mash and pepper sauce. Even though Molly loved fish, and was always trying to get Luke to try new dishes, he still loved his steak; so she started to peel potatoes to prepare the mash. She had butterflies in her stomach: she knew their talk that night would not be easy. She didn't even know where to start, but something had to happen, had to change. She could not feel guilty every time she had to work, she needed Luke to understand that. She needed someone to congratulate her when she got new offers, not someone who would sulk at how her catering might affect his weekend plans. Luke walked through the door at 7 p.m., and Molly could see he was surprised that the table was all set and the food almost ready. He made no attempt to give Molly his usual welcome-home kiss, but she said nothing, just poured him some wine.

'What's all this for?' Luke asked suspiciously, as he sat down and started to eat some of the fresh bread Molly had cooked while waiting.

'Well, I just thought we needed to spend a nice evening in together and talk properly.'

Luke said nothing as he buttered his bread. When Molly started mashing the potatoes he finally broke his silence.

'You know making mash or frying a steak is not going to make up for all this time we keep losing, due to your extra work commitments. I'm not that easily bought off,' he said sarcastically.

Molly was shocked by his tone, but sat down opposite him, and after a sip of wine replied. 'Luke, I'm not trying to bribe you with food. We need to talk, and I thought you might like this meal. There's no need to be cruel about it.'

'OK, Molly, I'm sorry for saying that. But let's be honest: you care more about food and your work than me nowadays.'

Molly felt like she was listening to a broken record. 'Luke, why are you acting like a spoilt child? You must understand that for the next few months my work will be very important. I need to work hard to pay my aunt back for being so good and taking me on, and I also need to start taking extra catering jobs on in order to get more experience and cash.'

'But what about us, Molly? I mean, one minute I've us booked into a scuba-diving course and the next you say you prefer a cooking course? Where does that leave our scuba holiday?'

'I don't know, Luke. I just have to do the cooking course. I'll try to get some extra scuba lessons in before we go away, I promise. But even if I can't dive that much when we are away you still can. It's not the end of the world.'

'It is to me, Molly. One minute you are not going diving, next you won't be coming on the holiday. I know how this will work out.'

Molly could not understand his childishness and bad temper. As she put the steaks on to fry, Luke poured himself more wine. Neither of them said anything until the steaks were cooked and Molly had served them with the mash and pepper sauce on the side.

'Thanks,' Luke mumbled.

Molly tried to change the conversation, and told Luke some of the funny things that had been happening in the café. He didn't seem that interested, but maybe that was just the wine, she thought.

'Oh, Molly, I forgot to tell you. Louise and Bryan have invited a gang of us down to their house in Brittas Bay the weekend after next. It'll be fun, spending time with our friends together. You haven't seen any of the lads in ages, what with your work and all.'

Molly ignored the little dig, but said she would love to go, maybe the fresh air and walks along the beach were just what they needed. It wasn't until she was telling Luke about Sarah's new man from Galway, that she suddenly remembered Sarah's sister Mel and the christening.

'Oh, Luke, I just remembered. I can't go to Brittas that weekend, I've Mel's christening party on the Saturday. I'm sorry.'

Luke slammed down his knife and fork. 'I knew it was too good to be true. You have no interest in me, our friends or holidays. Just forget it, I'll go alone. Good luck with the christening.' And with that he grabbed his jacket and walked out the door.

Molly looked at his plate: his steak and mash were only half-eaten. He had to be very upset to abandon his favourite meal. Oh God? What have I done? she worried. And as she cleared the plates she struggled not to cry.

71

Sarah sat in her back garden, her long legs stretched out, a sketch pad in her hand, trying to get ideas for Ali's wedding invite. She still couldn't believe she'd agreed to do it, but Ali's confidence in her had made it impossible to refuse. It was a lovely warm evening, and Hugh had dropped by, with the intention of taking her out for dinner, but before Sarah had had time to get her handbag, her mother had grabbed him.

'Well, with a man finally around the place, why don't we crack open the barbecue, and fling some steaks on? I can make a nice salad, and we've potatoes, too.'

It wasn't so much a question, as an order, so Hugh was now trying to get the ancient barbecue lit. Sarah laughed as she heard her mum explaining how it didn't matter that one of the barbecue legs had broken, and had to be propped up with a brick.

'We have cooked more burgers, steaks and marshmallows on this beauty than any fancy barbecue.'

As Hugh helped Sarah's mum prepare the food, Sarah sipped her beer. She knew better than to interrupt her mother's interrogation of Hugh. He might as well get it over with now, she thought. Her mum had been asking her questions non-stop about Hugh, and how their relationship was going. Sarah

187

didn't have all the answers, it was still early days, but she knew she liked Hugh, and enjoyed spending time with him.

Over dinner Hugh unwound and told them more about his childhood in Galway, summer days in Clifden, and part-time jobs in many of the touristy pubs and bars. 'I still miss the place, it's such a great city, and I make a point of going home as often as I can. Don't get me wrong, Dublin has its advantages: if it wasn't for living here and my discovery of the Stone Studio I might never have met Sarah!'

Sarah blushed, but secretly loved the way that Hugh was open, and not afraid to say what he felt in his heart. He was so different from most guys. Maybe it was because he was not from Dublin, or because he was confident and yet kind at the same time. As Hugh helped clear the table, and put the left-over salads into the fridge, Sarah's mum started washing some strawberries and whipping cream. Sarah felt totally relaxed. Maybe it is these beers, she thought, but having Hugh rattling around the kitchen with Mum feels normal and right. It calmed her, and as she watched her mum lead Hugh around the garden to show him her different plants and garden ornaments, Sarah was inspired to try a different design for the wedding invite. It just needs to be simple, she thought, simple and elegant. And so she began drawing the back of a bride and groom walking up the aisle, with their clothes and hair flowing, and yet intertwined. As she drew more she realized she was on to something, that Ali would like it. Hugh was inspiring her again, just the way he had when he'd left that blank canvas outside the art gallery. She put aside her beer and took out her paints and brushes.

72

Ali and Robin were on their way down to Kilkenny for the weekend. They were doing their ACCORD marriage guidance course in Kilkenny city at the weekend, and it started on Friday night, so they had both finished work early. But all the same, they were hitting all the Friday traffic on the M50.

'We are going to be late, Robin, I knew we should have taken a half-day off.'

'Ali, you know I've to start conserving my holiday days for the actual wedding.' Robin sighed.

As Ali fretted over the traffic, and tried to phone her mum to say they might not have time to go home for a family dinner before the course, Robin turned up the radio. Everyone was talking about the big football match on Saturday afternoon. It was a sore point for Robin: he was gutted that he would be 'locked up with a priest and crazy engaged couples' instead of watching the match in his local pub. He had no interest in doing the course, but Ali was excited, saying she had heard it was a very interesting experience and most couples really enjoyed it.

'Obviously they're a bunch of nerds,' Robin had remarked. But Ali had not laughed, so now, as they started slowing at the traffic tailback, he was trying to just go along with the idea of the course, despite having to miss the biggest football match of the year.

Finally they made it to Kilkenny city, and Robin managed to find a place in the Kilkenny community centre car park, and they rushed into the hall. Luckily the course had not started, so they grabbed two chairs and sat down. As people moved chairs and took off their coats, Ali could see that everyone was eyeing each other up. They were trying to see how old everyone else was, how anxious or bored they looked at having to do the course, and, most importantly, sizing up each other's engagement rings.

There were about thirty couples there, and a wide range of ages. Ali and Robin ended up beside one of the oldest couples. The girl introduced herself and her bored-looking boyfriend. She had a strong Kilkenny accent, and had begun telling Ali her wedding plans, when Ali asked how soon they were getting married.

'In two and a half years,' the girl exclaimed. 'I don't know how I'll get it all done by then.'

Ali could see Robin's face drop in shock, and before she could stop him he had turned to the girl.

'Why are you doing this course now, then, if you're not getting married for ages? It's crazy.'

The girl took great offence at this, and started sounding off about all the things she had to do – finding matching napkins and place-mats, making her own veil and typing her mass booklets, as well as losing two stone in weight – and how she wouldn't expect Robin to understand how great it was to be able to cross something off your 'to-do' list. And with that she turned her chair away from Ali, and begin chatting to another girl.

'Well done. No one will like us, Robin, if we behave like that.'

'We are not here to make friends, Ali, just relax.' And before Ali could say anything else, the course supervisors entered the room.

The two female coordinators introduced themselves and explained what would be happening over the course of the weekend. Robin was immediately surprised that there were no priests. He had thought it would all be about religion and God.

As if they could read his mind, one of the women said: 'I know some of you are probably surprised there are no priests here, because it was your local church which encouraged you to do this. Well, even though a priest will meet you all to answer any questions you may have about the ceremony or the law, we like the course to be run by people who are married and have experienced its ups and downs.'

As they explained the different areas that they would cover over the weekend – from children to money worries and in-laws – they also handed out booklets that everyone would have to fill in.

'But do not worry, your book will be secret, only seen by you and your fiancé.'

Thank God, thought Robin, as he flicked forward and saw he would have to answer questions on what first attracted him to his partner, and what he disliked about her family. There were also questions on sex, getting pregnant and arguments. This is going to be interesting, Robin thought to himself, and looked at the clock. Interesting, but long; he sighed.

Ali was fascinated by the course, she had always loved doing personality tests in magazines, and this was like one huge one, it was almost fun. She noticed they had to answer questions on the personalities of their parents; family traditions; things they would like to bring from each other's families into their own, new family; and things they wouldn't. It was also interesting to hear the supervisors talk about their own marital experience,

191

and offer tips on healthy relationships. If only Robin would enjoy it more. Ali saw him look at his watch again. He seemed to like filling out the questionnaires, but not be that bothered by what his answers meant, and not that concerned about the things they needed to change in their relationship. At the coffee break, she tried to bring this up with him, but was surprised when a girl she hadn't seen since she was about twelve came over and introduced herself. Herself and Ali had been in primary school together, and as the two girls swapped engagement stories, the boys comforted each other about how tough it was going to be tomorrow to miss the match. Robin enjoyed talking to the other lads on the course, and mentioned to Ali that a few were going for drinks later on.

'But we can't, Mum is waiting dinner for us at home, and we've so much to discuss, what with the marquee guy coming next week. We also need to start talking about the food with Molly.'

Robin looked annoyed, but said nothing, and just settled back into his chair as they started talking about 'Fertility Awareness'. He could see every guy in the room go red. What I wouldn't do for a pint! he thought. And he opened his booklet and squeamishly started answering questions on babies.

The course was over by nine thirty, and Robin and Ali headed back to Ali's parent's house. Ali was delighted to be home for a few days, it was so hard to do wedding things without her mum and sisters.

'Work is just getting in the way of my life, Mum,' she had declared the other day. Her mum had laughed, and said they would have plenty of time to discuss every little detail at the weekend, so the minute Ali arrived in from the course they started. Robin had barely taken his jacket off when Ali, her mum and sisters began discussing church music, desserts, first dance songs, and hair options. The dinner of steak, onions and potato gratin was yum, and he did like spending time with Ali's family, but this was all too much: an evening cooped up in a community centre talking about fertility and marital arguments, followed by hours of discussion about hair, dresses and marquee options.

Ali's dad could see that Robin was getting all hot and bothered, so the second the meal was over, he stood up and said: 'I am in dire need of a pint, and I'm taking Robin with me for company.'

Ali began to protest that they had to talk about flower arrangements, when her dad spoke again.

'Ali, pet, I'm sure you are clever enough to work that out on your own,' he said. And before she could reply, himself and Robin were walking down the long driveway and making their way to O'Reillys for some Guinness.

'Thanks,' Robin said.

'Robin, I don't know how you listen to that nonsense all day long, Ali must be driving you mad! I'm spending so much time out with the cows at the moment that I might as well move in with them, but I'd rather do that than be with those wedding-crazy women.'

Robin laughed, and, after a few well-earned pints, relaxed and began to enjoy listening to Ali's dad tell him stories about Ali when she was young.

Later, as they walked home, Ali's father stopped and turned to Robin. 'Robin, as much as Ali is driving us all a little crazy, she is a princess to me, an angel, and I would do anything for her. I know you would, too, and that's why I'm so happy you are going to be her husband. And if you would let me offer you two pieces of advice for a happy marriage then I'll leave all the rest of the wedding talk to the women.'

'Of course,' Robin said, suddenly sobering up.

'OK, the first is never sleep on an argument. And the second is: just realize that the woman is the head of the house, and runs it. If you can resign yourself to the fact that she will always be the boss you will save yourself a lot of arguments and stress.' And with that Ali's dad entered the house, and bid Robin good night.

When Robin got upstairs, he found Ali awake and reading a wedding magazine, looking stressed. He hugged her.

'I'm sorry I wasn't interested in the course tonight, Ali. I promise tomorrow I'll try harder.'

Ali looked surprised, she had been ready to have a fight with him over his lack of enthusiasm.

'OK, but we still need to discuss flower arrangements.'

Robin smiled. 'You're the boss, Ali, whatever you say goes.'

Ali was delighted, and started showing him pictures of what she wanted to get, and as Robin nodded off he silently thanked God for the weekend away and the marriage tips he had learnt. You were never too old for good advice, he thought, as he fell asleep to the sound of Ali talking about roses, lilies and daisies.

73

Ben was outside the hospital getting some fresh air, when Peter Jones, the fifty-year-old accountant who worked with his dad, came walking towards him. Peter was second in command at Joe O'Connor's accountancy firm, and was a dedicated man who enjoyed ensuring client accounts were in order, and that everything in O'Connor & Son ran smoothly. He had been a huge help, and run the whole business since Joe's heart-attack.

'Ben, how is he? I didn't want to visit him too early, but I had to make sure he was OK.'

Ben sighed. 'He's still not great, Peter. Dad has a long way to go before he is back to his old self.'

Peter sat down on one of the benches outside the hospital doors, his face serious, his hand smoothing the balding crown of his head.

'Well, then, we are going to have to talk, Ben. I can't run the whole company on my own. I'm swamped. I know we've two junior staff, but that is all they are – junior. I'm always overworked and now I've your father's clients as well. I can't do it long-term. I would do anything for your dad, but I do not want to run his beloved business into the ground.'

Ben didn't know what to say. Peter spoke again. 'You know, Ben, all your father ever wanted was for you to come and work side by side with him. Now is your chance. You are trained, you know how accountancy firms work. You could do this, help us out. Help your dad out.'

Ben was stunned. Did Peter expect him to drop his own job and life for a step backwards, back into accountancy, which he had tried and hated years ago?

'I can't do it, Peter. It's been years, and my heart is not in it. You could hire someone temporary. I'll help you find some-one.'

Peter's whole mood seemed to change. 'Ben, you don't understand. This company is your family's business: your dad worked long and hard for years to build it up, to support you all. Taking over is the least you can do.'

Ben knew that Peter was talking sense, but still, as much as he wanted to make his father proud, the thought of working in a stuffy accountancy firm again made him feel trapped. But before he could speak again, Peter had got up and was making his way towards the hospital.

Just before he got there he turned back and said: 'I have to attend my niece's wedding in England later this week, and I can't get out of it. I'll need you to start straight away, so I can show you the ropes before I head off. So I'll see you tomorrow at 9 a.m.' And with that he was gone.

Ben was still in shock when he finally went back in to check on his dad later. His mum came up and gave him a big hug.

'Peter told us you are going to help out with the firm, Ben. That is great news. It will be great to have you finally working with your father—'

Ben interrupted her. 'Mum, it is only for a few days, until I can find someone to help Peter out. I just rang Jeremy and explained the situation, but told him that this time next week, I'll be back working on the paper as a reporter.'

His mum looked disappointed, but said nothing. Joe stared

at Ben, and finally managed to whisper a sentence: 'I trust you, son. I know you will do your best.'

And what could Ben say to that? He headed off home to get his old suit out, and iron a shirt. He hadn't worn a suit in a long time.

The next morning Ben actually felt nervous. Even though it was his dad's firm, he had never worked there full-time. He had helped out a bit during college, but never been a permanent fixture. He didn't know what the staff would think of him. They probably hate me, he thought. Hate me for making my dad work so long and hard, while I swanned around in different jobs, and they are right, I'm useless. As he approached the front steps of the old Georgian building he was reminded about Joe's good eye for property. Even though Joe had had to borrow a lot of money when he first bought this office, he had just known the building would always be worth something, and he had been right. The accountancy office only used two floors, and they rented the top floor to a small public-relations firm.

Ben let himself in with his father's keys. He was early, so the office was quiet. Ben looked around, he hadn't been here for months. There were all the usual signs of activity – files, teacups, and faxes everywhere – but the furniture and art revealed Joe's impeccable taste. The furniture was all heavy old mahogany chairs and tables, while the walls were covered in some beautiful Markey Robinson and Evie Hone pieces.

'You can't expect a client to be impressed by a small firm, unless it not only looks the business, but can back that up with good and loyal work,' Joe always used to say. And Ben had to agree, the firm not only did a terrific job, but looked great. He walked up to the first floor, where his father's office was. It had a lovely view of the nearby park, and like the rest of the place, had some beautiful paintings. As Ben sat in the large leather chair, he saw that his father had put even more family photos around his desk and wall. There was one of Ben as a small boy, playing on a beach, others of family holidays, and a beautiful one of Ben's parents' twenty-fifth wedding anniversary, but the one Ben had never really noticed before was of his college graduation. He and his father were standing next to each other, with Ben holding his degree in front of him. Ben remembered that day so well, the relief at passing college, and yet the anxiety about entering the real world. His father had talked all day about how exciting it would be when they finally worked side by side. As Ben laid down the photo he realized that his father's dream had not only never happened, but probably never would either. How could Joe ever go back to work? Ben worried.

Just then Peter came in. 'It is great to see you, Ben, sitting where Joe normally does. It restores some balance to the office. Now, let me show you around. I am sure there have been some changes since your college days.' And with that Peter started filling Ben in on the work that had been done, and the work that still needed attention.

'We have some important meetings this week, Ben. I hope you are up to them.' Peter sounded as if he was issuing an order.

The day flew by, with Ben swamped by all the work he was supposed to do. He didn't even have time for lunch, and when Joe's secretary, Nora, asked if he wanted her to grab him a sandwich and coffee he jumped at the offer. As she handed him the sandwich, she asked after Joe and Maura. Ben filled her in, and also tried to get information out of her about clients, meetings and future projects.

'Don't worry, Ben,' she said. 'Your dad always hoped that one day you would walk through that door and begin working here, and he knew you would be very capable when you did. He had great faith in you, Ben. You just need to have some in yourself.' With that she was gone, leaving Ben to deal with a torrent of phone calls, faxes and emails. It was going to be a long week, he thought.

74

It was six o'clock in the morning, and Molly was wide awake and up baking biscuits in the shape of baby rattles and shoes. Why did I try to be different? No one will care what shape these are, Molly cursed to herself. This week had been a busy one at work, and she had spent almost every night getting prepared for the christening. As she was still getting used to this catering business, she was nervous and excited at the same time. Her mum had helped her prepare some things the day before, but it was Molly's cousin Eve who was going to help her serve the dishes today in Mel's house. Sarah had given her a spare key, so that Molly and Eve could set themselves up while everyone else was at the church. Sarah herself had been so excited all week at the thought of officially becoming baby Fiona's godmother. Molly was delighted for her friend, but had been very distracted with work and worries over Luke.

They had barely spoken since he had stormed out after their last fight, and then at the start of last week he had told her that he would be away for a few days on business. Luke normally tried to get out of having to go away for work, so she thought he must be trying to avoid her. He'd told her he was going to Cork for work, and intended to head straight on from there to Brittas Bay for the weekend with their friends.

After a few hours of sweating, frying, boiling and baking,

Molly jumped into the shower, as she wanted to change before Eve arrived and they prepared the rest of the food. As she dried her long dark hair in the bedroom she was surprised to see Luke walk through the door.

'You're back early,' she said, as he laid down his bag. He looked tired and pale.

'I know, I was just wrecked and couldn't sleep and decided to head home. I thought you would be gone by now.'

'Well, sorry to disappoint you, but don't worry I'll be gone soon, and then you can go back to ignoring me and our rotten relationship.' Molly was about to walk out the door when Luke gently took hold of her arm.

'Sorry, Molly, I didn't mean it to sound like that, I'm just tired. Sorry, but I need to talk to you, and maybe now is as good as any time.'

Molly sat on the bed, and Luke sat on the old restored chair they had bought for a bargain, and that they had intended to display. It was now covered with clothes, underwear and Luke's jacket.

'Molly, I love you. I know you don't think I do any more, but I do. I thought that you changing jobs would be the best thing for you and our relationship, too. But the last few months have been awful. I just can't help feeling jealous of the time you want to spend with food, ovens, clients and menus rather than with me.'

Molly went to interrupt him, but Luke put his hand up.

'Please, Molly, let me finish. I've been thinking about this all week. I don't know how we can change things. I'm sorry, but I can't see a solution. I just can't. And I don't think I can do this any more. I don't want to be with you – not at the moment anyway. I'm not happy.'

Molly felt as if her heart was stopping. She couldn't breathe, she was suffocating. As she stood up to get some air, she looked at Luke. His head was in his hands.

'I'm sorry, Molly.'

Molly was in shock. She felt she would never be able to speak again and a million thoughts went through her head. This can't be happening, she almost whispered. Eventually she managed to say something.

'Luke, I know we are going through a rough patch, but can't we work this out?' she pleaded. 'I promise things will change. Don't leave.'

But she could see in his eyes that his decision was already made, he was determined to go. He crossed the room to hug her, and as she let his arms comfort her, she let the tears out. Crying, she tried to reason with him, to explain that they just needed to talk more, understand each other more, and that they could work it out. Luke said nothing, then eventually spoke.

'Molly, I'm sorry. It's over.'

With that, Molly broke free of his arms. 'How dare you! How dare you do this to me hours before I've to cater for a massive function? How could you ruin this for me? You obviously planned this, wanted me to fail, how could you be so insensitive? A final act of revenge, was it?' she screamed.

Luke looked at her, shocked. 'Molly, I'm sorry, I didn't mean to tell you now. It just happened like this. I'm sorry. Let me help you prepare for the christening.'

'As if,' Molly cried, as she slammed the bedroom door and ran into the kitchen to check on the quiches.

After a few minutes Luke reappeared with his coat on. 'I should leave you alone. I'll be back later, we can talk more then.'

Molly looked at the face she knew so well, almost better than her own. Looked at the hands that had held her a million times. But the look in his eyes made her realize she didn't know him at all. How could he do this to me? she thought. As he left, he held her one last time.

'Sorry,' he whispered, as he kissed her forehead. He walked out of the door.

Molly touched the spot he had just kissed. His last kiss, she thought, as she sat on the kitchen floor and wailed. She sat there until the door bell rang and Eve's knocking made her sit up and try to wipe the tears from her swollen eyes. How can I go to work? she thought. How can I pretend nothing is wrong and cook my heart out when I know I've nothing and no one to come home to any more? She answered the door to her cousin, and began to cry again.

75

Sarah and her mum were running late for the christening.

'Sarah, I'm not going to be late for my granddaughter's christening,' Catherine Ryan shouted. 'I don't care what you wear, just come down those stairs and let's get going.'

Sarah cursed her mother as she looked under her bed for her shoes. Eventually she found them in her mother's wardrobe. I've got to move out, she thought. If Mum is borrowing my clothes – to go on dates, no doubt – then times have really got tough. But as she walked down the stairs she regretted thinking bad thoughts about her mum, who was standing in the hall, wearing a beautiful Louise Kennedy cream dress and a green wrap with matching bag and shoes. Her mum looked upset.

'Are you OK, Mum?' Sarah asked, as she locked the front door and opened the car door.

'It is just an emotional day, you know. I'm so happy for Mel and John's little Fiona, but also sad that your father is not here. I miss him so much.'

'I know, Mum, I know,' said Sarah. She gave her mum a big hug. 'You look great, Mum, and I'm sure after a glass of wine and some of Molly's fine food you will feel better. But we'd better get going now before Tom goes mad. I promised I'd collect "The Godfather", as he now refers to himself!'

Even though Sarah joked about Tom, she had really enjoying spending time with him this week, preparing for the
christening and chatting about what kind of godparents they
would be. ('Very cool' was their consensus.) Even though she
was very happy with Hugh now, Sarah couldn't forget all the
years she had secretly fancied Tom, so spending all this time
with him was fun. And when Hugh had said he wouldn't be
able to make it to the christening as he had to go home to
Galway, Sarah had at first been disappointed, as she had been
dying to introduce him to her family and friends. But later
she felt almost glad; it meant she could immerse herself in her
godmother role for the whole day, with Tom as her partner
in crime beside her. I don't fancy him any more, she thought,
as she drove the car up towards Blackrock, it's just fun! And
to make herself feel less uneasy she texted Hugh and said she
would ring him after the church service.

Her sister Mel looked beautiful outside the church, in a
gorgeous Coast black and white flower-printed dress. But as
Sarah approached her she realized things were not as rosy as
they seemed.

'Sarah, I'm furious with John,' Mel said. 'Fiona is after
spitting up all over her robe, and I told John to bring the spare
one, and he swore it was in the car, but it is not there. What
are we to do? Present Fiona to God and the priest covered in
sick? Help!'

Sarah looked at the ivory christening robe. It was stained,
and looked a lot less attractive than it had when Mel had
bought it the previous week.

'OK, well we don't have time to go home, so let's try to
gently wash the stain out, and maybe we could even turn it
inside out, no one would notice. And then you can change her
when we get back to the house and party.'

Sarah looked for a bottle of water but found none in the car,
or Mel's baby bag. OK, there is no other option, she thought.

She removed Fiona's robe, and dipped it briefly in the holy font at the entrance of the church. She managed to rinse the stain off, but not before her mother saw.

'Oh sweet Jesus, Sarah, what have you done? That is sacrilegious! God help us all. Fiona will go to hell for wearing that.'

Sarah ignored her mother and the stares of John's family. She tried to wipe the robe dry with a tissue before turning it inside out. Mel seemed relieved to see her again. As Mel re-dressed the almost-naked Fiona, Tom came up.

'Well done! Your first crisis as godmother was handled brilliantly, Sarah.' He gave her a congratulatory hug.

Sarah blushed slightly, but then gathered herself. 'We had better go into the church before Mum has a heart-attack.'

The christening was beautiful, and Sarah's eyes welled up to see her big sister so proud and happy with Fiona. John by Mel's side made them look the perfect family, off to an ideal start with beautiful baby Fiona. Sarah and Tom had to pose for what seemed like hundreds of photos with their goddaughter, but neither minded. The day was such a celebration of new life that Sarah felt almost light-headed with excitement, and in the car leaving the church really looked forward to the reception, and stuffing herself with Molly's food.

The house and garden looked spotless, and the guests were all welcomed with glasses of champagne as they arrived. Sarah went to find Molly, who was in the kitchen. She ran up and gave her a hug. 'Thanks so much for doing this, Molly, you are a star!'

Molly hugged her back, and then went back to slicing bread. She looked pale and tired.

'Are you OK?' Sarah asked her friend.

Molly looked like she was going to say something, then just smiled and said: 'It is your big family day out, so enjoy it. I'm fine. Now get out of this kitchen and let me and Eve get back to work!'

Sarah didn't need to be told twice, and was happy to leave the hot kitchen, and get back to the sunshine and more glasses of champagne.

Mel and John were as proud as punch of Fiona all day. She was in great form, and didn't mind being handed from person to person, and photographed every two minutes. John's mum seemed to be so much more relaxed, knowing her grandchild was safe in the eyes of God now. Mel was just glad they had managed to get it all organized in time; she often felt nowadays that with a baby everything took ten times as long to do and get ready. She was so happy to have Sarah and Tom as the godparents, and they both seemed delighted with their new jobs, and were fussing over Fiona all day. Molly's food had been a huge hit – everyone wanted seconds and even thirds – and as Mel helped Molly pass out the desserts, coffees and teas she realized the day had been a great success. She decided to put on some music to make it last. Baby or no baby she was staying up late tonight.

Sarah and Mel were knocking back the wine, and singing along to Robbie Williams when Molly came to say goodbye.

'Stay, have a drink,' Sarah offered.

Molly looked tired, and kept quiet, and before she could speak Eve came up and grabbed her.

'Molly is wrecked, Sarah, she just needs to relax and sleep, it has been a long day.'

Molly nodded her head.

'OK, Molly, but let's go for dinner some night this week, my treat,' insisted Sarah.

Molly thanked her, walked back into the kitchen, and started packing up her dishes, plates and containers.

*　　*　　*

'Molly was very quiet all day, wasn't she?' Tom remarked as he sat down beside Sarah.

He had met Molly many times with Sarah, but never seen her that silent.

'She was probably just tired. Anyway how are you, "God-father"?' Sarah laughed.

'I would feel much better if I could have a dance with you, Sarah.'

And with that Sarah and Tom joined Mel and John in the middle of the garden, shoes kicked off, just swaying to the music and laughing. Tom had his strong bronzed arms firmly wrapped around Sarah, and it felt very comfortable. Sarah was used to crouching when she danced with men – even Hugh, as he was smaller than her – but Tom was as tall as she was, so they danced easily together. They danced to song after song, Tom swinging Sarah around Mel's garden, his blue eyes staring right into hers. The intensity and closeness felt so right, and yet as Sarah danced, she suddenly felt guilty. She had done nothing, but her thoughts ran to Hugh, who was at home in Galway. And as if she was psychic she suddenly heard her phone ring, and knew it must be him.

'Sorry, Tom, I had better get that.'

Tom looked disappointed; the moment and mood had gone. He shrugged, ran his fingers through his sandy hair and then turned to start dancing with Sarah's mum. Sarah felt a pang of regret for ruining his mood, but then answered her phone and started telling Hugh all about the church and day.

76

Ali was at work, trying to type up a wedding booklet without her boss noticing. Every time Mary even looked her way Ali would quickly pull up some boring work document instead. Ali was trying to get organized, and the wedding booklet was one thing she knew she could get done ahead of time, although trying to pick the church songs, readings and prayers of the faithful was harder than she had thought. Robin had no interest, and just said she could pick whatever she wanted, even though she kept reminding him that the marriage guidance course had said it was important that both of the couple got involved in the wedding preparations.

'But let's be honest, Ali, once the man proposes with the ring he is out of the picture, it's the girl, her mum and sisters that seem to run the show,' Robin had said in the car the previous night. They'd been on their way to the cinema, and Ali had been trying to listen to a CD of church music.

Now Ali switched to studying the cover of her wedding CD, and trying to decide which song would be nice to light the candles to. It reminded her that she still hadn't chosen the prayer her sisters would read out. Mary, her boss, hadn't referred to Ali's wedding once since Ali had told her what days she needed to take off for the wedding and the as-yet-unbooked honeymoon.

'She must be jealous of you, Ali,' Ali sisters had said. 'Just ignore her. Either that or try to set her up with someone! Maybe if she had her own boyfriend she wouldn't be as mean!' Ali was seriously considering it, but she didn't know who to choose as Mary's date. Suddenly Mary walked to her desk; Ali just managed to hide the CD cover in time. Mary threw down the last contract Ali had worked on.

'Ali, I'm sure you can't think of anything but weddings nowadays, but you must remember to be professional. This contract went out unsigned, don't let it happen again.' And with that Mary turned on her heels and headed out of the door.

Ali looked at the document, and wanted to scream. Work is ruining this wedding, she thought tearfully. But then she looked at the clock. It was almost time for lunch, and she was meeting Molly today for a sandwich. At least that would be fun, Ali comforted herself as she started to redraft the contract.

Molly had said she would bring food from the café, and as Ali waited in Merrion Square she couldn't wait to see what it would be. Everything from Heavenly was yum! Molly arrived with two tartlets – one mushroom, one feta cheese – and two chocolate cupcakes.

'Oh my God, they look divine, Molly. Did you make them yourself?' Ali stared at the heavily iced cupcakes, which had Smarties hidden throughout the bun and icing.

'Yeah, I made about forty today! I've single-handedly eaten about a hundred Smarties, too.'

Ali started tucking into the mushroom tartlet.

'How did that marriage course go? Was Robin bored out of his brain?' Molly asked.

'At first he hated being there, but then by the second day he seemed to enjoy it, and found it interesting to talk about children and in-laws and all.' Ali laughed. 'But it was serious, the talk about kids. I mean, Robin and I have discussed them before, but never in such detail, but you could tell some of the other couples hadn't broached that subject before. It was weird: at one stage you had to turn to your partner and ask them if they would be prepared to adopt or do IVF if you couldn't have kids naturally. It was all very serious. Of course Robin said yes, but I heard one guy say: "I'd never want to bring up a child that wasn't my flesh and blood." How backward is that? It was awful for his poor fiancée. I thought everyone nowadays was up for adoption. Luke wouldn't mind if you guys had to, would he?'

Molly tried to pull herself together as she put down her chocolate cupcake. 'Luke and I have broken up, Ali. It's over.'

Ali looked shocked, but Molly was determined not to cry any more. She had spent the last few days in floods, and was desperately trying to maintain some composure.

'What? I don't believe you, Molly. You just had a bad fight or something,' Ali said as she gave her friend a hug.

'Yes, a fight we have had over and over again. We have been arguing for ages. I don't really know what happened, Ali. He just couldn't understand my new work commitments, and we fought about them more and more. I didn't think it would end like this, but Luke is gone.'

'Maybe he'll change his mind,' Ali said, trying to be supportive.

'I don't think so. He collected all his clothes from the apartment the other day, and we are meeting up at the weekend to discuss larger items like the furniture we bought over the years. I hate it, Ali, but what can I do?'

Ali didn't know what to say, Molly and Luke had seemed such a perfect couple. She had never imagined them breaking up. She spent the remainder of their lunch trying to console her friend. When she got back into her office and saw all the wedding magazines and booklets on her desk, she just pushed them aside. She wasn't in the mood to think about her own wedding and happiness today, when one of her best friends was suddenly single, and so heart-broken. God, Ali thought, I totally forgot Molly was doing the catering for the wedding. How painful it will be for her to see a loving couple and hear everyone talking about happily ever afters! I hope she will still be able to cope, though, because the date is so close now, that if she can't do it I'll have to cook the food myself. Ali almost laughed, picturing herself trying to make her own wedding cake the night before she had to walk up the aisle!

77

The next day Ali's parents were coming up to Dublin to help her make a final decision about her wedding dress. She just could not decide between two options. One was from a small boutique run by a Frenchwoman, in Sandymount. It was detailed, lacy and very slimming. The shop-owner had picked out some beautiful ivory shoes and beaded jewellery to go with it, and she really did have a good eye; everything she had chosen was perfect. Ali loved that dress, it was very elegant and the whole outfit was ideal, but she still couldn't stop thinking about the first dress she had tried on, the two-piece from The Wedding Boutique. It was cream, and had a fitted bodice that laced up at the back, and a beautiful full-bodied skirt. The dress was very simple, but it was the fit and cut that Ali had fallen in love with. It was like something you might see in an American bridal magazine. She had already found some jewellery in Brown Thomas that would go with it perfectly. How hard it was to choose the right dress!

Ali's parents wanted to talk to Robin and Ali about some final booking details for the marquee, so it was decided to combine this with a final trip to the bridal shops. Ali had agreed to meet her mum and dad after work in the shop in Sandymount. Ali had been held up in work, so she started to get anxious at the bus stop, waiting for a bus to arrive.

Finally one did, but as usual the queue was held up by people searching for change. How could people wait for a bus for half an hour, and then be taken aback by having to pay? Ali thought. Why couldn't they be ready, instead of waiting until they were at the head of the queue before taking off their backpack, searching for their wallet, and slowly counting out their change in pennies? It was ridiculous. Ali sighed with exasperation as she finally got a seat, and rang her mum to warn her she would be late.

Ali arrived a little hot and bothered, but as soon as she entered the bridal boutique was calmed by its atmosphere and by its owner, Madeline. The shop was small, yet filled with beautiful paintings, photos and bridal accessories. It was all cream, and smelled of perfumed candles. The Frenchwoman took one look at Ali and offered her a chair, to 'catch your breath', before continuing to make tea and coffee for Ali's parents. After a drink of water, Ali slipped into the lace wedding dress and fixed her hair. Then she stepped out of the changing room.

She saw a teardrop roll down her father's cheek. 'Oh Ali, your mother told me you looked gorgeous in all the dresses you tried on,' he said proudly. 'But Ali, pet, you look like an angel, an absolute angel. You are beautiful.'

Tears welled into Ali's eyes as she pictured the day her dad would walk her up the aisle. They all admired the dress, yet Ali still couldn't decide. It was a bit awkward telling Madeline that once again they need to 'think about it' as they left the little boutique.

'I don't know what to do, Mum, I love it, but I love the next dress, too.'

'Ali, they are all gorgeous on you. Let's just try this second one on, and get some dinner, and then we can decide.'

★   ★   ★

At The Wedding Boutique there was no coffee, tea or water, but Ali didn't mind. She made sure her parents were comfortable, before letting the sales assistant help her into the two-piece dress. The skirt had three layers, so she needed help. After slipping into some slingback heels and letting the assistant place a veil on her hair, she stepped out of the dressing room and walked over to her parents. This time they were both speechless. They gasped.

'That's it, Ali. That's the one,' her dad said at last, holding her mum's hand.

Ali looked in the mirror. 'But it's way more expensive, Dad, it's—'

Ali's dad cut in. 'I don't care how much it costs. That's the one, Ali, the one for you. You look like a princess.'

And before she knew it they had paid for the dress, with the assistant promising the alterations would be finished in three weeks' time. Ali bought some ivory low-heeled shoes and a beautiful ivory beaded veil; it was all perfect. And as Ali and her parents headed for dinner in a local Italian to celebrate 'the dress', Ali forgot all about the stress of work, and of buses and wedding arrangements – and just pictured herself walking up the aisle in that dream dress.

78

Ben was swamped with work. His desk was full of balance sheets, tax invoices, calculators and coffee cups. He had never realized his dad worked so hard. So much for the idea that if you ran your own company you were your own boss and could do whatever you wanted. Ben had been lucky to grab a bagel at lunchtime. The week had flown by, and even though he had tried to explain to clients that his dad was off work, and they had sympathized with him, yet somehow they had also still expected their work to be done on time and up to scratch. It had taken Ben a day or two to get back into the swing of things in the accountancy world but it was like riding a bike, once you knew how to balance an account you never forgot!

His father was coming out of hospital tomorrow. Maura was nervous about how he would cope at home, but the doctors had reassured her that if he had any problems she could bring him straight back in. They weren't going to take any chances with his heart. Ben was glad that Joe was coming out on a Saturday, because if it had been mid-week he wouldn't have been able to be there, work was so busy. He was determined to finish his work tonight by 6 p.m. and head straight for the pub. He hadn't seen any of his friends in weeks and needed to relax and have a few pints.

At six thirty Ben turned off his computer, locked the offices, and headed straight for The Bailey. The lads were already there and Ben just couldn't wait for a night of banter and pints. He pushed his way through the usual throng of after-work Friday drinkers, and found his friends. They were all delighted to see him, and happy to hear his dad was on the road to recovery, even if it would take him a while to get back to his old self. After telling them all about the hospital, the family business and being swamped at work the conversation returned to the usual male subjects: football and rugby. Ben was glad. It was nice to be able to relax and talk about something different.

By his third pint Ben had completely forgotten all the stress of the week and was laughing at his friend Philip's attempt to chat up some girls at the bar. But Philip did succeed in bringing two of the girls over to where Ben and the lads were sitting. Ben made room for them, and before long was chatting to the girls, who both worked on a well-known magazine and kept the boys entertained with funny celebrity gossip. The girls managed to persuade the bar manager that they would mention the pub in the next issue of the magazine in return for some free rounds of drinks, so before long Ben was not only having a great time but getting pretty drunk.

It is great to have a normal Friday night, he thought, as he put his arm around Nikki, who was blonde and very chatty. They walked on to Krystle nightclub. Nikki seemed to know everyone in Dublin, and managed to blag her way in to the nightclub for free, dragging Ben in with her. The night was only beginning in Krystle: the music was blaring and the club just filling up. As Ben's other friends filed in they all made their way to the smoking garden, while Ben and Nikki danced to Kanye West. After some shots and free champagne Ben was flying, and felt himself drawn more to Nikki. She obviously felt the same way, and before long they were grabbing their coats and hailing a taxi. As Nikki sat beside him in the taxi and leaned in to kiss him, Ben made a drunken but mental note to thank Philip for his bar bravery earlier. If it hadn't been for him, Ben wouldn't be on his way back to a gorgeous blonde's flat. Life is good, Ben thought, as he paid the taxi man and headed into Nikki's apartment, holding her by the hand.

79

Life is a nightmare, Ben thought, as he searched for his mobile phone. It had been ringing for ages now, but it had taken about ten rings to wake Ben from his drunken slumber. As he fumbled amid jeans, socks and underwear for his Nokia, he thought his head would explode. He hadn't been this hungover for a long time. Finally he found the phone and answered.

'Where are you, Ben? Do you know what time it is? Your father's blood pressure will be sky-high.'

Ben looked at his watch, it was twelve o'clock. Crap, he thought, his mum was right, they were supposed to be in the hospital by 11 a.m. to collect Joe.

'Where are you, anyway?' Maura O'Connor almost shouted down the phone.

Ben looked around at Nikki who was unconscious on the bed. Ben didn't have a clue where he was, maybe Donnybrook, but he could be anywhere. The night before seemed like a dream.

'Mum, I know I said I would drive, but could I meet you at the hospital? I'll be there as soon as I can.'

Maura agreed, and once she was gone Ben stood up to find the bathroom: he needed a shower before collecting his dad. Nikki awoke as Ben tripped over her boots.

'Hi,' she croaked. 'Big night, hey? Are you OK?'

Ben sat down on the bed. 'Sorry to sound like a prick, Nikki, but I've to be somewhere ASAP, so if you wouldn't mind I need to shower and then leave.'

Ben waited for her to be annoyed, but she smiled at him.

'No problem, Ben. I'm off to Spain later this afternoon with the girls for a week of sun and fun, so no bother. Do you want me to order you a taxi?'

Ben nodded as he headed for the bathroom, he felt kind of weird. He hadn't had a proper one-night stand in ages, and usually felt a bit guilty after, but Nikki didn't seem to care. Somehow that made Ben feel like he was the one being used. He tried to think it through in the shower, but the cold water forced him to realize just how bad his hangover was, and as he got dressed again and tried to make himself look presentable Nikki called out that his taxi had arrived. He walked to the door, and Nikki handed him a piece of paper with her number on it.

'In case you ever have an urge to dance your heart out to Kanye West again, Ben. I had a great time last night, see you!' And with that she gave him a quick peck on the cheek and closed the apartment door.

Ben was half in shock, not sure what to make of the situation. Maybe all magazine girls were like this, blagging drinks and free entry to nightclubs, followed by one-night stands; or maybe she did like him. Ben really didn't have time to think about it as he rang his mum to tell her he was on the way. Today was going to be a big day, and Ben needed to be there for his dad.

As Joe walked into the kitchen his eyes swelled with tears.

'I didn't think I would ever see that crazy parrot again,' he said with a smile, as Ben helped him into a chair. Maura set about making them all coffee.

Mango starting squawking away, delighted with all the attention Joe was giving him. The dog was going berserk too – tail wagging, jumping up and down all over Joe. Ben's head was pumping, his hangover seeming to get worse. Maura started to unpack the groceries they had picked up on the way home from the hospital.

'Maura, I'll never take any of your meals for granted again, that hospital food was like cardboard. I've been dreaming of your homemade lasagne and shepherds pie!'

'I thought you might like me to make them.' Maura smiled as she turned the oven on and decided they all needed a big lunch to celebrate Joe's return home.

Ben helped Joe unpack his bags, and change into some new clothes.

'Everything smells of hospital, Ben, it's horrible. Can you put my dirty things straight into the wash, please? I don't want to be reminded of that odour again.'

Ben looked at his dad, realizing how hard it must have been for him to be stuck in that hospital thinking he was going to die. He gave his dad a hug.

'I'm so glad you are home, Dad.'

Joe hugged him back, then slipped on an old jumper and trousers. The clothes hung off him: in the few short weeks he had been ill he had lost a huge amount of weight. Ben was shocked at how old and sick he suddenly looked.

'Ben, I'm very tired. I think I might go for a nap before lunch is ready. Wake me when that lasagne is cooked, I can't wait.' Joe smiled as Ben helped him into the bed, but Ben knew it must be hard to have to be helped to do the simplest things.

If he can barely get himself dressed or into bed, how will he ever go back to work? Ben worried. He closed his parents' bedroom door, and decided to lie down himself. As his hangover seemed to clear Ben's mind began to fill with worries about his dad's health, his ability to return to work, and the future of his company.

80

Molly picked up her box of cookbooks and headed for the front door. Luke stood in the kitchen, and didn't offer to help her with the last box. She stared at him.

'You know, Luke, you could at least look me in the eyes as I leave.'

Luke gazed into the big brown eyes of his ex-girlfriend and sighed. Neither spoke, and eventually Luke picked up the blue Nigella Lawson cookie jar.

'This is yours. You might as well take it. I never really liked homemade cookies anyway.'

Molly felt like hitting Luke over the head with the heavy jar, but then thought that would be very un-domestic-goddess-like, and instead picked the jar up and took one last lingering look around the apartment. After many discussions Molly and Luke had decided that it would be better for Luke to keep the one-bedded rented apartment. Molly knew how much he liked it, and she also knew that on her salary there was no way she could live there by herself. So, instead, she was returning home. Her mum kept saying she didn't mind, but Molly knew that by the time she was thirty her parents had hoped she would be getting married, or buying a house – not moving back home. As she looked around the brightly coloured rooms she felt a lump in her throat, remembering the first day they had moved in. They had been so excited finally to be living alone, and as they had unpacked boxes and eaten take-out pizza Luke had yet again told her how much he loved her, and how he couldn't wait to spend the rest of his life with her. That day felt like a dream now. As Molly took one last look at their small balcony and remembered cramped yet fun barbecues and beers there on sunny days, she felt her life was slipping out of her grasp. She felt lost: life without Luke, without a partner, felt so alien at her age. Molly didn't know how she would cope. All her friends had partners, and life normally revolved around double dates, or nights out with them all. Now she would be the lonely single girl, living at home with her parents. It couldn't get any sadder.

Luke politely walked Molly to the front door, and Molly had to stop herself from begging him to change his mind. But she knew he wouldn't, and a part of her didn't want to take him back anyway. What he felt and thought about her now was breaking her heart. She handed him her apartment key.

'Thanks, Molly,' he said, as he took it. He tried to shake her hand. It was so cold and businesslike, Molly thought broken heartedly.

Luckily Molly's hands were too full, so instead he just gave her a quick kiss on the cheek, but it was still cold and awkward. Molly didn't know what to say, and so just walked out of the door and headed to her mum's car, which she had borrowed and was now full of her clothes, CDs and junk. She looked back to say goodbye to Luke, but the door was closed. So that's the end of that, Molly said to herself. She squashed the cookbooks and cookie jar into the boot, and headed home, but she was only two minutes up the road when she had to pull over. As the tears poured out of her she thought of the one thing that she had left with Luke in the apartment – her heart – and with that she cried until she knew she had to go home and face her parents.

81

Molly heard a knock at her bedroom door. Her mum's head appeared.

'Can I come in, Molly?'

Molly pulled her pyjamas on. After years of living with her boyfriend she was finding it hard to get used to living at home with her parents, and their habit of dropping in on her unexpectedly.

Molly could barely remember getting into bed the previous night. She'd been crying all night and had hardly slept a wink. She'd heard the milkman and newspaper man arriving at 7 a.m., but she must have finally dozed off after that. Molly's mum sat down on her bed. She had a plate of toasted cheese, ham and tomato sandwiches in one hand and a can of Coke in the other.

'I thought you could do with this, pet,' she said. She hugged Molly while she gulped back the Coke.

'My favourite,' Molly said. She sat up in bed and tucked into the roasting-hot sandwiches.

'I take it it didn't go too well with Luke last night, then?' her mum asked, as she opened the curtains. The room was strewn with boxes and bags from Molly's apartment.

'We're still broken up, if that's what you mean, Mum,' Molly said quietly.

'I'm so sorry, pet, I really am. I just don't understand what went wrong. I know it is none of my business, but I still think Luke must be a bit jealous of your cooking. But he'll get over that, you'll see.'

'I'm not sure that he will.' Molly sighed. She tried not to shout out that she knew it was totally over, and that Luke didn't give a toss about her any more.

'Maybe Luke was right,' she said. 'Am I obsessed with work and my career? I should have seen how unhappy all those long hours I worked were making him. It's funny because he was the one that encouraged me to leave the bank and follow my heart, and then, when I did, I guess he didn't like it. But still, no matter what anyone says, he hurt me. He really hurt me, Mum.'

'I know he did, pet,' Molly's mum said, giving her a kiss. 'You have your work cut out for you in this room, Molly, but why don't we forget about it today, and just head off somewhere? Just you and me, spend a Sunday afternoon like we used to. We could go to Brittas Bay for the day if you liked?'

Molly looked round the room that was frozen in time from when she moved out years ago, with its Hello Kitty cushions, college accountancy books and massive U2 poster on the back of the door.

'OK, Mum. Let me get dressed and I'll worry about this mess later.' And with that Molly decided she had cried enough in the last twenty-four hours, and that a day spent in the sunshine with her mum would be the perfect medicine for suddenly becoming single.

The beach at Brittas, County Wicklow was full of young families, with kids running everywhere, delighted after months of winter and heavy clothes to be feeling free in their swimsuits and T-shirts. Molly and her mum walked to the centre of the beach and found a nice spot that was a bit quieter and had less children, kite-flying and football matches. Brittas brought back such happy memories for Molly: her grandad had owned a mobile home here when she was little, and she used to love visiting him for the whole summer, where it always seemed to be sunny, and the days were full of swimming, playing and barbecues. Whole days were spent just building sandcastles, or having picnics. Molly and her brother used to especially love spending bank holiday weekends here, when all the local summer kids would be allowed to travel around in a trailer on the back of a local tractor and be taken on a tour of the mobile home park. Molly used to feel so proud waving to her parents as they passed her grandad's mobile home; and in the evenings, after each child received a chocolate bar and can of Coke, they all used to head to the big campfire on the beach. It was a memory Molly would never forget.

'Are you thinking about Luke?' Molly's mum asked as she put on her sunhat and sunglasses.

'No, I'm actually thinking of Grandad and all the summers we spent here on this beach.'

'Oh, they were the simple days then, there was no going abroad, and trying to take screaming kids on a long-haul flight. No, with Brittas we could hop in the car once your dad was finished work on a Friday, and be down in time to make dinner and have a glass of wine in McDaniels pub. I never saw you and your brother so happy as all the days you spent in the water, and running around on the beach.'

Molly smiled. 'Remember the summer Hurricane Charlie hit and we had to abandon the beach and try to make it back to Dad in Dublin? I thought we would die.' Molly laughed.

'Don't laugh, Molly, how do you think I felt, trying to drive back in that storm with you and your brother complaining because we couldn't stop for chips and you had forgotten your armbands? I'll never forget that! But I suppose that was the only stressful day we had here, the rest of the days were just full of relaxation and fun. I do miss your grandad and that mobile home, though. Maybe when you have kids you can buy a place down here yourself, and we can relive those summer memories.'

Molly forced a smile and tried to push ideas of Luke and their never-to-happen-now marriage out of her mind. Instead she opened a cooler box that she often used to transport catering food, but which was now full of treats for the beach. She had been in no mood to cook before they left, so instead they had stopped off for supplies on the way into Brittas. Molly really was reliving her younger beach days, by tucking in to a Tayto crisp sandwich, followed by Coke and a Magnum ice-cream. As they ate she saw a group of guys carrying surf boards into the water; they were all joking, smiling and enjoying the sunshine. Molly thought one of them looked like Scott Williams, and for a moment they exchanged glances, and he seemed to smile and nod at her. It can't be him, though, Molly thought: he would never be exciting or relaxed enough to go surfing. It must be someone else, she thought, licking her ice-cream, and watching the guys having what seemed like lots of fun.

Herself and her mum ate up the rest of their snacks and then just napped in the sunshine. When she awoke Molly could feel her skin tingle with sunburn, so she took off her shorts and T-shirt and ran for the sea. The water was freezing! It always was in Ireland, but the coldness made her feel awake and alive, and as she swam back and forth, glancing back at her mum, who was sunbathing and reading a magazine on the beach, Molly thought: I can do this, I can get over Luke. The day at the beach had not only given her a tan, but hope – and that was exactly what she needed.

82

Sarah was going to mind baby Fiona for the day while her sister Mel went into town, to go shopping. And as Sarah's days off were often in the middle of the week, Mel was delighted to be able to shop on a quiet day in town. Sarah had been so excited about having Fiona all to herself! Her godchild was so good, and seemed to spend most of her time either sleeping or just laughing. Sarah thought as it was such a beautiful day she would take Fiona for a walk down to Sandycove beach, and maybe pop into Cavistons in Glasthule to buy some food. Hugh had said he might be able to drop by for lunch; Sarah hoped he would, as she was dying to show baby Fiona off to him.

Mel came into the kitchen in a whirlwind of stress and baby accessories.

'This is Fiona's milk, some spare clothes, spare diapers, spare bottles, spare soothers, spare wipes, spare sunhats, spare—'

'Stop it, Mel, I'll be fine. I've looked after her before. You just enjoy Grafton Street and being baby-free for a day.'

Sarah literally pushed Mel out the door, but not before Mel turned. 'Fiona is perfectly healthy, but just watch out when you change her, her stomach has been a little upset lately. But she was fine last night, so I hope she will be OK for you today.'

'No problem, Mel, she looks fine to me. I'll see you later tonight.'

And with that Mel was gone and it was just Sarah and her godchild. Sarah made sure every inch of Fiona that was remotely exposed was well-covered in sun cream, as the day was getting hot. She herself was in a simple summer dress she had picked up in Zara, and was delighted it was finally hot and sunny enough to wear. When she had made sure she had everything Fiona needed she locked the house and headed off towards Sandycove beach. The walk would do them both good. Sarah pushed the pram and received some doting glances and nice compliments from other women on how cute Fiona was, and she felt proud that being a mother came so easily to her. Maybe one day herself and Hugh would be walking their own baby to Sandycove.

When they arrived at the beach, Sarah made sure Fiona was in the shade and happy before pulling out a bottle of water and a sketch pad. As she took a drink of the cold refreshing water, she looked at her previous sketches for Ali's wedding invite. She was almost finished, and was meeting Ali at the weekend to hand over the last proof, so Ali could take it to the printer. Sarah still couldn't believe her idea and sketch would be seen by all of Ali's friends and family. She was delighted with herself, but also nervous about what people would think of her invite when they opened the envelope and saw her vision of an 'ideal bride'. Ali kept reassuring her that everyone would love it, and be jealous that she had such an original and one-off wedding invite. Sarah wasn't so sure, but this project had encouraged her to get back into art, and the last few weeks she had spent a good portion of her wages on canvases and new paints, and started losing herself in evenings full of painting and colour.

After an hour of sketching and chatting to Fiona, Sarah started to get hungry, so she packed up her belongings and headed towards Glasthule village. Cavistons was a family-run business renowned for its fresh deli-style food, with everything from fish to homemade lasagnes and cheeses on offer. Many a person held a dinner party in South Dublin, and tried to pretend the food was all their own, while everyone knew it was from Cavistons! Sarah stocked up on fish, bread, cheese, some quiches, a salad, and a bottle of pink lemonade, and began the walk home. Hugh had texted her to say he had a meeting near Monkstown so would be able to swing by her place for lunch with herself and Fiona.

Sarah hadn't realized how tiring it was to push a baby and buggie while walking and holding bags heavy with food, and by the time she got home to Monkstown she was in bits, and needed a quick lie-down, before refreshing herself for when Hugh arrived. No wonder mothers always looked wrecked, Sarah thought, as she caught a reflection of herself in the mirror. Her beautiful sundress now clung to her with sweat, while her perfectly straightened hair resembled a bush. She no longer felt like a glamorous yummy-mummy and she quickly tried to fix herself, and Fiona, before the doorbell rang, and Hugh arrived. When she opened the door he was standing there with a bunch of fresh flowers. He gave her a kiss and hug, and she ushered him in to the sunny kitchen and opened the pink lemonade.

'How was your meeting?' she enquired.

'It was great, business is going very well at the moment, must be all this glorious weather. It makes people happy to spend, spend, spend!'

Sarah was glad things were going well for Hugh: he was a good man and deserved to do well. They had only been together a short while, but it felt like years, he was so calm and laid-back. And their relationship was effortless: there was no hassle, no mind games, just a proper grown-up rapport. As Sarah and Hugh chatted about summer plans and some up-and-coming art exhibitions that Sarah's gallery was having, and that Hugh thought might be interesting, Fiona gurgled away. She was happy just basking in the sunshine and enjoying the attention that Hugh gave her. Hugh devoured the lunch and after her long walk Sarah herself really enjoyed the mushroom quiche and fresh bread. As they ate Sarah couldn't help observing how the three of them looked like the perfect family, and she began to fantasize again about herself and Hugh's own children. I'm such a girl, she thought, dreaming about children, when we haven't even been on a holiday or moved in together yet! As she listened to Hugh talk about some new film he wanted to see Sarah could smell something bad. It was awful, and Hugh must have noticed it, too.

'I think Fiona might need a nappy change,' Hugh laughed.

Sarah picked her niece up.

'God, I only changed her before you came, but I suppose Mel did mention her stomach was acting up a little. But don't worry, you finish your lunch and I'll change her inside.'

Hugh stood up.

'No, Sarah, you organized this beautiful lunch, I'll change her. I've plenty of experience from my own nieces and nephews. You finish your lunch.'

Sarah smiled. Hugh was so sweet, and obviously trying to impress, and to be honest she was happy to let him change Fiona. It was so cute to see him pick her up and chat to her. Just as Sarah was showing Hugh into the living room where Mel had left all of Fiona's clothes and spare nappies, Sarah's mum walked in the door.

'Oh, don't you make the perfect family picture,' she said as she laid down her handbag and went to give her grandchild a big kiss.

Sarah was mortified that her mum would say that out loud.

'I thought you were out for the day, Mum?' Sarah half-shouted.

'Oh I am, but I just wanted to pop home and grab my togs, as it's such a nice day myself and Mrs Flynn from next door thought we would ditch playing bridge and head to Grey-stones beach for the afternoon. Don't worry, I'll be out of your hair in a few minutes.'

While Hugh undressed the baby Sarah started to pick out a new outfit for her, as she had seemed a little hot in her other babygro. Sarah's mum was cooing over Fiona, and as Sarah looked over she heard a weird sound coming from Fiona's stomach. Hugh had taken Fiona's nappy off, and seemed to be leaning in to give her a kiss. Sarah stood up and was about to warn Hugh to be careful, when suddenly she heard the noise again. Before she could say anything Fiona's little plump bottom lined up perfectly with Hugh's mouth, and just as he went in for the kiss, Fiona's stomach gave an extra-loud rumble, and, as if in slow motion, baby poo flew out and landed all over Hugh's face.

Sarah dropped Fiona's clothes, and there was a dead silence. Sarah looked at her mum who was literally frozen. No one spoke until eventually Fiona started gurgling. She was the only person who found this funny. Sarah couldn't move, she was so mortified: how could baby Fiona do this to her? Surely Hugh would never set foot in this house again, or go near a baby, for the rest of his life. Hugh still hadn't moved, or said anything. He finally turned around, and as Sarah saw the full extent of what Fiona had done, she couldn't help giggling. Seeing Hugh covered in baby poo was suddenly hilarious. She felt like she was in a Ben Stiller comedy film, it was so funny. But as she tried to stifle another giggle, and tears began to roll down her face, she could see Hugh was not finding it remotely amusing, although it was hard to read his face as it was covered in Fiona's waste.

Luckily, Sarah's mum seemed to know what to do. She almost carried the shell-shocked Hugh upstairs to show him where the shower and bathroom was. As she did so, Sarah picked up Fiona. She didn't know whether to shout at her or not. Could a baby understand what it had done? Probably not, she thought. Instead she changed Fiona and put her back into her pram. As she heard the shower start running, Sarah's mum appeared back in the kitchen.

'I think I need a drink,' she said. 'Do we have any wine left?'

'Mum, it's two p.m.,' Sarah answered.

'Sarah, my granddaughter has just pooed all over not only a guest, but your only potential husband. Things don't get much worse than that.'

Sarah said nothing, just uncorked a bottle of Sauvignon Blanc. She couldn't help but replay the whole incident over and over in her mind, and every time she did the look on Hugh's face just kept making her laugh. She didn't mean it to, the whole thing was a disaster, but it was funny too. It really was.

Sarah's mum put down her wine glass.

'Sarah, stop that. Do you want Hugh to never see you again? No matter how funny it might have been, that poor man is in shock. How could you knock his confidence like that by laughing? I mean, he has to go back to work. Imagine going back to work after that! Not the best lunch break he has ever had, I imagine.' But even as she spoke, she herself started to giggle.

It set Sarah off, too, and before they knew it even Fiona had joined in, and all three of them were laughing and reliving the moment. Sarah never heard Hugh walk back into the room. He looked at her sternly.

'I need to get my jacket, it is on the chair. I'd better go back to work.'

Sarah suddenly got serious, and as she showed Hugh out to the door, put her arm around him.

'Hugh, I do not know what to say. I'm so sorry. How can I ever apologize enough for this awful explosion? I'm so sorry.'

Hugh looked at the ground and didn't say much. 'It's not your fault,' he mumbled.

But Sarah could sense he half-blamed her for his fertilized face. After an awkward hug goodbye, he turned to her.

'I meant to ask you if you wanted to go to Galway this weekend, to meet some of my family?'

Sarah wanted nothing more than to say yes – anything to please him after this afternoon's disaster – but instead had to turn him down.

'Oh Hugh, I had today off because this weekend we've that new exhibition opening on Saturday and I need to work all weekend. I'm sorry, maybe we can go another weekend?'

Hugh looked even more deflated.

'It's OK, forget it. Sure, I can talk to you at the weekend.' And with that, he was gone.

Sarah felt awful all evening, but when Mel arrived back from town and asked how her angel had been Sarah couldn't help but laugh as she told her the story. And before long they had both finished off the bottle of wine that her mum had opened, and were alternately laughing about the story and feeling horrified and embarrassed. When Sarah went to bed she felt terrible about Hugh, and texted him, asking if he would allow her to treat him to a fancy meal out on Saturday night. She didn't hear back from him for hours, and feared the worst, feared he would dump her, all because of her niece. But eventually he replied: 'Will Fiona be there?'

Sarah laughed, he was obviously starting to see the funny side of things. She hit the reply button on her phone.

'I promise you, you will never have to see Fiona again. It's just you and me.'

And luckily he replied saying he would love to go for dinner, but please could she never mention the incident ever again? Sarah promised she wouldn't. And as she nodded off she felt so relieved that he had been mature enough to let the whole disaster pass, and not let it ruin things. She swore to herself she would never bring it up again, or tell any of her friends, but just as she did, she heard her mum start laughing downstairs, and knew she must be remembering it. And before long Sarah was off laughing herself. She would never forget her day of babysitting.

83

Ali was wide awake and up and dressed by eight o'clock on Saturday morning. It was only a matter of weeks until the wedding, and she could no longer sleep from the stress of everything that had to be done. It was hard to get organized, as so many of her wedding suppliers were in Kilkenny. She just had to trust that her mum and dad were capable of dealing with the hands-on enquiries. She had a massive 'to-do' list, which she now carried with her everywhere. At least the dress is organized, she thought to herself. The dress was the one thing that kept making her smile; she couldn't wait for Robin to see it. Although Robin himself was driving her half-mad: he just didn't seem to care enough about half the wedding decisions, and kept saying she was the boss and could decide. Ali thought this was a cop out, and knew he just didn't want to tear himself away from the TV or football. But today he had no choice, they had to go to town to book their honeymoon, and while they were in town they had to collect the invites from the printers. After that, they were going to head to Molly's, where she would cook some sample dishes for them to choose between for the wedding. And after that they had to go to a few venues to check out different bands. It was going to be a busy day. And tomorrow she wanted to write and post all the wedding invites.

She turned to Robin and tried to wake him.

'Get up, Robin, we've to get going.'

Robin looked half-dead.

'What time is it?' he croaked.

'Eight o'clock, so let's get going.'

'Eight o'clock? Ali, are you mad? It's the one day of the week when we can lie in. Let's go back to sleep for two hours, and then I promise I'll be wide awake.'

Ali stood up and pulled off the duvet.

'Get up, Robin,' she shouted.

That woke Robin, and as he stormed off into the bathroom, he mumbled to himself, 'We should just have got married in a drive-through in Las Vegas.'

Ali didn't bother replying. Instead she picked up the holiday brochures that she had been thumbing through for weeks. They just couldn't decide where to go. Robin quite fancied Thailand, but Ali was nervous of all the drugs and tsunamis, and even though Robin had said she was mad, she didn't care, and instead was trying to push him into going to the Maldives.

They were outside the Tropical Places travel agency just as the shutter was coming up.

'You two must be eager to get away,' laughed the travel agent. She unlocked the front door and showed them in.

Ali explained about their honeymoon, and when they wanted to go, and how they couldn't quite decide on their destination.

'Don't worry, that is normal. Most people go on many holidays a year, and never give much thought to booking a trip, but the minute they have to book their honeymoon they freak out! I suppose it's the one holiday that must be perfect. But don't worry, we'll find you somewhere; and trust me, no matter where you go you will enjoy it. Everyone loves their honeymoon, it's the going back to normal life that makes them sad.'

Ali looked at Robin, and felt bad for shouting at him earlier. It was his wedding and honeymoon, too. She had to try to remember that, and remember the honeymoon would just be the two of them, and they had to pick somewhere they both dreamed of.

'So let me know your thoughts,' the chatty agent said. And with that they spent a good half an hour going through the different options. It wasn't until the travel agent mentioned Hawaii that they both sat up and asked her to give them more details.

'There are many islands within Hawaii, but having been there myself a few times, I would totally recommend Maui. It is the second largest of the islands, and not as built-up as the popular Oahu. Maui really is drop-dead beautiful: the beaches are white, and the sea is so warm. There are so many activities, too: snorkelling in the coral reef, surfing, kayaking, day adventure-trips to volcanos – and, of course, you can visit many of the other Hawaiian islands if you want.'

'Tell us more,' Robin laughed.

'Well, you fly into Kahului airport, and I would advise you to head to Ka'ananapali beach, near to the town of Lahina. As you travel this road the smell of pineapples fills the air, because they grow them over there. Lahina is a very laid-back town, but has plenty of restaurants and bars, and the Ka'ananapali beach area is where I'd recommend you stay. The whole island is amazing, and is full of things to do.'

As she showed Ali the brochures Ali just knew she wanted to go, Hawaii seemed so tropical and exciting. She turned to Robin, who squeezed her hand.

'Let's go to Maui!' he said.

'And, of course, you know the flights to Hawaii stop in either New York or Los Angeles. Would you like to stop off in either of those places? It won't change the cost of the flight. You will only have to pay for your hotel.'

Ali couldn't believe what the travel agent was saying. To be able to have a five-star beach holiday on a tropical island, and also get in some shopping in New York, followed by celebrity sightseeing in LA, would be a dream come true. There was no discussion, they were going, and so they booked the Waldorf Astoria in New York for two nights on the way over, and a hotel in LA for two nights on the way home from Hawaii. Signing the booking forms, Ali couldn't stop smiling. The honeymoon was going to be a once-in-a-lifetime trip, and as they thanked the travel agent and headed to Bewleys for some breakfast Robin gave her a kiss.

'Hawaii, here we come!' he shouted.

84

After a full Irish breakfast and plenty of tea, Ali and Robin were fired up and ready to collect their wedding invites. As they walked along Abbey Street to the printers they couldn't stop talking about Hawaii.

'It is going to be the best honeymoon ever,' Ali gushed.

Robin was delighted they had found somewhere they both liked and were excited about. He was picturing himself surfing on the beaches of Maui, when they found themselves outside the little printer's. The shop was busy with people collecting birthday, wedding and party invites. Eventually Ali and Robin's turn came, and the woman behind the desk handed them a large box. Ali ripped it open and was almost overwhelmed. The invitations were so beautiful. Sarah's artwork was a masterpiece. The printer had chosen paper that suited the design perfectly, and the gold-sheeted envelopes echoed the golden hair of the bride on the card.

'These are amazing. Wait until everyone sees them,' Robin said, as he examined the cards. He gave Ali a hug.

'Everyone has been complimenting us, and asking where you found that artist,' the shop assistant said.

'She's my friend,' Ali answered.

'Well, aren't you lucky to be friends with such a talented

artist! Tell her she should set up shop as a full-time wedding-invite designer. She could make her fortune!'

Ali agreed with the lady, and as she paid Robin picked up the box and headed for the door.

'Another thing to cross off your to-do list, hey, Ali?'

Yes, Ali thought, but she was still in shock about the invite. To see it in print made the whole wedding so real now. People were actually going to be invited to their wedding: it really was happening.

They arrived at Molly's parents' house by 2 p.m. Molly answered the door looking a little hot and bothered.

'Sorry to be so stressed,' she exclaimed. 'I wanted to have everything ready for you by now, but our dog escaped and I spent an hour running around trying to catch him. Then I had forgotten I had left the bread in the oven, so that was well and truly burnt by the time we got the bad dog back home.'

Ali and Robin sat down in the kitchen.

'Molly, it is only us, don't be so worried. We can't wait to try your work!'

Molly calmed herself down, and poured them all glasses of lemonade.

'OK, well, as we discussed before, I've prepared two servings of every course you are going to choose from. I've kept the menu simple, as weddings have to cater for a wide range of ages. For starters I've narrowed it down to either a cold seafood platter or else Caesar salad.' Ali and Robin's mouths were watering as Molly served them the two dishes.

'What fish are in this, Molly?' Robin asked as she handed him the cold seafood platter.

'Quite a lot, really. There is fresh salmon, Boston prawns, oak-smoked salmon, Bismarck herring, fresh anchovies and crayfish tails, and it's all on a bed of salad leaves with saffron fusion. Like the salad, I can serve this with my mum's special homemade walnut brown bread.'

Robin tucked in, and was delighted by the taste.

'This is unreal,' both Ali and Robin agreed as they sampled the fish.

'It's so different, and it is lovely to have a cold starter. It's August so it will probably be quite hot, and fish and brown bread will be perfect. Nobody will be expecting such a glamorous starter from us. Let's go for the fish,' Ali added.

Molly was happy that her friends liked the dish: she had worked so hard the last few weeks getting it right.

Next, Molly served them the tenderest beef Robin had ever tasted. And with it a mixture of green beans, baby carrots, roasted potatoes and spring-onion champ.

'It will be a lucky man who marries you,' he said as he wolfed down the lean slices of sirloin.

Molly laughed, but could see Ali giving Robin a dirty look for mentioning men. All her friends were careful not to mention men, Luke or future plans at the moment. Molly ignored the awkward moment, and started to serve them another option, which was a rolled stuffed loin of pork with an apple and walnut stuffing.

'They will both be served with the same vegetables and all, it is just whether you prefer beef or pork,' Molly said, giving Robin more potatoes and gravy.

Ali and Robin discussed the advantages of both, and in the end both agreed they preferred the tender sirloin.

'Great, so now we have dessert.' Molly laughed as she whipped some cream.

They both gasped when they saw pastry slices layered with a hazelnut praline filling and served with yummy hot chocolate sauce.

'But then, as it's summer, we could go for juicy Wexford

Amanda Hearty

strawberries with freshly whipped cream and a homemade vanilla ice-cream,' Molly added.

Ali could feel her mouth watering as she ate the pastry, but it did it again when she tried the fresh strawberries.

'Oh, I don't know, these are both great,' Ali said, in-between more mouthfuls of both desserts. Molly laughed. She was starting to tidy away the dirty pots, pans and plates.

'I do love praline and chocolate,' Robin said. 'But I think after a big meal on a hot day there is nothing like strawberries and cream. I know everyone loves strawberries, while some people don't like pastry and chocolate, so maybe the strawberries are better, Ali.' Robin turned to his future wife, who now had chocolate sauce all over her face.

'You are probably right.' Ali sighed as she scraped the chocolate sauce off her plate.

'Don't worry, Ali,' Molly said, pouring her some more lemonade. 'On your wedding day I can sneak you in a pastry slice, just for you. You are the bride, after all. Just don't tell anyone else!'

Ali hugged her friend.

'You are the best, Molly, and such a great chef. Thanks so much for doing this job.'

'Thank you both for believing in me, I appreciate it.' After that all three moved out to the back garden to catch some sun, and Ali filled Molly in on Hawaii and showed her the wedding invitations.

After two hours soaking in the sun and catching up on gossip, Robin stood up.

'We'd better get going soon, Ali, we've those bands to go and see.'

'Why don't you come with us, Molly?' Ali asked. 'We're going to see three different bands tonight, ones we want to check out for the wedding. They're all having gigs in various bars, so they invited us along to hear them play. It might be fun.'

Molly was about to say no, but remembered even her mum and dad were going out tonight. It would be so sad to stay in on a Saturday night, alone and single.

'OK. Just let me wash all this flour and chocolate sauce off!'

85

Ben walked in from work to hear his mother and father talking in the kitchen.

'I just don't want you going back to work, Joe. You almost died. You can't push yourself so much again. Ben will take care of things.'

Ben's heart sank. Work was exactly what he had wanted to talk to his parents about tonight. As his second week of working for his father's company had come to an end he was hoping to tell his parents that he really had to go back to work on the newspaper. His friend Jeremy had been a great help, but he had said he really couldn't keep the job open any longer. Ben set his briefcase and suit jacket down and headed for the kitchen. His father was sitting at the kitchen table, and even though Ben and Maura were doing everything they could to make sure he rested and ate well, he looked ten years older than he was. Pale and thin, he was like a ghost. Ben still got a shock every time he saw him. The doctor had said that recovering from a massive heart-attack and surgery could take months, but nothing ever prepares you for the sight of your father being too weak to be able to dress himself properly, or walk up the stairs.

'How was work? How did that meeting with Andrew McCarthy go?' Joe asked Ben enthusiastically.

Ben could see the pride in his father's eyes at the thought of Ben attending meetings on behalf of the company and dealing with clients.

'It all went very well, Dad, don't worry. Andrew was asking after you, and said whenever you're ready for a round of golf to give him a call.'

'Golf? Sweet Jesus, there will be no golf, Ben. Do you want to kill your father off?' Maura half-shrieked, as she prepared a chicken casserole.

'Don't worry, honey, there will be no golf for a while. But maybe we could swing by the clubhouse for a pint one day, Ben!' Joe whispered the last sentence to his son.

Ben knew how much his dad must miss golf and the social interaction he relied on work and the golf club for.

'So, how is everything going in the office? I suppose everyone can't believe you have finally joined the company. I'm so proud of you, Ben,' Joe said. He patted Ben's hand and smiled at him.

Ben didn't know what to say, and instead excused himself and went up to change. After dinner Ben was in the living room watching *The Rugby Club*, a weekly rugby programme he loved, when his mum came in.

'How is work really, Ben?' she said kindly, as she passed him a cup of tea and a slice of apple tart with cream.

Ben sat up and turned the TV off.

'I don't know what to say to Dad. I told you both I was only helping the company out for a week or so, and then we would have to get someone in to take over until Dad went back. But now he seems to think I've agreed to work there for ever.'

Maura looked at her son.

'I can't force you to work for the company, Ben, but please don't fling away this chance to run your own company and make your father proud, just because you want less responsibility and a carefree life. Your father is a long way off going back to work, and I do not want you upsetting him by chucking in the job and heading back to that newspaper. You are old enough now to start thinking about your own future and how your decisions affect us.'

And at that moment his father walked into the room and their conversation was over. As Ben turned the TV back on and watched his father struggle to lower himself into a chair, he realized he had no choice. He texted Jeremy: 'You free for a pint tonight? We need to talk.' Jeremy texted him right back, and they agreed to meet in Stillorgan in half an hour.

After many pints and a long discussion, Ben and Jeremy both knew what Ben had to do.

'Thanks for all your help, anyway, Jeremy. You're a good friend, and I hope you're not in trouble with the paper for keeping my job open. I'll really miss it, but I've to help my dad, it's the only option.'

Jeremy looked at his oldest friend.

'Ben, I'm proud of you. Of course I'll miss seeing you around the office, but it's great you're growing up.'

'"Growing up?" You're the married one now,' Ben laughed.

'It's not about being married or not. You're grown-up when you start thinking about others' feelings, and notice how your actions affect them. And sometimes that means doing stuff you don't want to do. So you, my friend, really have grown up. Watch out! You'll be getting married next!'

Ben laughed, taking over a company was enough for him for one day. Finding a girl to marry was another day's work. As they left the pub and Ben began the walk home, Jeremy turned.

'I might get Martin in accounts to give you a shout next month. The paper is getting fed up dealing with the overpriced stuck-up snobs we use at the moment, and they've been thinking about putting the audit out to tender.'

Ben thought having a newspaper as a client would certainly be more interesting than all the old fogies he mostly dealt with at the moment.

'I would love that, give me a call any time.'

Maybe being an accountant won't be so bad after all, Ben thought, as he walked home.

86

On Saturday morning Ben was eating Nutella spread straight out of the jar, and helping his mum unpack groceries in the kitchen, when his dad asked him what meetings were coming up the following week. Ben saw his mum look at him, concerned. He had not yet told either of them his decision about work.

'Well, actually, Dad, that is something I want to talk to you about.'

Ben's mum walked behind Joe, and put her hand on his shoulder. She didn't know how he would take the news that Ben was going back to the newspaper.

'It's about all those meetings and clients. I think it is about time I had some business cards printed up. I mean, how can I spread the word about our business when I don't even have a business card to keep in my wallet?'

A look of relief spread over Maura's face, while Joe beamed with joy.

'Yes, son, we must get on to that straight away. Let me show you my card.' And with that Ben and Joe were deep in a discussion about cards, new letterheads and email addresses. Maura gave Ben a big hug. She had always known that one day he would grow up and do the right thing. Now it had happened, and he was becoming the man of the family, and she couldn't have been prouder.

Ben spent the afternoon discussing work and clients before his dad got too tired and needed to lie down. Ben had been nervous about committing to taking over the company, but after seeing the excitement in his dad's eyes he knew he was doing the right thing. He grabbed some beers from the fridge: he was off to a barbecue at a friend's house, and was looking forward to an afternoon of burgers, beer and relaxation. As he picked up his sunglasses and wallet he suddenly thought he would text that girl Nikki. She had been great fun, and maybe she would like to see him after the barbecue. By the time he got into his car, she had texted him back to say she would meet him at 10 p.m. on Dawson Street. It's going to be a great night, Ben thought to himself, as he plugged his iPod into his car and blared the Foo Fighters the whole way to his friend's house.

The barbecue was great fun, and everyone there was delighted to hear about Ben taking over running the family business from his dad. As they drank beer and sang along to Razorlight Ben knew he had made the right decision. After some drinking games and some more dancing he realized it was after 10 p.m., and he was late meeting Nikki, but she didn't seem to mind. He grabbed a taxi to town and met her outside Samsara.

As they headed into the bar for a drink Ben ran straight into Laura. It was quite a shock: he hadn't seen her for so long, not since before his dad got sick and his life had changed. She looked startled to see him, too.

'Hi,' Ben said. He gave her a kiss on the cheek.

She smiled, and accepted the kiss, even though he knew she must still be fuming that he stood her up on a date.

'I meant to ring you many times, I really did. I'm so sorry about that night.'

'It's OK, Ben. Robin and Ali explained to me about your dad being sick. I did text you but I'm not sure if you ever got it,' Laura said.

Ben silently cursed himself for not replying. He had received her text, but with all the panic of the hospital he had never even replied. She must hate me, he thought.

'Sorry about that, too,' Ben mumbled.

Laura looked great: she had a good tan, her brown eyes sparkled, and her long dark brown curly hair fell over her face. She smiled back. 'Don't worry about it,' she said, looking at Nikki. 'I'll let you get back to your date. I hope your dad is OK.' And with that she was gone.

Ben turned to Nikki, who had begun chatting to the bouncer, telling him she knew the owner and persuading him to let them go upstairs to the VIP section. The bouncer was charmed by her, and led them straight there. It was good to skip the queues at the regular bar, and be served drinks at their table. And it was fun, too, to chat about anything and everything with Nikki, who looked amazing tonight, and was so laid-back and full of fun. But it still took Ben a few more drinks before he could forget about Laura and what might have been.

87

On Monday Molly was busy making sandwiches when Ali asked her to meet up for lunch. It was a quiet enough day so Molly agreed. As the girls sat down inside another local café for a lasagne, Ali told Molly how herself and Robin had to make the final decision on the band for the wedding.

'You were there, Molly, what do you think?'

Molly thought back to ten days earlier, when she had gone with Robin and Ali to see the three potential wedding bands. The first had been called The Breakfast Club, and had been an eighties band. They'd played all the hits that were famous when the girls were young, and they had certainly got the crowd going – Molly hadn't wanted to leave the dance floor – but she didn't know if they would alienate the older crowd at the wedding. The next group, called The Golden Oldies, were awful, and Robin had made the girls leave before the fourth song. They had played corny numbers, and when 'Come On Eileen' had been followed by 'Sweet Caroline', Molly had known that they would be way too cheesy for Ali's wedding. The last band had been called Set List, and even though Molly had been slightly drunk by the time they arrived at someone's thirtieth birthday in a private room upstairs in Kielys, she could see the band were very good. They tried to play a mixture of older classic tunes and some new ones from U2 and the like. The band were also very cool-looking and had been really nice to talk to after the gig, when Ali and Robin had asked questions about their availability and cost.

'I do think Set List might be the best, Ali.'

'Oh, great, I'm so glad, because I agree with you, and think we should book them. But I was also hoping you would say that, because Will, the lead singer in the band, rang me today to ask if we still wanted them for the wedding. They are getting booked up and needed to know. He also asked me for your number. You made a big impression on him the other night.'

Molly blushed; she didn't know what to say. The singer had definitely been cute, and obviously talented, but she and Luke had only broken up a few weeks ago. How could she even think about dating?

'I think it's way too soon, Ali. I'm sorry. Please don't give him my number.' Ali said nothing, and instead started chatting about her upcoming hen party.

As Molly walked back to work after lunch she couldn't stop thinking about the singer, Will, and the thought of dating again. Even though she wouldn't admit it to anyone else, there was a small part of her that got lonely and kept wanting to ring Luke. Sometimes she longed to forget about the arguments and promise to be the girlfriend he wanted. But she would always see sense in time, and turn her phone off. Even if she didn't want him back, though, how could she date so soon? Luke had been her life for years, had been the person she woke up beside every day, and now the thought of kissing or even holding hands with someone else made her feel uneasy. The last few weeks had been hard, and she swung between missing Luke and feeling she was better off without him, and needed to find a guy who would appreciate her work and understand her passion for it. Living at home was also a rollercoaster: she loved having her mum there to constantly chat to and cook with, but other days it drove her mad when her mum kept asking her if she would be home for dinner and what she would like to eat. Her mum couldn't understand that some days Molly wanted to be able to meet a friend at the last minute after work, or was in the mood for Eddie Rocket's and not beef stew. Often, too, Molly had eaten enough at work, and just didn't feel like a big home-cooked meal. *If I hear my mum complain one more time that she bought an extra chicken breast for me that will now go to waste, I'll eat one raw just to please her!* Molly thought to herself. As she walked into Heavenly she could see things had picked up. She quickly tied up her dark hair, put on her work apron and headed for the hot kitchen.

The following afternoon Molly had a huge order to deliver to Sterling Bank. They had a client conference, and so herself and her cousin Eve had to deliver not only all the usual orders, but a selection of sandwiches, quiches and tarts to the large conference room. As they walked into the bank, Molly told her cousin about the singer of the band, and him asking for her number.

'Wow, sounds exciting, go for it!'

'Eve, I think it might be too soon,' Molly said, not sure that Eve would understand.

'Molly, I know you must miss Luke, and much as I always got on well with him I have to say I think he treated you badly. This rock star might not be the guy for you, but don't close yourself off from meeting guys just because Luke was too foolish to see you were the perfect girl. You have to get used to going out and meeting new people. Just think about this Will guy, and if nothing else it could be fun to go and see him play. We could be his groupies!'

Molly laughed as she entered the conference room and left the picnic baskets full of freshly cooked food on the large mahogany table. Next they began to hand out sandwiches to their usual customers. As they approached Scott Williams's desk, he put down the phone and smiled at Molly.

'How is my favourite cook?'

Molly smiled back politely, and handed him his usual boring sandwich. She had been embarrassed around him ever since he had dropped her home that day.

'I'm fine, Scott, thanks. Your office is certainly busy to-day.'

'Oh yeah, we've had all these big clients with us all week, and it's been one long round of meetings, but this weekend we are having our annual summer barbecue, and inviting not only them but all our best clients and suppliers. You should come,' Scott said. He handed her an invite.

Molly read that the bank were having a large barbecue with music and games at the Royal Dublin Society club that Saturday.

'You are one of our best suppliers, you know! And maybe you would like to come, too,' he said to Eve, who had suddenly appeared beside Molly.

Eve read the invite.

'We would love to. I'm always up for a barbecue. It will be fun.'

Molly could have kicked her cousin, there was no way she wanted to go a barbecue with Scott Williams, but it was too late. Scott was already telling Eve the best time to come.

'Not too early as it's all kids and face-painting then, but not too late as we'll all be too drunk to enjoy your company!'

Eve laughed, told Scott they would see him in a few days, and walked out of the office with Molly.

'Before you say anything, Molly,' she said, 'the barbecue will be fun, and he is a good client of ours, so we are going. We've no other plans for Saturday night, and I don't want you staying in moping over Luke and baking cookies! I'm sure with the lure of free barbecue food André will want to come as well.'

Molly liked Eve's boyfriend, André, and knew that at least if he was there Eve wouldn't spend the whole barbecue trying to set her up with new guys.

'Fine, but we'll just pop in for an hour, and then go. I don't want to spend my Saturday night talking about sandwiches with clients.'

88

On Saturday afternoon Molly was in her bedroom trying to decide what to wear. A barbecue was a tough challenge. She didn't want to be too casual as there were going to be a lot of potential clients there, but she didn't want Scott to think she was dressing up for him, either. I need something in-between a deb's dress and a bikini, she laughed to herself. Eventually she decided on a pair of white cut-off trousers and a blue Roxy string top, along with white wedge shoes and a pair of very fashionable oversized sunglasses propped on top of her long, thick dark hair. As she put on a beaded bracelet she had picked up in Mexico years ago she heard Eve beeping her car horn outside. Molly felt a bit nervous heading off like this: she was used to just hanging out with Luke and her own friends, and was not the best person at meeting new people. But it was too late now, so she shouted goodbye to her mum, and headed out to the car. Eve was driving and André was turning up his favourite CD, *Moon Safari* by Air. It was the only French band Eve would let him listen to, so it got played a lot! Molly squeezed into the back of Eve's black Mini.

'You look great, Molly,' said André. 'No wonder you have rock stars falling for you.'

Molly gave Eve a dirty look. Why had she told André about Will?

'He is not a rock star, and no one is falling for me, but thanks anyway, André.'

They were in the RDS within minutes.

'Wow!' exclaimed Eve as they handed the security man their invite, and started to realize that this 'barbecue' was about more than just burgers. Not only was there a professional kitchen set-up with tables of buffet-style food, and plenty of kids running around with their faces painted and balloon animals trailing behind them, there was also a small funfair, and Molly could see the head of the Sterling Bank on a bumper car. There was a lively band belting out Van Morrison's 'Brown Eyed Girl', while the beer tent seemed to have hundreds of men in boardshorts and sunglasses crowded around it.

Molly, Eve and André made their way to the queue for the burgers.

'Wow, the bank must be doing well to be able to throw this kind of party,' Eve exclaimed, as she filled her plate high with chips, salad and chicken kebabs. Molly was impressed, too: the food was simple enough, but perfect for the throngs of kids and families, and the funfair and music were totally unexpected. André found them a table right in front of the band, and as they half-swayed, half-ate their food to some U2 hits, Scott Williams appeared out of nowhere wearing beige chinos, and a crisp white shirt. His skin looked very tanned.

'Molly, it's great to see you.' He smiled as he introduced himself to André.

Molly tried to swallow back her burger, which she'd rammed into her mouth. Eventually she was able to smile back, and thank Scott for his generous invite.

'No problem, sure if a bank can afford to throw a party like this, then the more the merrier! I think you would have cooked a better burger, but it is your day off, I suppose.'

'Oh, she would, Scott. She really is the best cook in the world. Molly, you should cook Scott something special, rather than making him a sandwich, someday,' Eve added.

Molly glared at Eve. Scott Williams was nice, but he was just a client. What was Eve playing at? But Scott didn't comment on Eve's proposed dinner date, and instead told André that they were starting a game of tag-rugby soon if he was interested. The word rugby was like sweet music to André's ears, and before the girls could say anything he and Scott had walked off to the back fields to get kitted out.

Once Scott left, Molly was able to relax again, and herself and Eve made their way over to the funfair. Molly hadn't been on a big wheel for years, but Eve persuaded her and before long they were high over Ballsbridge, overlooking the whole of Dublin. The sight was beautiful, but Molly's thoughts turned to Luke, and she wondered where in the big city he was, and what he was doing. Eve chatted away about her summer plans and her proposed trip to André's family in the South of France. Molly half-listened but couldn't stop herself thinking of Luke, or rather the lack of Luke, and wondering what would happen that summer. She knew Eve was right, and she had to move on from Luke and open herself up to new people, and in particular new guys, but it was hard. Hard to have the confidence to get out there and meet new men. Molly knew from her single girlfriends that there might be guys out there, but not many of them were good. It was going to be tough.

'Molly, are you listening?' Eve said, breaking into her train of thought. 'I was just saying that Scott seems like a very generous and sweet guy, to invite us all here.'

'Yeah, it is a fun way to spend a Saturday afternoon, but I'm sure he invited plenty of other people, not just us – his sandwich makers,' Molly said.

Eve said nothing, and instead steered Molly towards the

bumper cars. They spent thirty minutes banging into each other and the many teenagers who seemed hell-bent on trying to crash into as many people as possible. Molly was dizzy with all the spinning, so decided to take a break, and headed for the candy floss stand. As she ate the light and fluffy sugar candy, she saw André and Scott trying to shoot little plastic ducks. She joined them.

'Oh, Molly, maybe you can help Scott here. I can't bring myself to hurt these little ducks!'

André thrust the plastic gun into Molly's hand. Molly was reluctant at first, but before long was having a great time as she and Scott worked together to try and get as many ducks assassinated as possible, in order to win prizes. Eventually she was laughing so much she could no longer play, and handed her gun to some little children. The man behind the stand asked Scott what prizes he wanted.

'You did all the work, Molly, you pick.' Molly chose a large teddy bear and a Hello Kitty plastic watch.

'It is great to see all the long hours I work earning the bank money go into buying such superb things for everyone.' Scott laughed and picked up the teddy bear.

Molly wrapped the watch, around her wrist. Scott smiled as they walked back side by side to join Eve and André, who were dancing to the band.

'Who wants drinks?' Scott said, heading for the bar.

As they sipped their beers Molly realized that Eve was right: she had just needed to go out and do new things. Her life with Luke was over, she needed to be open to different experiences and people. The day had been so much fun, and Molly was delighted Eve had forced her to come. Just then she got a call from Ali, saying they were going to see Set List one more time tonight, and did she want to come? It would be a chance to see that guy Will again, and earlier Molly would have said it was too soon, but today had taught her change was necessary, so she texted Ali back and said she would be in town as soon as she could. She went to say goodbye to Scott but couldn't find him. So, as she wished goodnight to her cousin and André, she asked them to thank Scott on her behalf. She started to walk out to Anglesea Road to catch a taxi to Temple Bar, and suddenly saw Scott deep in conversation with a beautiful young girl. Their heads were bent together, so Molly decided not to disturb him. That must be his girlfriend, Molly thought, as she flagged down a taxi.

89

Sarah was having breakfast with her mum before going to work in the gallery, when the post arrived.

'There is one for you, Sarah,' said her mum, handing her a large gold envelope. Sarah opened it up and actually gasped. It was Ali and Robin's wedding invitation with her drawing on the front! Seeing her work in print made it feel so real, made her feel like a real artist.

'Sarah, it is beautiful, well done. I knew you still had that artist inside you, wow,' her mum said as she hugged Sarah and stared at the invitation.

Ali had included some spare invites in the envelope, and a cheque for Sarah's work. Sarah had felt uneasy being paid, but Ali had insisted. Sarah stood one of the cards up on the windowsill, and when the sun shone in on top of it, she felt like it was an invitation to her own wedding, she was so proud! The whole way to work Sarah just kept smiling; she was chuffed with herself, the invite looked so professional and beautiful. As she opened up the Stone Studio she received a text from Molly congratulating her on the 'most original and stunning wedding invitation ever!' Sarah was delighted, and as she unpacked the day's new canvases and paintings she started to imagine that one day someone would unpack her work and hang it on the walls of a gallery like this one. It had been her

263

dream once to be a full-time artist. Maybe it could be again, she thought, as she began photographing and cataloguing new pieces for the gallery.

By lunch Sarah had all the new work ready to be hung, and was waiting for Clodagh to come in. Clodagh was helping her get prepared for the gallery's latest exhibition, which was opening that night. Sarah grabbed a sandwich and coffee in the newsagent's next door, and as she ate she flicked through the property section of the daily newspaper. She would still like to grow up and finally live in her own place, but it was hard to find somewhere she liked and could afford. It was too early to talk to Hugh about buying somewhere, and all her friends either had places or, like her, couldn't afford to leave home. As she circled places she might look at over the weekend Clodagh walked in.

'Still trying to move?' Clodagh said, as she noticed the newspaper.

'I wish,' Sarah sighed.

'Well, at least you have a full-time job. Imagine how hard it is for me. I would love to move away from home, but being a student who works part-time means nothing to a bank, especially when they hear I'm an art student. Nobody wants to lend money to artists, we might be creative but we are too unreliable, too much of a risk. I can't even get a meeting with my bank manager! I should have studied accountancy or something boring and reliable like that.'

Sarah laughed, but she did feel sorry for artists. She knew how hard it was to spend days, weeks, months on work, and then for it not to sell. It was a tough life, and money was always a problem, and if she became a full-time artist she would have to cope with that. But now she needed to spend the afternoon getting this evening's exhibition up and running.

90

The gallery was filling up, and with a David Gray CD playing in the background and the wine flowing, there was an air of excitement about the unveiling of the gallery's new collection of pieces from an up-and-coming French artist. Sarah was just handing out some exhibition brochures when she got a shock: Maggie McCartney, the gallery's owner, was walking in the door. The months of living in her villa in Marbella had obviously paid off. She looked great: tanned and healthy. She walked up to Sarah and gave her a big hug.

'Sorry to surprise you like this, Sarah darling. I swear I'm not trying to spy on you! Just this morning my husband had to come home to Ireland for some business, and at the last minute I thought to hell with it, I'd come too. I knew we had this exhibition tonight, and to be honest a few days away from paella, siestas and chorizo will do me good!'

Sarah was very surprised to see her boss, but was instantly relieved that the gallery was packed and looking impressive.

'Thank God we hoovered earlier,' whispered Clodagh, as she poured wine for their guests. Sarah laughed her agreement. Maggie will find nothing wrong with this place, she thought. The evening was a huge success, and not only did the gallery earn a hefty commission and sell many pieces, but the artist promised to do more for them, and to spread the word to his other artist friends. Clodagh finished tidying up, and then headed home, leaving Maggie and Sarah sitting down enjoying a glass of wine.

As Sarah filled Maggie in on Hugh, and her sister's new baby, Maggie thanked her for running the gallery so well, and always keeping her informed of what was happening. 'You have such a great eye, Sarah. Some of these new pieces are great buys for us, well done. I actually have the name of a new artist I want you to contact. If you have a pen there I'll write his name and number down.'

Sarah opened her oversized handbag to search for a pen. She had to unload her iPod, diary and wallet to find it, and as she did so the wedding invite fell out. Maggie picked it up.

'Wow, who did this? It's beautiful. Is this a wedding you are going to?'

'Well, yes I'm going, but I also designed that invite. It's my work.' Sarah blushed.

Maggie looked shocked.

'Sarah, this work is completely different from your old pieces. It's far more commercial. I love this kind of free illustration, and you've a great sense of colour. I could sell this! You know there is a growing market for illustrative work like this, and I'm always on the lookout for new artists. You are an untapped treasure.'

Sarah didn't know what to say, but Maggie did.

'Please tell me that there is more like this – lovely pieces to frame and sell. There are buyers crying out for work like yours.'

Sarah shook her head. 'Oh, Maggie. I'd love to work as a full-time artist, you know that, but it didn't work out for me years ago, and I wouldn't even know where to start, or how to fund myself.'

'You don't know where to start? Sarah you have already started. This is beautiful, so different,' Maggie exclaimed, as she placed the invite on a large glass table beside two large bronzes. Seeing her work on show alongside the sculptures, Sarah began to think: Maybe I could do this, maybe I should be an artist, a proper artist.

'Sarah, don't let your talent go to waste. Your work has really evolved, and I think maybe you have found your niche. I'd be delighted to exhibit your work,' Maggie encouraged. She went on: 'Well, you have a serious think about it. You could show here, let us sell your work. If you worked part-time for me, that would give you more hours to paint. Think about it, Sarah. Listen I've to go now, as hubby will be waiting! But I'll be back in Ireland again in a few weeks' time to attend a friend's sixtieth party, so maybe we can sit down and have a proper chat and see what your plans are then.'

And with that Maggie waved goodbye to her gallery and was gone out the door.

Sarah sat there for another hour, stunned, staring into space, dreaming about her future. Maggie McCartney, one of the top gallery owners, was offering to show and sell her work! Maggie was right, she shouldn't let any of her love for art be wasted, but she knew painting needed your full commitment, and even though she might manage to work the odd day at the gallery, she couldn't work full-time, or even part-time. She knew when you were in a creative flow, you just had to go with it, and serving wine at exhibitions wouldn't help. But then Sarah remembered what Clodagh had said about getting loans and mortgages from a bank. I'll never be able to move away from home if I give art a go, Sarah thought, as she locked the gallery and headed home. She fretted over whether to become an artist, or stay in the gallery and buy her own place all the way home. It was going to be a tough decision.

As she walked in the door at home, and took her suit jacket off, the wall in their hall caught her eye. On it her mum hung framed family photos: there was a photo of Sarah's parents on their wedding day, another of her parents at Mel's college graduation, one of their whole family in Italy in summer, one of Mel and John on their wedding day, and another of Sarah, Mel, their mum and baby Fiona on her christening day. But it wasn't these older photos that caught her eye, it was the brand-new frame in the middle that did. Right bang in the centre of all these proud family photos was Sarah's wedding invitation, framed and now hanging for the world to see. Her mum had been so proud that she must have rushed off to buy a new frame to show off Sarah's work. Alongside the photos of Mel and her achievements now hung Sarah's invite. Excited, she headed up to bed, but couldn't sleep. Between the new painting in the hall and Maggie's encouraging words, Sarah's head was filled with dreams of paints, sketches, canvasses and gallery exhibitions.

91

Ali was one stressed fiancée. She was in Kilkenny for the weekend, not only for her hen party, which was taking place tonight, but also because her two sisters Jill and Kate had yet to make a final decision on their bridesmaids' dresses. Her sisters had planned her hen for the Saturday, but Ali had driven down home the night before, so all three of them could get up and shop early, before all her friends arrived in Kilkenny for the big night. So they were now in a very fashionable boutique, with Jill in one changing room, Kate in the other, and Ali running between the two rooms trying to stop them fighting. Ali's mum was sitting in a large chair, with a cup of tea in her hand.

'Ali, I think we should let them wear their tracksuits. I've wasted enough time with those two. I mean, God help us all, when they actually have to get married and pick their own wedding dresses, I'll have a stroke.'

Ali sighed. Her mum was right, the whole idea of being a bridesmaid had gone to their heads, and both sisters seemed to be competing for best bridesmaid ever, yet somehow not actually helping Ali at all. Ali was looking at bridal shoes when she heard Jill shout.

'You only picked this dress because you know it won't suit me. You want me to look fat on the day, Kate.'

'I want you to look fat? You are the one wanting us to wear yellow corsets, which you know will clash with my fair hair,' Kate shouted back.

Ali looked at the boutique's owner, but she didn't seem fazed.

'I have seen it all before,' she said softly as she poured Ali's mum more tea.

'I can't take this, Ali, my nerves . . .' Her mum sighed.

Ali raced towards the dressing rooms.

'What is wrong with you girls?' she shouted.

'Jill wants to show me up on the big day,' Kate shouted.

Jill was about to answer back when Ali turned on them both. 'I picked you both as my bridesmaids because you are my sisters and I love you, but let me tell you this, if you don't start realizing that it's mine and Robin's day, not yours, then I'll ask mum to be my bridesmaid. Now, stop arguing and get into those dresses.' And with that she walked out of the dressing room and grabbed some tea from her mum.

She heard nothing for five minutes, but then suddenly her two sisters appeared out of the dressing room, looking sheepish yet stunning in two matching ballet-length pink satin dresses.

'Do you like them, Ali?' asked Jill in a whisper.

Ali knew her sisters were scared of her, and although she sensed it wouldn't last for long, she decided to exploit it a bit longer.

'I do, but I want to see the champagne version of it on both of you, too.'

Kate seemed about to protest, but abruptly stopped, and walked back into the dressing room.

'Well, Ali, it's funny how well threats work on the two of them, isn't it?' her mum laughed.

The girls appeared again in knee-length champagne dresses that had large white ribbons around the waist, and a high neckline.

'I like those too, but I think the pink ones were nicer, try them again,' Ali ordered.

The girls turned wearily on their heels and reappeared a few minutes later, and when they did Ali knew the rose-pink ballerina dresses were the ones to go for. The girls looked stunning, and the fit of the dresses suited their now slimmed-down bodies. The cream waistline bow and matching cream satin shoes made them look so grown-up and beautiful. The girls also knew they looked good, and for once stopped fighting and gave each other a hug. The shop owner looked relieved and started to tot up how much the outfits, shoes and matching bags would cost. Ali didn't have much time to celebrate finding the dresses, as she had booked to have her hair done in a local hairdresser's, ready for that night's hen party.

She waved her sisters goodbye and headed towards the city centre, and only as she got comfortable in the hairdresser's chair and told the stylist what she wanted done, did she realize that she was going on her hen in a few hours' time. Her last official night out as a single girl! Weird, she thought, but as the hairdresser began to wash and then cut her hair, Ali forgot all about her hen and instead enjoyed having some time to herself, away from work, bridesmaids and wedding talk.

92

Ali, her two sisters, a few of her cousins, and twelve of her friends were all meeting at 6 p.m. in Kilkenny's newest and hippest hotel. Her Dublin friends were all staying there for the night, and had heard the place had opened a fabulous cocktail bar. They were not wrong, the bar was amazing, and as Ali walked in she felt she had walked on to the set of *Sex and the City*. There were beautiful people and Manhattan cocktails everywhere. The bar was all glass, with funky chandeliers and oversized chairs, it was like something from a film. Ali was greeted by a cheer when she walked in, and she saw all her friends had reserved an area and were surrounded by cocktails and feather boas.

'Well, Ali, I knew that L-plates wouldn't be your style, but when we saw these pink feather boas last time we were in Dublin we had to stock up,' laughed Jill. She was trying to be the perfect bridesmaid and sister by holding Ali's bag, and at the same time struggling to take a picture of Ali being greeted by her friends and also ordering Ali a Frozen Strawberry Daiquiri.

Ali settled into a comfy couch and looked around at her friends. She had invited a selection of her old school friends – who hadn't had far to travel, as most of them still lived in Kilkenny – and then she had her Dublin friends, and girls she had met in college. She had agonized over whether to have her hen in Kilkenny or Dublin, but when all her Dublin friends had said they would be only too happy to spend a night in such a fun city as Kilkenny Ali had been delighted and let Jill and Kate make the plans.

So here they were having cocktails with their pink boas, swapping stories about how they had met Ali. They had dinner booked in an Italian at 9 p.m. Jill knew the owner, and so they had been given their own small function room upstairs, where they could make as much noise as they wanted. Ali had been nervous about the hen, as growing up near Kilkenny city she was well used to seeing hen and stag parties that looked tacky and messy and gave her city a bad name, but her friends had assured her that they knew she was a bit hesitant. They had promised: 'No L-plates, or tacky veils!'

Robin, on the other hand, had enthusiastically embraced his stag party in Edinburgh, and himself and twenty lads had taken off for Scotland the day before. Ali had received one text from him yesterday to assure her his eyebrows and hair were all still intact, but that the lads had taken all his clothes, and only allowed him to wear a clown outfit! Ben had actually texted Ali a photo of Robin earlier, and Ali had had to laugh at the photo of him at the bar in a polka-dot jumpsuit, a red curly wig, and big red sponge nose! She was glad he was having a good time, but still slightly nervous that he would end up chained to a lamppost naked in the middle of Edinburgh. But for tonight she had to forget about that, and get back to drinking and having a good time with the girls.

She was on her fourth cocktail when Jill clapped to get everyone's attention.

'Now, Ali, we've a few surprises for you. A stripper!'

Ali went pale, she had specifically said no strippers.

273

'Only kidding, sis! I know that would be your worst night-mare, so we've some gifts for you instead.' And with that Jill and Kate pulled out a large bag that had been hidden under a seat.

Ali was surprised, she had thought her sisters were so pre-occupied with their dresses and losing weight that organizing a dinner out tonight would have been enough. Kate stood up.

'OK, sis, the first gift has taken us weeks, and it is due to your friends' hard work.'

'And ours,' Jill added as she handed Ali a large thick rectan-gular parcel that looked like a book.

Ali unwrapped the paper, and stared in shock. It was not a book, but what looked like a red-bound thesis, like the one she had had to submit when she was finishing college. Yet this one had on the front: 'To Ali, aka the future Mrs Kenny . . . *This is Your Life*'. And like the old Eamon Andrews show, the red book was exactly what it said, a book all about her. Ali started flicking through the pages. It was filled with photos of her as a baby, as a child, in college and at the engagement party. It was also filled with stories and memories that each of her friends had typed up and submitted, along with some funny and embarrassing photos. Her sisters had put in pictures of her favourite food, drinks, TV programmes, films – even the movie stars she used to fancy! The whole book was just about her, it was amazing. They had even included copies of her Leaving Certificate results, her Girl Guide badges, and photos of the day she became a qualified solicitor. She had to laugh at all the photos of her with cows and chickens. Those farm photos made her look like a real country child, but she treasured them and appreciated how much time and effort must have gone into finding them.

'Ali, you have no idea how much time we've spent scanning, typing and printing, trying to get that book ready. Mum and

Dad were driven demented! It was hard trying to get everyone to send their bits about you in on time, and we didn't have the book ready for the binders yesterday, but once we'd chosen the dresses today, we ran over there and got it done, thank God.'

All Ali's friends were dying to read the book, and see what memories and photos everyone else had included. Ali began to feel very emotional: she realized how good her friends and sisters were to have gone to all this trouble for her.

After they had all had a good look through the book, Jill ordered more cocktails and got everyone's attention.

'OK, now it's time for some of the fun gifts,' she said. She started pulling out lots of little wrapped parcels.

'Myself and Kate thought we would ask each of your friends to buy you a little inexpensive gift, something that would remind you of a funny or good time with them. And you have to guess which gift goes with what person!'

Ali's sisters handed her the first gift. It was a little toy cow and a pair of flip-flops. Ali didn't know what it meant, or who it was from. And then it came to her: when she was eleven herself and her best friend Liz had decided to have a picnic on the farm, but because they had wanted it to be private they had wandered further and further from the farmhouse until they were in the neighbour's fields. And then, as they set up their lunch of crisps and red lemonade, a bull had come out of nowhere and charged at them! Ali and Liz had manage to outrun the bull, and climbed over the fences to safety, but Liz had lost her brand-new sandals along the way and been in big trouble when she got home. Ali pointed to Liz, who was laughing so much she had tears rolling down her face!

Next was a Take That CD and a bottle of sun lotion. Ali knew who this was: her old school friend Jenny. After their Leaving Certificate they had gone to Majorca on holiday and spent the whole time listening to Take That's latest CD and sunbathing, although Ali had got badly burnt on the first day and looked like a lobster in every photo! After this there were gifts that made her laugh so much that she attracted the attention of the whole bar, who were all dying to know what was so funny. The girls tried to explain the gifts to the barman, but they were giggling too much. All the same, he still gave them free sparkling wine to celebrate Ali's night.

After a few more cocktails they all headed for dinner. The meal was gorgeous, and made even more special by the table-mats that Jill and Kate had got printed up: all old photos of Ali. The night was perfect, Ali felt so special and cared for by all her friends. They laughed and drank, and eventually ended up in a local nightclub, and as they danced to Beyoncé Ali felt blessed to have such good sisters and friends. She only hoped that Robin was having such a good night too, and that he was still standing – even if he was wearing a clown suit!

93

Ben was just out of a big meeting with a client when he got a text from Nikki, asking if he wanted to meet up. Ben did like Nikki – she was great fun, gorgeous and so chatty – but he didn't know if their relationship was going anywhere. I'll reply later, he thought as he sat back down at his father's desk, which was now his. It was amazing how quickly things had changed. In the last few days Ben had officially become the boss of the company, and he could see how differently the staff and clients now treated him. He was no longer Joe's useless son, but a grown-up man running a small yet successful accountancy firm. As new letterheads, business cards and office signage got printed Ben really felt that there was no turning back, he was here to stay. Sometimes on the bus into work he felt like jumping off at Jeremy's newspaper and offering to report on the latest football match, but he knew what he had to do, and looking after his father's company was it. It wasn't all bad, though. With his new increased salary Ben knew he would soon be able to buy a place of his own, but it depended on how his dad was doing. He couldn't leave his mum alone with his father right now. His dad was still so weak, and would be for quite some time. His dad's illness had changed Ben's life hugely: not only was he now working as an accountant again, but his social life had been affected. He missed seeing his friends as much as he used to, but he hoped that could change as his dad recovered and he stopped feeling guilty every time he left the house.

Ben turned on his computer and checked his emails. Most of them were from clients and colleagues, but there was one from his friend Philip saying that the lads had all taken up tag-rugby for the summer and even though Ben hadn't been able to join earlier, did he want to play tonight, as one of them was pulling out due to a broken leg? Ben was delighted: getting back into rugby and seeing his friends would be great fun. He replied immediately and told Philip he was well up for it.

The rest of the day flew by and Ben was happy to head home and tell his dad that he had had another successful day at the office. Maura had gone out for a few hours, so Ben and Joe cooked dinner for themselves – steaks and mash. As they chatted about rugby, work and books Joe suggested they let Mango out of his cage for a few hours.

'That poor parrot doesn't get out half as much as it should.'

Ben closed the kitchen door and windows and then let Mango free. The bird went mental with the freedom and flew all over the kitchen squawking and swooping around Ben and Joe. Joe couldn't stop laughing, and Ben was delighted to see his dad enjoying himself. So much so that he didn't hear his mum open the kitchen door and walk in.

'Can you help me with these groceries, Ben?'

'Mango!' Ben and Joe both shouted together, but it was too late: the crazy bird had made a dive for the kitchen door, and as Maura had left the front door open so she could bring in the groceries, Mango headed right out of it.

'Oh, Ben, quick! Do something,' shouted Maura.

She flung Ben her pink golf jacket.

'Catch him in that. Run quickly, your dad will die if anything happens to that bird.'

Ben ran out of the house, barefoot and just in shorts and an old T-shirt. He tried to keep his eyes firmly on the multi-coloured bird, but it was hard as he also had to watch the road and pedestrians. Some local kids were fascinated by seeing Mango fly through the air, and the bird squawking crazily only encouraged them.

'What is he trying to say?' the kids asked.

'*Freedom*, probably,' Ben mumbled, as he tried to avoid them. He ran wildly down the road with his mum's fluorescent pink golf jacket waving from one hand. Mango suddenly made a move to turn into Foxrock village, and at this stage Ben was well out of breath and his feet were killing him. Suddenly he heard a car beeping at him: he slowed down and saw it was Laura. She had oversized sunglasses on, and her long curly hair tied back, and looked great.

'Ben, are you OK? Where are your shoes? Why are you carrying that pink coat?' Ben turned red. This was mortifying: once again he had run into Laura while he was with one of his crazy pets and while wearing horrific clothes. He tried to catch his breath and explain to Laura about Mango's jail break.

'Are you visiting your friend again?' Ben asked, while keeping an eye on Mango, who was now perched on top of the local petrol station screeching at everyone who came in or out of the shop.

'Yes, I'm on my way to collect her, as we've got tag-rugby tonight in Blackrock.'

'So have I,' Ben exclaimed. He couldn't believe the coincidence.

Laura didn't seem that excited that he would be playing tag-rugby with her, but she still got out of her car.

'Come on, let's get that crazy bird down,' she said.

Ben said he'd appreciate the help, and they made their way to the petrol pumps, where they called to Mango. Laura ran inside the shop, bought some nuts and seeds and laid a Hansel and Gretel trail to her car, thinking Mango might fall for that. At first Mango was too busy lapping up the attention of the passing customers, but eventually the lure of the food got to him, and he started to swoop down to eat some of the seeds, and after a third try Ben managed to catch him. Ben quickly bundled the now pink-polyester-covered bird into the back of Laura's car.

'Thanks so much, Laura. Sorry for holding you up,' Ben said.

'No bother, it was fun. Sure, why don't I give you a lift down to the rugby club? I just need to collect my friend and we can be on our way.'

Ben agreed, and they pulled into his house to drop the now-exhausted jailbird Mango off.

When Ben walked into the kitchen Joe started laughing, while Maura seemed annoyed.

'I am never leaving you two alone again, if this is the kind of thing that happens. That poor bird, how could you?'

Ben ignored her, and ran upstairs to grab his rugby boots, hoodie and wallet. He wanted to change, as he hated Laura seeing him in his worst shorts and T-shirt, but knew it would look too obvious if he reappeared in his good jeans and jumper. Anyway, she probably doesn't care, Ben thought, as he walked back down the stairs. I messed up with her, and I don't know what is going on with Nikki, so it is probably best to forget what could have happened and get down to the rugby and enjoy it.

Ben, Laura and her friend made small chat in the car, but once they got to the rugby club Laura seemed happy to wish him good luck in his matches and leave him to it. He saw her once or twice during the evening, but didn't get to speak to her. It was great fun, though, and Ben enjoyed having a good sports work-out, even if he was a little unfit. The lads had pints and barbecued burgers after, and Ben was glad to get back into the swing of things with them. As he left later he went to wave Laura goodbye, but she seemed engrossed in conversation with some guy. Well, I can't blame any guy for liking her, Ben said to himself as he headed home. It was only then that he remembered that he hadn't replied to Nikki's text that morning.

94

Molly was running late for work. She was dying with a hang-over, and if she didn't get Coca-Cola soon she would die. As she sat on the bus she brushed her dark hair, and doused herself in perfume, anything to cover the smell of Bulmers cider. She would never normally have arrived late for work or hungover, and she was worried about what her Aunt Fran would think, but things had just gone pear-shaped the night before. A week and a half ago, after she had left Sterling Bank's summer party, she had gone with Ali and Robin to see Set List again. She had been a bit nervous, about seeing the lead singer Will again, but the beers at the barbecue had loosened her up, and she had known that she had to go out and make her own fun, or else life would pass her by. The gig had been packed, and Molly had rocked to all their songs, and by the end herself and Ali had become hard-core fans. After the gig they'd joined the band for drinks, and even though Molly and Will had talked and gently flirted all evening, nothing had happened. Will had had lots of girls surrounding him, all wanting a piece of the main singer, and at first Molly had been embarrassed to find herself competing for his attention, but by the end of the night it had just been Ali, Robin, Will and Molly, and after getting some burgers at 3 a.m. they had all headed home. And even though Molly had gone home alone, with just a peck on the cheek from Will, that had suited her. She hadn't wanted things to move too quickly. All the same, she had thought about him all week. He had taken her number, and she hadn't heard anything until Saturday, when he had asked her to come along to his gig. Unfortunately, Molly had been in Kilkenny, at Ali's hen party so she hadn't been able to. Then, yesterday, he had told her about a free outdoor festival Set List were playing at in Temple Bar. Molly had managed to persuade Sarah to join her, and they had both a fantastic night, and heard many unsigned yet brilliant Dublin bands.

It was fun to be at an outdoor festival, and as they had danced around in the balmy evening Sarah and Molly had probably had one drink too many. After the gig Will had got the two girls backstage, where there was a free bar for the groups and their friends. Again there had been plenty of girls hanging around Will, and he had seemed to enjoy the attention, but later on in the night had only talked to Molly. He told her how, as a up-and-coming band, they had to take any gig they could, and that included weddings, even though it wasn't really their 'kinda thing, it's hardly rock 'n' roll!' But they needed money to pay for recording-studio time, and weddings helped them practise, and 'practice makes perfect', laughed Will. He looked very young, but Molly didn't mind: he was fun, and being a musician made him even more attractive. Sarah eventually wanted to leave, and Molly hadn't known what to do. She'd hoped Will would want her to stay, but she was also nervous at being alone with a new man. But when Will heard that Molly was going to leave, he begged her to stay, and even though Molly guessed it was the free Budweiser rather than him speaking, she had agreed and Sarah had left alone. Although Sarah had first asked her if she knew what she was doing.

'This is unlike you, Molly. Are you sure you are not trying to get over Luke too quickly?'

Molly had put aside her own fears and replied that she wanted to move on, get on with her life — and for now Will was her stepping stone to being single again. When the free bar finally came to a stop, Molly followed Will to an after-gig party in a trendy nightclub. At this stage she had become very drunk, and lost all her inhibitions, and so became queen of the dance floor, while Will — who was slightly too cool to dance — watched from the side while ordering her more beers. Luckily one of Will's band was sober, and had been driving and had suggested at 2 a.m. that she might want a lift home. By then, Will had also been in a bad state, and had been encouraged to squeeze into the little Micra. As Molly had sat beside Will, with two guitars squashed in on top of her and guitar leads piled on her lap, she had leant her head on his shoulder. Before she knew it she had been kissing him and it had felt great, so great that she had almost been tempted to take him up on his offer and go back to his flat, but luckily his band members had thought she needed to sleep her drink off, and had made sure she got dropped right at her door. Will had walked her up the driveway and they had stopped for a long kiss before they had heard honking, and Will had been called back to the car.

Molly had felt great when she got to her room and undressed, but the minute she had lain down she had started to feel slightly sick, and had had to sit up and drink plenty of water. And as she had sat there alone, in the dark, feeling queasy, she had known that she'd taken things too fast. Yes, she needed to create her own life now that her comfortable couple lifestyle with Luke was gone, but maybe she had been too forward, had moved too quickly, too soon. Sarah had been right, it wasn't like her to follow a musician around, even if he was very cute. Molly loved staying in, cooking, chatting, going for walks and to the cinema. Hanging out with young musicians in a grubby nightclub wasn't what she was used to. But then living at home with her mum and dad wasn't what she was used to, either. Molly had felt sick all night, but it hadn't just been the beer that had kept her up, her thoughts had kept flicking to Luke, Will and her future. Eventually she had fallen asleep, and she would have slept all day if her dad hadn't woken her up and told her she was late for work, and now she was stuck on the very slow-moving bus and feeling stressed. She finally made it to the door of Heavenly, but almost felt like leaving again when she saw how busy the café was. All she wanted to do was sleep. Her cousin Eve rushed up to her.

'Where have you been?' she asked, concerned. Molly quickly filled her in, but didn't have time to answer her questions about Will, as she knew she needed to head for the kitchen and apologize to her aunt.

Fran had been swept off her feet all morning, trying to get her own and Molly's work done, and when Molly finally walked through the door, Fran had known from one look at her and from the smell of beer, that she was hungover. She knew it had been hard for Molly recently, finding herself single again, but still she didn't have time for this.

'I am sorry, so sorry,' Molly said, as she put on her apron and started chopping tomatoes.

Fran had been prepared to have given out to Molly, but could see she was in enough pain as it was. She looked as white as a ghost.

'Just don't let it happen again, Molly. Now help yourself to a Lucozade, and let me heat you up this muffin.'

Molly thanked God her aunt was so kind, and promised herself that no man would make her jeopardize her career again.

95

Later that night Molly was at home, trying to unpack all her boxes of clothes, CDs and other junk. She had been avoiding it for weeks, mainly because she kept thinking that moving home was only a temporary solution, and that if she didn't unpack it wouldn't become real. But she knew now that she needed to move on, and wise up to the fact that she was single and back to living at home. As she unpacked flip-flops, slippers and boots she found her old photo albums. Molly had always been really into photos, and even though Luke wasn't he had finally realized, like most guys, that he might as well just give in and let her take photos of him on holidays, rather then upset her. She loved having memories in photo form: being able to flick through an album can take you right back to a beach, and to soaking up the sun and having that feeling of being endlessly happy. As Molly looked through the albums, they reminded her of holidays, parties, Christmases and weddings, but in every page there was Luke staring out at her. Was there any point keeping these photos now? Molly wondered. Would Luke want any of them? Would he care? Would she find someone new to create a photo album with? Molly put the albums back into their box. Then she got up and put the box in her brother's old room. She couldn't handle them today, she didn't need to see them again for a long time.

She spent the rest of the evening trying to sort out her new bedroom, and as she set up a shelf for all her cookbooks she decided to cook something. It would help her unwind, and after hours of looking at clothes, CDs and photos that all reminded her of Luke and that part of her life that was now over, she wanted to just head for the kitchen and make something. Her dad was reading the newspaper when Molly entered with the Avoca cookbook in her hand.

'How are you, pet?' he asked, putting down his glasses.

Molly didn't feel like talking to him about Luke, Will, work or all her worries, and instead said she was fine.

'Dad, I'm in the mood for cooking, so let's see what we've in the press. What do you feel like?' Molly said as she opened cupboards, jars and the fridge.

'Something sweet to go with this tea would be nice!'

Molly knew just the thing, and opened the book to page forty-five, where the famous Avoca recipe for their Mars Bar squares was. It was a very simple dish, but so yummy, and Molly knew her dad loved chocolate. As she melted the chocolate her dad filled her in on family news and stories from work. Molly felt at ease: being in the family kitchen chatting and cooking was her dream night in. A million times better than last night, she thought, remembering the reality of the sweaty nightclub and the groupies hanging off the band. What was I thinking? she wondered. Will is nice, but that isn't my scene. As she served her dad the chocolate and Rice Krispie squares, he gave her a hug.

'I could get used to this, Molly. Not just being served up delights, but just having you around. I know it must be hard to move back in with us old fogies, but I love having you here, Mars Bar squares or not.'

After cleaning up, Molly went to bed and for once she wasn't thinking about Luke, but about her family and how lucky she was to have them. And even though she was back in a room that still had her My Little Pony stable and Glo-Worm doll, for now she couldn't imagine anywhere better in the world to be.

96

Sarah and her mum were trying to weed the garden.

'It's too hot, Mum,' Sarah protested.

Sweat was pouring down her face, her long blonde hair was matted from the heat, and there was grass stuck to her long bare legs. Sarah's mum collapsed into a garden chair and tried to cool herself down with an iced tea.

'Sarah, we're almost finished, and once I plant those new flowers the garden will look perfect for tonight and my guests!'

Sarah had agreed to help her mum prepare for the Midsummer's Eve drinks party that she was giving for her neighbours and friends. Sarah's parents had always had one, it was a family tradition, but after her dad died, no one had had the heart to throw it any more. But now Sarah's mum had felt the time was right to have an enchanting party again.

'Dad would have loved being here today, getting it all ready,' Sarah said, as she tried to splash water from the small garden fountain on to herself.

'Yes, he would, he loved nothing more than a party. Are you sure you don't want to stay yourself?' said her mum.

Sarah had always enjoyed parties at home, but she knew tonight was her mum's night, and so herself and Hugh were going out for dinner and drinks – and more than likely she would stay over at his.

'No, I'm fine, Mum, you enjoy yourself. I'm going for dinner, that's if I don't die from digging up dandelions.'

They spent the next few hours tidying the garden, planting some new bedding flowers, and setting up the wooden garden furniture. They then moved into the kitchen, where they prepared little snacks of chicken satay, sausage rolls, salmon and brown bread and mini-kebabs. Sarah then had a shower and slipped her long thin body into a new brown and cream cotton dress from Jigsaw.

Once her mum's first guests had arrived, Sarah wished her mum well and drove up to Hugh's flat. He lived in a very modern apartment in Dundrum, near the shopping centre and the Luas tram line. The furniture was all dark wood and minimalist, apart from the huge amount of art pieces on the walls. They didn't all go with the apartment, but Hugh was always saying that one day he hoped to move back to Galway. Sarah hoped this wasn't true and pretended she hadn't heard whenever he mentioned his home city. She knocked on the apartment door, and Hugh welcomed her with a big kiss and some flowers.

'I haven't seen you all week. I missed you,' he said, as he took her overnight bag and her coat.

'I missed you, too. It's just that work is busy and I've been trying to work on some of my own pieces. I'm so sorry.'

'No problem, let's just get going for dinner. I thought we would try that new Thai restaurant in the Beacon hotel, as it's close and supposed to be very funky.' He locked the apartment behind them.

The hotel was very modern, with oversized couches, glass walls and unusual lighting: the bar glowed blue, and the chairs all changed colour as you sat on them. They decided to have a drink before their meal. Sarah still couldn't believe how well things were going with Hugh. He was very relaxed, and was such interesting company. Even though he worked in finance, he had a huge interest in the arts and Sarah could talk to him for hours about theatre, art exhibitions and films. They had settled into a nice routine of dinners, cinema, and lazy Sundays in bed. He was always asking her to go to Galway to meet his family, but it was hard for Sarah to get a weekend off work. She knew, though, that she would have to soon, or else she would come across as rude. They both had two Coronas before sitting down to enjoy their Thai curries. Over dinner Hugh once again talked about Galway.

'Next weekend my two best friends are having an engagement party. They have this house in Salthill right on the water. It will be great fun, and it will give me a chance to show you the true Galway, not just Quay Street and the touristy bars.'

Sarah saw the excitement in his eyes. Even though she was due to work the next weekend, she knew Clodagh, who had now finished college for the summer and was always looking for extra work, could cover it, so she agreed.

'Great,' Hugh said, as he smiled and ordered more wine. 'Wait until you meet my parents and friends! And you just have to meet my cousin Pat, he loves art, too. They will all love you, they can't wait to meet you.'

Sarah was happy he was excited about the proposed trip, but as he planned the weekend, and she heard him name all the people she would be meeting, she began to get nervous. Hugh seemed so determined this would be a perfect weekend and everyone would like Sarah. She hoped he wouldn't be disappointed.

97

After work on Tuesday Sarah was just telling her mum about her upcoming weekend trip to Galway, when the doorbell rang. Sarah answered it and was surprised to see John and Tom at the door. They both gave her a kiss and headed for the kitchen.

'Your mum asked me to pop in and see if we could fix your shed door. She said it keeps sticking,' her brother-in-law John said, as he headed out to the garden.

'Are you here to help, too?' she asked Tom, who looked great in a pinstripe suit and blue shirt.

'No, not in this suit! I just popped into Tom after work to drop back a DVD of his, when he roped me into coming here, with the promise of a pint after.'

'Well, let me get the alcohol rolling, then,' laughed Sarah. She opened the fridge and pulled out some beers. Tom relaxed and took off his suit jacket.

'So tell me about this wedding invite that is spurring Mel to think you are the next Monet!'

Sarah blushed, but showed Tom the invite.

'Well done, Sarah,' he said approvingly. 'It looks fantastic. I don't know much about art, but you obviously have great talent, good luck with it.'

Sarah appreciated his honesty, and knew that paint-by-numbers was about as arty as he and his brother John got. At least he was trying to be supportive. While John and Sarah's mum were busy over at the shed, Tom and Sarah chatted about their godchild, Mel and John, and the latest Quentin Tarantino film. Tom was so relaxed and just a regular Dublin guy, he didn't have an interest in the arts like Hugh, but he was happy to have a beer and chat about sport or Sarah's family. Eventually John made it back into the kitchen having fixed the shed door.

'Why does my brother get the beers while I do all the work?' John asked, as Sarah handed him a cold Budweiser.

'It's because Sarah thinks I'm the best-looking, of course. Charming and single, who could resist! Isn't that right, Sarah?' Tom joked.

Sarah felt herself blush again. She was mortified by Tom's remark. She had Hugh now, and tried to think of him rather than the lads who were now teasing each other about their fashion sense.

'Well, did you hear about Sarah?' Sarah's mum said as she opened a pack of Bakewell tartlets for the boys. 'She is off to meet Hugh's family this weekend in Galway. I'm telling you, John, we could have another wedding to be planning!'

Sarah didn't think she could blush again so soon, but she did. Why did mum say that now, right in front of Tom and John? she thought, fuming. She tried to change the subject to baby Fiona, which always worked with her mum, but she still felt awkward, and was glad half an hour later when the lads excused themselves and headed to Dalkey for a pint. Sarah went to bed feeling guilty she wasn't prouder that Hugh wanted her to meet his family in Galway; but she just didn't want everyone thinking she was about to be married – it was a while away yet.

98

Ali couldn't believe her wedding was only a few weeks away! She felt time was speeding up. The last few weeks had been a blur: of finalizing wedding songs, trying to write wedding speeches, and buying clothes for the big honeymoon. She was up to her eyes in contracts; she had barely seen Robin all week, because she had to work so late every night. Her boss was really piling it on her. It seemed to be her tactic in order to make sure Ali had time for work and nothing else when she was in the office. Ali thought this unfair: everyone knew brides had to do some wedding jobs between nine and five. How else could she research Hawaii online, or print off rough copies of her wedding booklet? She knew her interest in work had been poor recently, but the wedding just did consume all her thoughts and actions. Her aim this week was to get her wedding booklet finalized and printed. She needed two hundred copies, though, so it would be hard to print them while her boss was snooping around. She would have to do it after work hours, or during lunch. Just then Mary walked in, her nun-like bun looking tighter than ever.

'Ali, we've a case that we've to take and to do free of charge. I'm against it, but the powers that be say we have to. They say we need to be seen to be doing some pro-bono work, it's good PR for the firm. I'm going to pass the client over to you, there is no point wasting one of the senior partners on a freebie job, but don't forget you need to be up-to-date with all your own work, too. Just try to do this case as quickly and cheaply as you can.' And with that she tossed Ali a file with information on the case.

Ali would normally have been curious about the job, but she happened to be online chatting to a travel expert in Hawaii who was recommending places for her to eat at and visit. She placed the file in her 'to-do' pile and ploughed ahead with the online chat, all the while looking deep in thought, so that Mary wouldn't suspect anything.

It wasn't until the next day, when Ali got a message that a Mr Fleming had been trying to contact her that she knew she had better flick through the case notes and then call him right back. She was meeting a make-up artist in Brown Thomas at 1 p.m., to discuss make-up options, so she decided this guy better be quick on the phone, she had things to do.

She opened the file and started reading about him. He was forty-two, lived in Dublin and had two kids. His problem was the custody of and access to his children. Ali wasn't sure how her company were supposed to help, as family law was not really their area, but the more she read the more she slowed down and started taking notes. It seemed Paddy Fleming and his then girlfriend Trish had had two children while they lived in a nice-enough estate in Lucan. Things had been going well until he was laid off in work. He had found it hard to get a new job, and as time went by he had become more disheartened, and had begun betting a little and drinking too much. Even so, he had still looked after the kids all day and had never drunk around them. But with him unemployed, it hadn't been long before his girlfriend had found someone new and had upped and left him. She was now married and living in a well-to-do area in South Dublin, and had prevented almost all contact between the kids and her ex-partner. As they had never been married he didn't have many legal rights, and the fact that Trish could now afford a great solicitor meant Paddy couldn't surmount all the legal barriers she had set up. Ali didn't know what to think about the case: she had heard of this kind of thing happening before, but she wasn't sure there was much she could do to help the man. As she went to close the file she saw a letter that Paddy had enclosed. Along with it were some photos of what must have been him and his two young children. The kids were the spit of him – blond hair and fair freckled faces – and in the photos they were all hugging and laughing, and Paddy was beaming with joy. You could imagine how hard it would be for him, not to be allowed to see them. She put the photos down and read the letter. In it Paddy described how he felt, and how not having the kids was sucking the life out of him, how they were all he cared about, how Trish had exaggerated his drinking and betting and made him out to be a lowlife scum, and how she had bamboozled his legal team until they couldn't fight her any more. Paddy said he just wanted one last chance to be a part of his kids' life. Ali picked up the phone and rang him, and after two minutes of talking to the soft-spoken man she knew what she had to do. She rang the Elizabeth Arden counter in Brown Thomas and cancelled her long-awaited appointment, and agreed to meet Paddy in a local bagel bar for lunch in an hour's time.

Within five minutes of talking to Paddy, Ali knew she had to do her best to help him. He held his head in his hands as he explained how the child custody meetings had been full of lies. How he had turned down many jobs, as they would have meant being away long hours from the kids, and how he couldn't have done that, he was a hands-on dad and needed to play, talk and eat with them every night. How, when he finally had got a good job, Trish hadn't cared: she had met someone richer and 'better class' and had grabbed the kids and gone. How Trish didn't even work herself now, and yet had a nanny to look after their children: 'She never did like getting her hands dirty.'

'I would gladly look after them every day, but even once a week would give me hope,' Paddy whispered.

As Ali headed back to the office, she rang an old classmate of hers who used to specialize in family law and they agreed to meet for drinks after work. Ali used to dream of cases like this, but after years of conveyancing and checking the legality of planning permissions she had forgotten what it was like to help someone who really needed it. As she saw her wedding booklet on her desk, she felt embarrassed. I've been so caught up in the wedding that I've forgotten what's important in life, she thought guiltily. She was so lucky to have a man who truly loved her, and would never do to her what Trish had done to Paddy, and she was lucky to have great friends and family who would help her out. Paddy had no one. She remembered what her boss Mary had said to her about doing the case as quickly and cheaply as she could, and she knew she wouldn't be able to spend her whole working day on it, but she knew it needed that. I'll just have to work after hours on it, she thought. She had planned to spend her evenings working on the wedding, but this afternoon had made her feel guilty about that, so instead she copied her wedding booklet on to a CD, and ran down to the local printer.

'It will cost a good bit to proof it and print out two hundred copies, you know,' said the sales assistant.

'I know,' Ali said as she reached for her credit card, 'but I've more important things to do than wait for copies to print.' And with that she headed back to the office and to the long night of work that lay ahead of her.

99

Ben was at home in his living room trying to show his dad how to play Tiger Woods Golf on his PlayStation 2.

'How do I pick the nine iron, Ben?' asked Joe.

Ben didn't have a clue, he was only used to playing soccer, rugby or car-racing games, but as Joe couldn't play golf or even go for a pint nowadays, Ben had thought it would be nice if they could do something together apart from watch TV or eat. So when he had seen the new Tiger Woods computer game advertised he had raced into HMV to buy it, knowing how his dad missed the excitement of playing real golf. Ben was trying to read the game manual as Joe picked Padraig Harrington as his player, and Augusta as his golf club of choice.

'Well, I never thought I would get to play in the US Masters,' Joe laughed.

Ben eventually worked out how to tee off and so they started. It took Joe a while to get the hang of using the game controller, and for him to realize that actually swinging the controller like it was a golf club would not help Padraig win anything! Maura had a friend in for a cup of coffee, and Ben went into the kitchen to get some biscuits for his dad, but just before he opened the door he could hear her talking about him.

'Ben is just so responsible now, such a grown-up. I knew he had it in him, we are both so proud of him.'

Ben couldn't believe it. All he had ever heard for years was how he had to 'grow up' or 'get real', and now at last his mother was boasting about what a man he had become. He was chuffed. He knew playing computer games might destroy this brand-new grown-up image, but as he headed back to the living room laden down with chocolate chip cookies and tea he didn't care. He was learning you could be a grown-up and have fun, too.

After an hour of trying to play golf against the likes of Ernie Els and Phil Mickelson, they decided to call it a night.

'Don't worry, Dad, you will get the hang of it soon,' Ben said, as he unplugged the TV.

'Oh, I'm not worried, Ben. Sure, don't I have all day to practise while you are out at work slaving away,' Joe laughed. 'But tell me, Ben,' he asked, 'how are you really finding being back working as an accountant?'

Ben wasn't so sure what to tell his dad. Yes, there were days when he loved being his own boss, and felt chuffed at getting work off to clients on time, but there were other days, too (a lot of other days), when it was hard to be responsible for the whole company, for all the staff, their wages, the office, the clients, and make sure the business ticked over as well as his dad had done for the last twenty-five years. He decided to be honest and tell his dad, tell him he had up and down times.

'That's just life, son. Not every day will be the same, but that's the fun of it, also. Life would be boring if every day was the same – if every meeting was alike, every round of golf equal, every person similar – that's just the way it is. If the positives weigh up the negatives, that's the main thing.'

Ben knew his dad was right, and he was gradually getting the hang of the company, and realized he was the envy of many of his friends, who only dreamt of running their own businesses.

'I know, Dad, and I know I should have said this a long time ago, but I'm sorry. Sorry for just not realizing how important me entering your business was to you, for just not getting it. But I get it now, I really do, and I'll make you proud.'

'You already have, son,' Joe said, taking another biscuit. 'I just wish you had someone special to share all the joys with, a nice girl. What about that Laura girl? She seemed nice.'

'I messed up there, Dad. It's over. I've been seeing someone else, but I'm just not sure about her.' Ben stopped before going into much detail; he loved his dad but didn't feel too comfortable telling him about Nikki.

'Well, Ben, life is too short to be with someone you're "just not sure" of. The second I met your mother I just knew, and I still know. Every day I thank God for her. She might drive us all demented sometimes, but I couldn't live without her.' And with that Joe headed up to bed, leaving Ben sitting thinking about work and girlfriends until way past his bedtime.

100

The next day Ben was meeting Nikki for lunch. Between rugby, helping out at home, work, and catching up with his friends he hadn't spent much time with her lately. But as usual she was so laid-back Ben couldn't tell if she cared or not. Ben had always thought he would want a girl who was like him – laid-back, not overly dying to hang out all day long, not looking for much commitment – but now that he had exactly that he realized he would prefer someone who really made him feel they were glad he was there. But Nikki was always busy: as she worked on a popular magazine, she was always at the latest launch party, or promotional event, or just checking out celebrities. Ben had been to some of the events, and they were great fun, with lots of free drinks and food – but he felt they were both holding back on spending much time alone, just one-on-one.

They had agreed to meet at a local Italian, which served quick yet tasty lunch dishes. Ben ordered the spaghetti carbonara, Nikki the tuna Niçoise salad. She looked fantastic in a tight-fitting skirt and black shirt, with her hair tied back and sunglasses perched on her head. Ben could only spare forty-five minutes for lunch, but tried to catch up as much as he could within that. He told Nikki about his dad and work, while she told him that the captain of the Irish soccer team

301

had been spotted out drinking the night before a match. It was interesting to know, but as Ben tried to turn the conversation to more personal things she just talked faster about people he didn't care about. It was frustrating, but he kept thinking she might just be nervous; they didn't really know each other that well. Even the few times he had stayed over at her place after a night out, they had normally ended up having breakfast with her flatmates and chatting to them. Ben knew something was missing, but then as Nikki walked him back to his office and gave him a hug and kiss he forgot all his worries: lunchtime kissing! She handed him an invite to the launch party of a new aftershave the next Saturday in Krystle nightclub.

'It will be fun! I've to work for the first hour or so, as we want to get pictures of celebs, et cetera, but after that I'm free to dance the night away with you.' And with that Nikki was gone.

Ben took the invite and thought to himself, Well I can't turn down a free drinks party, and sure, we can see how things go on Saturday. But as he walked back to his office, he kept thinking of what his dad said about knowing you had the right girl. Ben wasn't sure about Nikki.

101

Molly and Sarah were having dinner and drinks in the 40 Foot bar in Dun Laoghaire, after working up an appetite by walking the harbour pier. Sarah was telling Molly how she was off to Galway the next day, once Hugh had finished work.

'Are you nervous about meeting his family?' Molly asked.

'Of course! But he's met all of mine, and after the way he "met" baby Fiona I suppose it is only fair to give his family a go,' Sarah replied. As she sipped back her Heineken shandy, Molly laughed.

'Well, as long as none of them poo in your face, it should be fine!' And with that the girls collapsed in fits of laughter, until their food arrived. Although Sarah suddenly felt a pang of guilt for telling her friend about the baby Fiona and Hugh poo incident, as she had promised Hugh she would tell no one.

'I got a text today from that guy Will, saying he was going to the gig of some rival band on Saturday night and did I want to go,' Molly said, keeping Sarah up to date on her love life. Sarah didn't say much.

'You don't like him, do you?' Molly asked her oldest friend.

Sarah put down her fork.

'It is not that, Molly. I want you to be happy, especially after the shock of breaking up with Luke, but I still just don't know about Will. I'm sure he is talented and fun, but he is so different from Luke or any other guy you have dated. Are you sure you know what you are doing?'

'No, I don't, that's just it. The other day, after that gig, when I was so hungover I thought I would die, I was ready to forget all about Will. I thought: Yes he is cute, and fun, and so different from me, but it's too different. But then when I got that text today I thought: Is this it? Could he be the only guy out there who likes me? And if he is then I'm stupid not to give him a chance. I don't want to be single and living at home for ever. I love my job, but I need more than work.' Molly stared out of the large glass window at the harbour and boats.

'Molly, there are tons of guys who like you. You just need to open your eyes – and your heart – to them. Don't settle for the first guy you meet after Luke. Trust me, there will be others.'

Molly didn't know if she agreed with her friend, but she decided to drop the conversation. Instead they talked about what they would wear to Ali and Robin's upcoming wedding.

The next day at work, as Molly was making homemade Caesar dressing, Eve came into the kitchen.

'You have a visitor!'

Molly wiped her hands and tried to smooth back her hair, as Eve smiled and pushed her into the café. There stood Scott Williams with a large teddy bear.

'You forgot to take him with you after we massacred those ducks at the funfair,' he said, passing Molly the fluffy cream and brown stuffed bear.

Molly was confused for a few moments, then remembered how she had won the Hello Kitty watch and a teddy bear at the Sterling Bank party. She had actually been wearing the watch ever since.

'I tried to find you later on in the night to give you the bear, but you must have sneaked off. Anyway, I thought you might like the little guy, and, besides, a single guy with a big teddy bear on his bed isn't that attractive!'

Molly laughed, but also noticed how he had said single. She was sure that that night when she had left he had been deep in conversation with a beautiful girl.

'Thanks, Scott, and as a single girl living at home with her parents, having a big teddy bear on my bed to cuddle up to is perfect, and couldn't make me any less attractive, so I'll take him.'

She thought she saw Scott smile when she said she was single, but she wasn't sure if he mightn't have been laughing at her.

'I meant to give him back to you sooner, but I kept forgetting the furry guy, and then I was away all last week surfing with friends in Portugal.'

Molly now understood why he had a tan and bleached hair, but she couldn't help looking surprised when he said surfing.

'You look surprised, Molly. Let me guess, you think I'm some boring banker, who eats the same sandwich every day and loves counting numbers and working on spreadsheets? Well, there are plenty of things you don't know about me, Molly. I'm actually quite like Mr Benn – you know, the old children's cartoon character.'

Molly smiled to herself. Maybe he was like that old cartoon she had loved when she was a kid.

'I might wear my banker clothes and look boring all day, but you can't imagine the adventures I have after hours.'

And with that Scott, aka Mr Benn, was off, leaving Molly standing flabbergasted in the middle of Heavenly holding a very large bear.

102

On Saturday afternoon, with nothing else planned for that night, Molly thought she would give Will one more chance. She put on her jeans, a T-shirt and boots, and with her hair tied back headed on the bus into Smithfield to where the gig was. As she approached she could see a big group of girls and guys queuing to get in. She had received a text from Will saying he was inside, and to meet him at the bar. The queue was quite large, and while she was waiting Molly looked around and recognized some of the same girls she had seen at Will's other gigs. One girl kept staring at Molly. Molly didn't know who she was, so she just ignored her until the doorman let her in and she headed for the bar. Will and the band were all there, drinking and laughing. Will gave Molly a hug and introduced her to another band. Will loved being the centre of attention and was happy sitting around with the big group, while Molly would have liked to have got to know him a little better. When they talked on the phone it was always about his band and their gigs, he never asked about Molly's job or her life. And every time she suggested they hang out with her friends he always had an excuse, from guitar practice to checking out rival bands. Has he any real interest in me? she wondered. They all had a few beers and just before the music began Molly headed for the bathroom. As she got into another queue, she again noticed the girl who had been staring at her outside. The girl and her friends were all fixing their make-up and chatting. As Molly entered a cubicle she overheard what they were saying.

'Did you see that small girl with dark hair is here again?' she said to her friends.

'Girl?' one of the friends laughed. "You mean woman! She looks ancient, she must be in her thirties!' she said as they all giggled.

'How sad is she? I mean, not only should she get someone her own age, but AS IF she is the only one seeing Will. Lauren said Will brought her to a gig in Eamon Dorans last week, and I know his ex is still always hanging around as well. That dark-haired girl must be deluded if she thinks Will is hers.'

When she was sure that they'd gone, Molly pushed her way out of the cubicle, trembling. She had never been so embarrassed. Was I just a bit of fun for Will? she asked herself. Was I just like these other girls, a sad groupie for a pretty average wedding band? Well, I've got to get out of here, she thought. I'm too old for this. Forget Will, they can have him, he only cares about music, drink and himself, anyway. I just want to be at home. Molly walked as fast as she could from the bathroom to the main door.

'Let me stamp your hand, love, so you can get back in later,' a bouncer said to her.

'Trust me, I won't be back, ever,' Molly said, and with that she legged it to a taxi rank, and climbed into a cab.

As she sat in the back, she realized Sarah had been right: Will had been the wrong guy all along. Molly texted her mum to say she would be home in time for *The Tubridy Show* and that maybe they could make some brownies.

103

Sarah woke up to the smell of bacon and frying sausages, and for a second she couldn't remember where she was. Then she heard Hugh snoring and remembered she was in Galway. They had arrived last night, and gone straight to Hugh's parents' house. Hugh had his own house in Galway, but as he lived in Dublin had been renting it out the last few years, so he had thought it would be nice if Sarah and himself stayed with his parents. 'So you can get to know them!' he had said encouragingly. Sarah had been a bit stressed, and the whole way down hadn't been able to stop worrying about what his family would think of her, and wondering if living with his mum and dad for a whole weekend would be too intimidating. She had wished they could turn the car around and she could have spent the afternoon painting in her garden, but they had ploughed ahead and arrived down in Galway by 10 p.m.

Hugh's parents lived outside Galway city, in a lovely house overlooking the sea. His parents were quite old, but very friendly. Hugh's mum had had some dinner prepared for them, which they had eaten quickly, as Hugh had wanted to make it down to the local pub to catch up with his brothers and friends – 'And to show you off!' he had said proudly to Sarah. Sarah knew Hugh was a good man, and from the brief dinner she had understood where he got his attractive manner from: both his parents were interesting, friendly and not over-the-top. Their house was also full of amazing art, and Sarah had suddenly seen why Hugh had become so interested in it himself. Drinks in his local bar had been fun, too. Sarah had met his brothers before at The Galwegians' rugby match, so she had been happy to see their familiar faces, but there had been so many other people to meet that her head had spun from all the names and faces. But there had been live music, and between that and the beers Sarah had had a good night. Hugh had promised Sarah that on Saturday he would take her round 'his Galway' before they headed off to his friends' engagement party.

Sarah heard a knock at the bedroom door.

'I have breakfast ready whenever you want to come down,' Hugh's mum said softly.

Sarah didn't reply: she felt awkward at sleeping in the same room as Hugh under his parents' roof. When she heard his mum make her way downstairs she shook Hugh.

'Wake up, your mum is waiting for us for breakfast.'

Hugh mumbled something, he looked and smelt very hungover.

'You go down, I need more sleep,' he eventually managed to say.

No way am I eating breakfast alone with his parents, it's too early in the day and our relationship for that, Sarah thought. Instead she threw off the duvet and made him get up. They both flung on clothes, Sarah hastily tied back her long blonde hair and applied some make-up, and then they headed down to the kitchen, which smelled of cooking. Hugh's mum had put on a big spread: the table was covered with sausages, bacon, eggs, tomatoes, mushrooms, toast, orange juice and tea. Hugh was suddenly wide awake and tucking into the fry.

As his mum poured Sarah tea, she asked what their plan was for the day.

'Well, I want to bring Sarah to Moran's on the Weir for some lunch, and I want to show her around the city, and we might pop down to the beach for a swim as well, it's a warm day,' Hugh said between mouthfuls of toast.

Once breakfast was over Hugh and Sarah showered, changed and hit the road.

'I must show you the new Kenny's Art Gallery in the city centre. You know the famous bookshop closed down? Well, it is now this great gallery, you will love it,' Hugh said, as he drove along beside the water and headed to the city.

It was a beautiful day and Sarah was really beginning to relax and look forward to the rest of the weekend. As they strolled around the gallery Hugh held her hand: it felt right, he was gentle and yet a man's man too. Then they headed to a small gift shop to buy a present and card for the engagement party later. Sarah also popped into a Brown Thomas to see if she could find any nice wedding gifts for Ali and Robin. Hugh bought a new shirt, and before long it was lunchtime.

'Wait until you eat at Moran's! It is this famous pub, about nine miles from the city. It is simply decorated, but as it is right on the water it has the freshest and tastiest fish you have ever eaten. It is always packed at weekends but I booked a table for us so we should be fine.'

Hugh was right: the pub was jammed, packed with locals, and tourists who had heard good reports about the food and atmosphere. Their table was outside, and was so close to the water that Sarah kicked off her flip-flops and dipped her toes in while they waited for their oysters to arrive. Sarah had a beer while Hugh stuck to Club Orange.

'I feel like I'm abroad. It is so beautiful here,' Sarah said, admiring the view over the water and sipping her beer.

Hugh smiled and put his arms around her. 'So now you can understand why I love coming back here so much?'

Sarah nodded.

'Galway is great, so stunning,' Hugh said. 'There isn't anywhere like it, it's my home. That is the reason why I've wanted to talk to you about something.' He took his sunglasses off. 'Sarah, I'm moving back to Galway.'

Sarah put down her beer glass.

'I miss the city, the buzz,' Hugh went on. 'Dublin is great, but my home is here. I've got enough experience in my job to start out on my own. I've got some investors and I'm looking at offices in the city. I've told the tenants who rent my house that they have two months to find somewhere else, but I'm hoping they might be gone before that.'

Sarah didn't know what to say. He seemed to have everything all planned out. When did he make these decisions, and why hadn't he told her? But before she could ask any questions the waiter served their lunch.

'But, Sarah, the other reason I wanted you to come down here was to meet my family, see my kind of Galway. I want you to move here with me, move to Galway.'

Sarah almost choked on an oyster. 'What?' she managed to splutter.

'Sarah, I know it's only been months, but I feel like we've known each other for years. I knew the first time I saw you in the Stone Studio that you were the one for me, and the last few months have been great. I just know you would love it here, what with the art galleries, the sea, the people – so what do you say?'

Sarah looked at Hugh. At her age she had begun to think no prince was going to come and sweep her off her feet, that she would be everyone's 'single friend' for ever, but then Hugh

311

had come along, someone she had only seen as a client, and there under her nose had been a prince all along. The last few months had been great: he was kind, enjoyed spending time with her family, was supportive of her art, clever, and a real grown-up man. But to ask her to leave Dublin, leave her friends, family, job and life to come here and set up a new life with him? Sarah didn't know if she could do it.

'Hugh, I don't know what to say. You've caught me off-guard,' Sarah said honestly.

'That's OK, Sarah, I just got a bit over-excited. Of course you need to think about it, but I want you to know I'm already in love with you, and if we could set up a new life here in Galway surrounded by all this beauty I'd be the happiest man in the world.'

So no pressure, then, Sarah thought sarcastically to herself. He is only saying that I'm responsible for making or not making him the happiest man in the world. Suddenly the world-famous fish didn't taste of anything, Sarah was in too much shock to eat or drink. She had a dreamboat of a man asking her to move in with him, and that would make any girl delighted – and in part it did, yet she couldn't stop thinking of her home, of Dublin. What am I going to do? she asked herself.

104

Sarah had found it impossible to concentrate all day. She couldn't, even when Hugh showed her his old school, took her to meet his brothers' families, pulled her a pint in his cousin's pub, showed her where his own house was, brought her to where he hoped his new office would be, and finally brought her home to get changed before the big engagement party later.

'I know this might all seem a bit rushed, Sarah, but the time is right for me to start out on my own, and I can get good offices for a great price, and it just feels perfect to me. I know I should have told you sooner, but I thought it would scare you off, and until I knew for sure I didn't want to say anything to you or anyone.'

Sarah could understand all of that, and as she dried her hair and put on her make-up she knew she should say something more encouraging to him, but she felt too tired to speak.

'Sarah, I know you may not have an answer for me for a few days, but just remember we are not twenty-one. I'm thirty-six, so moving in with someone after a few months isn't unheard of. We are no spring chickens but I know we could be happy.'

Sarah took a breath – her heart was pounding under her ribs. Hugh took her hand.

'God, why do you think I'd been trying to get you to come to Galway for so long? I wanted you to see my life, before I asked you to make the big move. Don't make me wait too long for my answer, because I just can't wait to start planning the future!'

Sarah could see his excitement, and knew she was lucky to have a man who was so open, but for her it was still a shock. She gave Hugh a hug, and tried to steady herself before getting back to her make-up.

They ordered a taxi, and headed for the engagement party. High hadn't exaggerated when he had said his friends' house was amazing. It was right on the water, and when Sarah and Hugh arrived the smell of barbecue and the sound of laughter welcomed them in. Hugh gave his friends Richie and Joanne a big hug and kiss; apparently they had been going out for years, so everyone was relieved and excited to hear they were finally getting engaged. Hugh introduced Sarah, and as Sarah handed Joanne the engagement present she had brought with her for them, Joanne gave her a hug.

'Don't worry, I know you don't know anyone, but we won't bite! We've all been dying to meet the girl who has lovely Hugh so smitten!'

Sarah smiled, and immediately warmed to Joanne. Hugh handed Sarah a bottle of beer and introduced her to more of his friends. Sarah found Hugh's friends appealing, and as they all sat out, overlooking the sea, surrounded by hundreds of tea-lights and by delicious food, she couldn't help imagining this being her life in a few months, if she decided to move here. But could I do it? she thought to herself. Could I give up Dublin? She knew Hugh was trying to make everyone and everything seem perfect, in order to make Galway more attractive to her, saying how great his friends were, how much fun they all had, and how great the job market was. But she still didn't feel sure. It was a big decision to make, and one good engagement party wasn't going to force her into it.

After a few beers she knew she had to lighten up and just enjoy the party for what it was, and so when Hugh asked her to dance in the garden overlooking the glistening Galway Bay, with a Damien Rice CD playing in the background, she couldn't help feeling Galway might be the place to be – maybe.

105

Ali was in Weir & Sons jewellers on Grafton Street, trying on her wedding ring. Herself and Robin had ordered their matching white gold rings a few weeks ago, and were now just checking they fitted and looked right.

'I still can't believe I'm going to be wearing this for the rest of my life,' Robin exclaimed.

Even Ali agreed it was weird seeing him with a ring on.

'But I'm so glad you decided to get one, too, Robin. I mean, it is so odd when guys don't wear a wedding ring. It only means one thing when they don't want to . . . they want others to think they are still on the market. What a nightmare. I'm glad all girls will know you are taken, very much taken!'

Ali laughed as she glanced at the ring again. Just then her phone rang, it was her new client, Paddy Fleming. She talked to him for a few minutes, but could see the sales assistant and Robin were getting impatient, so she put him on hold.

'Robin, can you finish up here? I need to get back to the office.'

Robin looked a little disappointed, but nodded and gave his fiancée a quick hug.

Ali had been flat out busy in work since taking on Paddy Fleming. Not only had she plenty of other work to be done before she took time off for her wedding and honeymoon, but Mr Fleming's case was tough and required a lot of extra work. She kept trying to cut down the time she spent on it, but she was starting to feel so passionately about the case. Paddy was a genuine man, who was madly in love with his kids, and had proved how much he cared for them, and his ex-partner was breaking his heart. It wasn't fair, and Ali wanted to help. She wanted the chance to put things right – not only for Paddy, but for herself – to get back to realizing what her true principles and goals were. Ali knew she had gotten a little obsessed with the wedding over the last few months but now this case was making her understand what was important. Of course the wedding was, but she already knew herself and Robin were going to last for ever, and have a great wedding day no matter what. Mr Fleming had lost his reason for living, had lost everything, and it was this that had made Ali put aside her wedding planner and work late nights all week, in order to get as much done on the case before her own big day. As Ali went into a meeting with a family solicitor and Paddy she knew it was going to be another long night at work.

When Ali finally finished at 10.30 p.m. and switched on her phone there were four messages. One was from Molly asking if she could proof the menu before Molly got it printed for all the guests. Another was from her dad saying the marquee people needed to know where the band and DJ were going to play, and did they need an extra generator? Father Conway had left a message saying he wanted to check she wasn't getting too stressed before her big day. And finally there was a very frantic one from her mum saying that the florist had gone into hospital for emergency gall-bladder surgery and what were they to do? As Ali jumped on the bus she felt a bit panicky. She could handle most of the messages tomorrow, but even in her new state of wedding calmness, she knew having no florist was going to be tough. She waited until she was home and had a glass of wine in front of her before she rang her mum.

'Oh Ali, thank God. I'm up the walls here. I popped into Blooming Bouquets today to get some fresh flowers, as I was having the girls up for lunch, but when I got there it was closed. I didn't think anything much, and just got flowers in the local supermarket, but then over lunch I was informed that the florist had collapsed, and she is now in hospital and needs to have surgery. I don't know what we are going to do.' Ali could tell her mum was upset, and knew she had to calm her down.

'Mum, surely there's another florist we can get to do the bouquets, table arrangements and church displays?'

'Well, after lunch I rang the only other one near here and they could do the bouquets, but they already have two weddings on in Carlow on the day, so they can't do the table arrangements or church flowers. What can we do? All the ones in Kilkenny city are far away and cost God only knows what.'

Ali knew she was right, and that at only eight days to go the chance of getting another florist was slim.

'Well, Mum, you are great at doing arrangements. Maybe you could talk to the ladies in the church and between you all you could do the five ones for there?'

'Well, I suppose I could, Ali. I mean, I could buy flowers in that other florist and just do them myself. I wouldn't trust those church ladies, they are too old and blind to see what flower is alive or dead.'

Ali laughed, and was relieved they had that bit sorted out.

'But what do we do about the table arrangements? We've already ordered the fifty vases from the catering place.'

Ali didn't know what they were going to do, and was so tired from work she couldn't think of anything.

'Mum, I'm wrecked from work. I'll just have to sleep on

this, but we'll sort it out, I know it,' Ali said, as she began to head for bed and a half-unconscious Robin.

'Well, you certainly seem calm. Don't say you are changing to Buddhism or something days before the Catholic wedding of the year?' her mum asked.

Ali laughed. 'No, Mum, I just realize now that this wedding will be perfect whether we stress about it or not, so let's try not to.'

Ali wished her mum goodnight and fell asleep to thoughts of Paddy Fleming and flowers.

106

Ali was blow-drying her short blonde hair and trying to flick through the stack of wedding magazines beside her bed. She was hoping to get inspiration from them, anything to help her decide what to do about the wedding table-arrangements. As she flicked through pages advertising dresses, veils, car hire, photographers, caterers, musicians and much more it made her realize what a huge business getting married was. She found the section that carried features on people's weddings, and showed everything: from how they decorated the room to hair-styling ideas. As Ali admired a bride from Cork's beautiful hair and veil, she noticed the gorgeous table arrangements the girl had had at the Sheraton Fota Island in Cork. She had had square vases, very like the ones Ali had ordered, and in each she had had pink and cream roses. Ali had chosen a mixed bouquet of flowers for her vases, but now that her florist was out of action, she had a thought. Could they make the table arrangements themselves? The vases would be in this week, and they could order flowers from the other flower shop, and even though they couldn't do any preparation, Ali was sure her mum, sisters and Ali could manage to fill each square vase with the rose arrangement. It was simple yet beautiful. She ripped the page out of the magazine, flung on her striped black Zara suit and set off for work.

When Ali got there, she headed for the fax machine and sent her mum the page from the bridal magazine, with a note explaining what she thought they could do. Then she sat down at her desk, which was covered in files, faxes, empty coffee cups and phone messages. She had a lot of work to get through before the big day. She scanned her phone messages and saw there was one from her old college friend who worked in family law. Ali rang her back, and was delighted when Linda informed her that with all the information Paddy had supplied – and if they got more character witnesses involved – they had a winnable case. It needed a good bit more work, but Ali was determined to make this happen. Just then her boss came in and stood over Ali's desk. Ali informed Mary of the progress she had made with her cases, in particular the Paddy Fleming one. Mary just nodded, but then turned to Ali.

'Ali, as you know, I've to go to Cork for some court work this afternoon for a few days, and I thought in case I'm not back before you head off to Kilkenny for the wedding, that we would have cakes in the canteen for you today at 11 a.m. I presume you can make it?'

Ali was a little shocked; she couldn't believe Mary was organizing a celebration for her. She thanked her boss and looked at the clock. She had an hour before the cakes, so she got down to work. At 11 a.m. Ali grabbed her empty coffee cup and headed for the small office canteen. All the other office employees were there, and she walked into a big row of smiles. Ali wasn't that friendly with her work colleagues, but appreciated the cakes and wedding wishes. When Mary arrived everyone went quiet; Ali was not the only one scared of her. Mary stood up.

'Well, Ali, we want to wish you good luck in your marriage. I hope you and your partner are very happy. We got you a wedding gift, I hope you like it.'

And with that Mary handed Ali a small envelope, gave her

a half-hug and left the canteen. Ali put down her chocolate eclair and opened the card, which had been signed by the office staff. Inside was a five-hundred-euro voucher for Arnotts. Ali was shocked and so happy at the same time, and was already thinking of all the different things herself and Robin could buy – luggage for Hawaii being the first thing! Debbie from accounts sat beside her and poured her some more coffee.

'Mary was very good, you know, Ali. It was her idea for the collection and cakes.'

'Really?' Ali said, thinking Mary barely spoke two words to her most days.

'Yes, I don't think she's that bad, after all. I suppose she has had it hard,' Debbie said, biting into a doughnut.

'What do you mean?' Ali enquired.

'Do you not know? About five years ago Mary's fiancé was killed in a car crash only one month before their wedding. It was so sad. I had only just started here, but apparently she was a very lively fun person before, but I suppose tragedy will do that to you. She has had it hard.'

Ali felt so guilty. No wonder Mary never asked about my wedding plans, it must have reminded her too much of her own loss, Ali thought. She finished off her cake and headed back to her office. Mary didn't even raise her head when Ali walked in, but Ali stood over Mary's desk.

'Thank you, Mary, I appreciate your generosity and kind words.'

Ali would have said she was also sorry for Mary's loss, but she didn't think her boss would want her knowing her personal business, so instead she just offered Mary an eclair that had been left over in the canteen. Mary took it, and half-smiled at Ali, before pulling her cardigan tightly around her, fixing her ever-perfect hair bun and turning back to her computer. Ali got back to work, but couldn't help marvelling at how you could think you knew someone, and be entirely mistaken. But she didn't have long to ponder this before getting a call from her mum who had 'loved the pictures in the fax' and was all excited about the table arrangements and her plans for 'Project Flower Arrangement', which seemed to involve a lot of 'making your two sisters get up off their asses and begin cutting, tying and arranging the roses'. Ali smiled. She knew it was going to be hard work, but she also knew it was all going to be all right.

107

Ben was in Dalkey for dinner with his parents. It was his mother's birthday, but as Joe was still not feeling his best they had decided to delay any big celebrations for a few weeks and instead were in Nosh, drinking wine and enjoying the good food and atmosphere. As Ben tucked into his prawn starter he watched his parents as they hugged and his dad presented Maura with a new painting. Ever since he had started questioning his relationship with Nikki he had begun watching his parents more and more, and realizing what they had. He envied the love and respect they had for each other, and the interest they took in each other's thoughts and feelings. In the last few months Ben knew he had truly grown up: not only had his father's heart-attack made him go back into the family business, but his attitude to his parents and his behaviour had changed. It had been a real wake-up call.

As he poured his mum more wine, Ben's mind flashed back to Saturday night, his last date with Nikki. They had gone to a nightclub, and as she had tried to wrangle some celebrity photos for her magazine she had almost drunk her own weight in wine, and ended up too drunk even to talk to Ben. So he had brought her home, and while she slept he had watched TV, and regretted ever agreeing to see her that night. She had been away with work for the last three days, but Ben was planning to meet her later for drinks, and he knew that they needed to end whatever kind of relationship they had. Yes it was fun, but it wasn't right for Ben any longer. Ben's sea bass arrived, and he tucked into it and some potato gratin as his mum and dad laughed at stories of birthdays gone by. Joe was getting stronger and healthier every day. He was still a long way off playing eighteen holes of golf, but Ben and Maura were both relieved he was on the road to recovery. Maura was more relaxed about Joe's health and future now, and was beginning to enjoy having him around the house during the day – and Ben often came home to find them both sunning themselves in the back garden, or playing bridge.

After another bottle of wine, Ben could see Joe was tired, and as Ben had been drinking he couldn't drive his parents home. He arranged for a taxi to collect them, then kissed his mum goodnight and headed for the nearby pub where Nikki was waiting. Ben took a deep breath as he entered, and prayed Nikki wouldn't look too hot, as that would make this even harder.

108

'So, you are single again?' Jeremy asked Ben.

Ben nodded as he ordered two drinks for himself and his friend. It was a gorgeous evening, so Ben and Jeremy had met for a drink after work in a great beer garden on Harcourt Street. They spotted a seat and sat down to enjoy their pints.

'So, what happened?' Jeremy asked, lighting a cigarette.

'She was fun and very pretty, but just not that bothered about anything half the time. And the other half she was too drunk, or at celebrity parties. I don't know, Jeremy, she just wasn't what I'm looking for any more, I guess. I know that sounds very soppy,' Ben said, opening a pack of crisps.

'Soppy? Sure, I'm the married one, here, and soppy is my middle name! But you are right, time is too short to be wasting on people that aren't right.'

Ben nodded in agreement.

'Anyway, it was probably too good to be true,' Jeremy said to Ben.

'What do you mean?' Ben asked, puzzled.

'Well, you know, that you would get so grown-up, what with taking over your dad's place, and settle down with the woman of your dreams all in the space of a few months. That's too much growing up for you!'

Ben laughed, but still felt a little disappointed that he and

Nikki were over, even though he knew it had been the right thing to do. He decided to change the subject by teasing Jeremy. So he asked him when he was going to have kids and become a dad. 'That's the real grown-up married thing to do,' he laughed.

They enjoyed the rest of the night: catching up, drinking and watching football on the large outdoor flat screen TV. At 11 p.m. they headed for a late-night burger before heading home, and Jeremy asked if Ben wanted to go surfing the following weekend.

'Great idea, but I can't. I'm off to a wedding in Kilkenny,' Ben said. Only then did he remember he had no idea where his tuxedo was, and that he needed to get Ali and Robin a wedding gift.

'No bother. Sure, I'll see you soon, and maybe I'll help find a nice girl for you. What do accountants go for? Book worms? Tax consultants? TV licence inspectors?'

Ben playfully hit Jeremy. 'Just because you are an old married man now, doesn't mean you have to be jealous of single young men like myself!'

And with that, Ben hopped into a taxi and made a mental note to remember to find his tuxedo and good shoes for the wedding – and buy that present.

109

Molly was in Coast on St Stephen's Green, trying to find something to wear for Ali's upcoming wedding. Even though she would be busy working for most of the day, she was going to the church while her cousin Eve kept an eye on the food. Then, straight after the ceremony, when everyone else would be posing for photos and having a drink in the local pub, Molly planned to rush back to Ali's farm, change into her catering gear and get going on the food. It would be hectic, but Molly was delighted to be helping her friend and gaining the experience of catering a wedding. She realized how much she loved doing jobs like this: planning menus, being her own boss, and getting joy from seeing clients well-fed and happy. It gave her hope that her career and job prospects would improve in the future, and that maybe one day she would have enough money to live away from home.

She zipped up a short, white dress that had large black flowers printed all over it, and a wide black ribbon trim. There were matching shoes and a clutch bag. It showed off her long brown hair and dark brown eyes, and as she looked in the mirror Molly knew she had found the perfect wedding outfit, so she made her way to the till.

She was going to Kilkenny the night before the wedding, to get the kitchen and food set up. Ali's dad had booked her into a small hotel near the farm. He had also hired some local waiters to help serve the food on the big day. Molly was actually looking forward to getting away: she was so sick of alternating nights in with her mum with nights out with the girls – who all seemed obsessed with finding her a man. After the disaster with the singer, Will, Molly had been put off all men, and was just happy working and enjoying the summer sunshine, but she thought a few days away would do her good. She paid for the new dress and headed home. Tonight she was going to the cinema with her brother Patrick. He might be nearly thirty-two but he had almost died from excitement when he had heard *Spider-Man 3* was out, and when his girlfriend had refused to go, Molly had given in to her brother's obsession with comic-book heroes and booked for them to see it together, followed by a pizza in Dundrum.

When she got home she did a quick fashion show for her mum, who agreed the new dress was perfect, before her brother knocked on the front door. Molly grabbed her handbag, and after her mum had made Patrick promise to come for dinner the following weekend, they headed for Dundrum cinema. As she sat in the car, listening to Patrick rattle on about his job, his football team's disastrous relegation, and his plans for a holiday Molly realized how much she had missed male company. Even though she had her dad at home, and Eve's boyfriend André at work, she missed just sitting in a car listening to a man chat and drive. Her girlfriends were great, but they were all obsessed with men and weddings, while boys could chat about a good dinner, or *Star Wars* for hours. Molly laughed when Patrick asked if she could teach him some special meals to cook for his girlfriend who was getting sick of takeaway every time it was Patrick's turn to cook. When they got to the cinema Molly picked up the tickets while Patrick went hell for leather on the food and came back with huge cokes, popcorns, pick'n'mix and nachos.

'How will we fit dinner in after?' she laughed.

'Oh we will, don't you worry,' he said, as he handed his sister her share of the food. They found their seats and waited to see how Tobey Maguire was filling out the new black *Spider-Man* suit.

After the cinema Molly and Patrick had started walking towards *Milanos* for a pizza when Molly stopped dead. There, across the path, was Luke, walking hand in hand with a girl. Molly actually thought she was going to be sick. Patrick noticed them at the same time, and put his arm around his younger sister.

'Just keep on walking, Molly,' he said as he almost lifted her, and pushed her towards the restaurant.

Molly just stared at Luke, who hadn't seen her. He was laughing and chatting, and having the time of his life. When they sat down Patrick ordered a bottle of white wine, and it wasn't until he had poured Molly a large glass that he finally spoke.

'Molly, that must have been so hard for you. I'm so sorry, it's my fault we came to the cinema tonight. I'm sorry.'

Molly knocked back the wine and poured herself more.

'It's not your fault, Patrick,' she eventually managed to say. 'I just can't believe Luke has moved on so fast. I mean, yes, I went on a couple of kind of dates with that guy Will, but nothing in broad daylight, stone cold sober, and holding hands.' Molly spoke in shock, thinking back to all the millions of times she and Luke had held hands. It was a normal every-day thing that she had taken for granted, yet now that she had no one to do it with it seemed as priceless as gold dust.

Patrick ordered them each a pizza, not having to ask what his only sister wanted; he knew pepperoni was her favourite.

'Molly, I'm sorry, but maybe it will help you move on, you know?' Patrick said, looking worriedly at her.

Molly sighed to herself. Patrick was right. And Luke was a nice guy. He deserved to have someone in his life. He had never liked being on his own, anyway, so it did not surprise her that he had found a new girlfriend.

'Patrick, it is not that I'm still madly in love with Luke, and I know I've to move on. But it's just not as easy as that. It's so hard seeing the guy you went out with and lived with for years obviously madly in love with someone new.'

Patrick kept quiet, and then changed the subject and began talking about the movie trailers that they had seen, including a new *Superman* one. Molly smiled at him. He might be older than her, but he was still pretty childish.

After Patrick had dropped her home, she went to her room and saw the new dress laid out ready, and as she changed into her pyjamas she was amazed by how much could change in a day. A few hours earlier she had been so excited about her work, and the wedding, and her new dress, and now she only felt numb – all because she had seen Luke. Just when she had thought her life was moving forward she felt it slow down and begin to fall backwards. She couldn't sleep, so she went down to the kitchen for some water. Her mum was still up, watching an old black-and-white movie on TV. She turned the film off as Molly sank into a chair and began telling her about seeing Luke with someone new. When Molly finished, her mum put her cup of tea down and began to speak.

'You know, pet, I was heart-broken for you when you and Luke split up. After all those years you had together it seemed like such a shame, a waste. I was annoyed that he'd hurt you, and I knew how hard it must have been for you to move back home. But now, when I look back, maybe Luke was right. You did want different things. Maybe he could see that clearer than you could. I know you were not that happy when you had your old banking job, and I thought changing jobs would solve everything, but maybe it was just that you and Luke

331

were not meant for each other. You had such great times with him, and we loved having him here in the house, he was like family for years, but maybe it was fate. Maybe you and Luke were never meant to end up married. I know what I'm saying might hurt you, love, and I don't mean to take away from you what you had with Luke, but I want you to find someone now who is truly your perfect other half. You are as beautiful on the inside as you are on the outside, and trust me, some day you will find your perfect match.'

Molly wasn't sure what to say, and instead gave her mum a hug, made herself some hot chocolate and went back up to bed. But as she lay under her duvet that night her mind raced with thoughts. Maybe her mum was right: Luke and herself were not meant for each other. All along she had thought Luke was her soulmate, and that by breaking it off with her he had ruined her only chance at true love, but when she looked back now, she saw it differently. If Luke had been her perfect match, how come they hadn't seen eye to eye about anything? That they had always fought and hadn't just been happy for one another? She had seen her different jobs as the reason for their fights, but wasn't that just a cop out? Surely work didn't have that much influence on your love life? She suddenly felt so guilty. When she remembered how moody and depressed she had been when she worked in banking and funds, and how distant and obsessed she had become when she began working as a cook, she realized that it hadn't all been just Luke's fault. She had been difficult, too. She had used her jobs as an excuse for behaving unreasonably. Luke had simply been worried for her, and even after he had financially supported her new career, she had just spent all her time cooking, and taking on extra work and classes. No wonder he had felt hurt and upset. I didn't give our relationship a chance, Molly thought to herself. She sat bolt upright in bed, wide awake with the realization that she had made mistakes. She began to understand how her actions had contributed more to their break-up than she had realized at the time. Maybe Luke had had a better handle on things all along: he had known they were never going to get back to where they had started. They really had wanted different things, Molly admitted to herself.

As she sat in her bedroom all alone in the early hours of the morning, she began finally to have closure on Luke. She couldn't change the past, but she realized she could change the future. She realized, too, that as hard as it had been, she was actually glad she had seen Luke and his date tonight. It had made her own up to some hard truths about herself. She had not been easy to live with — always complaining about work, or being overworked and too busy — and now she knew she didn't want to make that mistake again. If and when she met someone new, she vowed not to repeat history. She would change.

And by the time she began to nod off, Molly was almost glad Luke had a new partner. She wanted him to be happy, and it made her dream that some day soon she too would have someone who would hold her hand and not let go.

110

Sarah was locking up the gallery and making her way home. She wanted to talk to her mum before she met Hugh for dinner tonight. The last few days, ever since she had returned from Galway, Sarah had not been able to concentrate. Hugh asking her to move to Galway had really thrown her. She didn't know if she was ready for such a commitment. She had spent a day writing up a list of pros and cons. Of course the biggest pro was moving to a city with the man she was falling in love with, and Galway wasn't that far away; but then the biggest cons were that she had a good job and her family and friends all here in Dublin. When she had called on her sister Mel the night before to discuss things with her, she had realized that if she moved she wouldn't be able to see her godchild quite so often or pop in to see her sister for chats. And then of course there was her mum. Sarah might complain about living at home, but her mum was her best friend, and it was hard to think about moving hours away and leaving her mum living alone. Sarah walked into the kitchen and caught her mum staring out into the garden.

'Are you OK, Mum?' she asked, putting down her handbag and helping herself to a biscuit.

'Oh yes, pet, I'm just thinking how when you and Mel were small the garden was so bare, and it has taken years to get it so colourful. But now that it is there will be no one here to enjoy it, what with your father gone, Mel married and now you moving to Galway.'

'Mum, I'm not definitely going yet, you know. I'm still not sure about it.'

'I know, Sarah, but it is weird. I know I've been pressuring you to be like Mel, to meet a man and settle down and have kids, but now that you are on your way to doing that I realize how much I'll miss you when you move. I'm not putting pressure on you to stay here, but I just want you to know I'll miss you, pet. I know I might drive you mad at home, but I do love you so much, and only want the best for you. But you had better make sure Hugh has a spare room in that big house of his in Galway, for all my visits!'

Sarah gave her mum a big hug, and sat down beside her. She started telling her what she feared if she moved to Galway.

'Not only may I not get a job, but me and Hugh haven't been together that long. What happens if it doesn't all work out?'

Her mum opened a bottle of wine as they both moved out into the garden to chat.

'No one can predict if you and Hugh will last for ever,' she said. 'But you will know in your heart if Hugh is the one for you, and if he is you must do whatever it is to make sure you hold on to him. Good men are hard to come by.'

Sarah knew her mum was right, but it still hadn't helped her make up her mind. She looked again at her list of pros and cons. If she stayed in Dublin, yes she would have her friends and family but she was still a long way off affording to buy anywhere. At least in Galway Hugh already had a house, so she wouldn't have the pressure to save, and instead could focus on her painting and on working at what she really wanted to do. She also knew she needed change: she was getting too old to be stuck in the rut of living at home and working in just the Stone Studio. But she had thought her big change would be moving out of home, or being able to finally cut down her work hours in the gallery to focus on her painting, not moving half-way across the country. As she sat in the garden she realized what inspiration she had taken from it, from her mum, from the local beach, and from Dublin itself. She knew she had many more paintings in her if she stayed here; would Galway give her the inspiration she needed? Sarah knew she wanted to give her art another chance, but was a move away from everything she knew the right choice to make now? Just then Sarah got a call from Hugh saying he had to take a new client out to dinner and could they postpone until tomorrow night? Sarah was actually relieved; it gave her another twenty-four hours to make her decision, the biggest decision of her life. She immediately rang her sister and asked if Mel could spare the time to walk the Dun Laoghaire pier with her. She needed some advice.

She arrived at Mel's an hour later, and found John holding Fiona while Mel tried to find her runners.

'So, any decision on Galway yet?' her brother-in-law asked. Sarah shook her head.

'We will all miss you so much if you go. Mel will be in bits! But it is your life, Sarah, you must make the decision on your own. Hugh seems like a good guy, although Tom was disappointed when I told him you were off.'

'Tom?' Sarah said in surprise, thinking John's brother wouldn't give a toss if she moved.

'Yeah, although maybe it is because he worries he will be left with all the babysitting duties if you go!'

'Oh, the babysitting, of course,' Sarah said, giving her god-child a kiss. Just then Mel arrived in the kitchen, and the two girls headed off for their walk.

Sarah told Mel all her fears about moving, but also discussed the positives, like being with Hugh and starting afresh. Mel nodded that Hugh was lovely, and his house and friends all sounded great.

'It is hard for me to give you an unbiased view, because Mum and I will miss you so much, but I realize that when you meet the man of your dreams you have to go for it. I mean, if John had lived in Galway, I would probably be there now. But I suppose you need to work out what is important to you, and if it is Hugh and Galway, then off you go.'

Sarah nodded, but was still unsure.

'If only he was happy to live in Dublin, then I could have my family, my work, my friends and him,' she said, as the girls got ice-creams and sat down overlooking the waves and boats.

'Well, that would be perfect, but we are not living Disney-style lives here,' Mel joked.

'But if I don't go to Galway, I'll end up where I was months ago . . . single, and no nearer to being able to leave home.'

Mel looked at her younger sister.

'Don't worry about living at home. All you need to do is sell a few paintings and then you could at least afford to rent somewhere, while still maybe saving a bit. I know Tom is looking for a new room-mate in his house.'

Sarah thought about moving in with Tom, but realized it wouldn't work: she knew she still slightly fancied him.

'No, I couldn't do that. Either I move in with Hugh or else I'll stay with Mum for the next while.'

'OK, Sarah. Listen, I know your decision is hard, and I do like Hugh, but if he really wants you to give up your life here in Dublin then why hasn't he asked you to marry him? Is it fair to ask you to abandon your life here for a relationship that might not even be a long-term thing?'

Sarah didn't know what to say to her sister. She wasn't expecting Hugh to ask her to marry him after such a short time together, but was her sister right? Should he be promising her more than just a good time in Galway? And as she went to sleep that night, what Mel had said earlier about finding the man of your dreams kept replaying in her head. Was Hugh really her Prince Charming?

111

Sarah didn't sleep all night, and by 8 a.m. she was sitting on Sandycove beach with her sketch pad and pencils. As she watched the waves she remembered the story of *The Little Mermaid*, that her dad used to read to her at night. A tear came to her eye as she wished her father was here now to give her some advice. Giving in to an impulse, she decided to visit his grave, jumped into the car and drove out to Shanganagh graveyard in no time. It was early, so there were no other visitors. She bought some flowers and made her way over to her dad's spot. She sat beside his headstone and just started telling him about Hugh, her dream of going back to art full-time, how her mum was, how baby Fiona was getting so big – she talked for what seemed like hours. By 11 a.m. she knew what she wanted to do. She took out her mobile phone and rang Clodagh, the part-time student from the gallery, and arranged to meet her there within the hour. By the time Sarah arrived in Monkstown and at the studio, she had already been on the phone to Maggie McCartney, the gallery owner, ending her call with a promise to one day visit Spain. It was time to talk to Clodagh.

By 7 p.m. that night Sarah was feeling much more positive about her future, and as she ordered some wine while waiting for Hugh to arrive she finally began to relax. She knew she had made the right choice. Hugh arrived straight from work, so he looked very handsome in a grey suit and bright blue shirt. He gave Sarah a kiss and poured himself some wine. He looked a little nervous, so Sarah knew they had to just get the Galway talk out of the way.

'Hugh, I'm sorry that the last few days I've been sounding so uncertain about moving to Galway, but you have to understand that my life has always been here in Dublin, surrounded by my family and friends. But when I met you I knew I had met a great man, so it made my decision very hard.' She took a swig of wine.

'Hugh, I knew I needed change, and your encouragement has helped me go back to being an artist. Painting again has been the biggest change I've made in years, but I never imagined that I might have to make another change, and move counties. But then, today, I suddenly saw how to do everything I wanted and be happy. I talked to Maggie and Clodagh, and Maggie has agreed that I can work three days as the gallery manager, and the rest of the time I'll paint, as long as I promise to give my work solely to her to sell in the Stone Studio. So I'll still be the gallery manager, but Clodagh will now have a permanent job as my assistant. She's broke after college, anyway, so is delighted at the pay rise. As I now only need to be in Dublin three days a week I can spend the rest of the time with you in Galway. It is perfect.'

Sarah gave Hugh's hand a squeeze as she poured him some more wine, but Hugh's expression did not reflect her good mood.

'Sarah,' he said, leaning forward and looking serious, 'I've been mad about you for ages, and the last few months have been great, but I'm thirty-six now, I'm too old for long-distance relationships. I want and need someone I can come home to every night. I want that person to be you! Even if you were only gone for three days, that would be too much. I can see you still want to stay in Dublin, and you're not ready to give up your life here. And I can't compete with that, I don't want to compete with that. I want someone who wants to be with me twenty-four hours a day, no matter where I live.'

'But I will be with you,' Sarah replied.

'Sarah, I can't do this half-hearted attempt at moving in together. I want us to start our lives as one, and be together full-time.'

Sarah was taken aback. She had thought her idea was perfect. She began to feel angry, but then, as she looked at Hugh's expression she realized he only wanted them to be together seven days a week because he loved her. And even though Sarah thought he was a great guy, and they shared so many interests, she could see now that he might be a prince, but he wasn't the right one for her. If he had been, she would not have hesitated when he had asked her to move: she would have moved to Outer Mongolia if necessary. But no, instead she had got caught up in how the move would affect her job, her family, her art; even though she had known those elements shouldn't really have come into it. She did love Hugh, but not enough. And a part of her thought back to what Mel had said. If he really wanted her to move to Galway would Hugh not have asked her to marry him? Maybe they both weren't 100 per cent sure.

'I'm sorry, Hugh, but I can't do it,' Sarah said. Her throat choked up with emotion.

Hugh didn't look up from the table, he just called for the bill. They'd only had wine.

'Hugh, I don't mean to hurt you,' she babbled. 'I just don't know what to say. I can't help how I feel.'

Hugh nodded slowly and gave her a hug. 'I know, and even though I feel heart-broken right now I'm glad I finally got up the courage to ask you out all those months ago, because it has been great. If you change your mind you know where I am.'

Sarah felt heart-broken herself. She was saying goodbye to so much, but when you know something is right you just have to go with your gut instinct, and trust it. When she got home she was glad her mum was out for the night, as she barely made it to her bed before bursting into tears. She was mourning the relationship, even if in her heart she knew that breaking up with Hugh was the best thing to do.

112

Today was Ali's last day at work before the wedding; that evening she was heading home to Kilkenny. The marquee was going up, and she had been receiving text messages all day from her sisters saying the cows were all very put out by having to give their field up for the next few days, and seemed to have been getting their revenge on everyone by leaving cowpat after cowpat all over it. Ali's mum had rung to say she was mortified when Father Conway had popped by to make sure everyone was OK, and, while admiring the marquee, had slipped and fallen right into the biggest cowpat of them all.

'God will never forgive us for that, Ali, and even though I'm getting his suit dry cleaned, I don't know how we are going to look him in the eye on the wedding day. Your father will have to triple his usual church donation.'

Ali felt sorry for the priest, but was too busy at work to stay chatting to her mum. This morning she had a big meeting with two other solicitors and an official from the Department of Family Affairs. Paddy Fleming's case was really looking up. Ali had put in long hours and it had paid off; the solicitor that Paddy had had before her had been doing the work pro-bono, too, and hadn't looked into the details of the case properly at all. Ali knew this meeting today could end up with Paddy getting more access to his children and more joy back in his

343

life. Even though Robin had complained he hadn't seen Ali properly for the last few weeks, Ali thought that with all her luck and happiness at getting married it was only right she should help someone less fortunate. And, as she kept reminding Robin, they would have the whole honeymoon to catch up! Ali quickly grabbed her case file and headed downstairs, where the meeting was about to start. Paddy had bought a new suit, and at Ali's suggestion had cut his hair. He looked very presentable. As they entered the room she squeezed his hand.

'Trust me, this will work out. You will see your kids soon.'

After two and a half hours Ali and Paddy were finally able to relax. The Department of Family Affairs agreed Paddy had a case, and a very successful family law specialist, Ray Moore, had said he would take the case over from Ali, now that she would be away for a few weeks. They still weren't guaranteeing Paddy full access, but it was a start. Ali walked the men to the door, and as she said goodbye to Ray Moore, he handed her his business card.

'You have done great work here, Ali. I'm sure you are very settled here in this firm, but if you would like a career helping the less fortunate, give me a call. Now, you won't make the money like all these private solicitors, but will sleep easy at night knowing you are making a difference.'

Ali thanked him, and as she stared at the card decided that the minute she was back from America she would give him a call. She had entered law to do work like this, and the last few weeks, although hard, had given her great pleasure. She could also do with never seeing her boss Mary again! And, anyway, she thought, change never hurt anyone.

She walked Paddy to the bus stop, and as she gave him a hug he said: 'Ali, I can't thank you enough. Robin is a lucky man to have found you. Good luck on the big day. I got you something small, I hope you like it.'

Ali took the small package from her client, opened it, and was surprised to find a Christmas tree decoration inside.

'I know Christmas is a long time away, but when the kids were small I started buying them each their own inscribed ornaments, and you should have seen their excitement each year as they hung their own piece on the tree. Maybe you will start that tradition in your family, too.'

Ali looked at the silver star. Paddy had inscribed it with her and Robin's names and their wedding date.

'It is beautiful, Paddy, thank you so much.' Paddy walked off quickly, but Ali stared at his thoughtful gift for a long time.

113

Molly was busy trying to help her aunt in the café, and get herself organized for her biggest catering job yet. She was heading down to Kilkenny the next day for Ali and Robin's wedding. Her cousin Eve was going to come down to help with the cooking, but even so Molly felt the pressure was really on her. Although Ali was her friend, and kept reassuring her that she was sure Molly would do a good job, Molly also knew that a wedding was the biggest day in people's lives, and she didn't want to mess it up. As she put some scones into the oven her aunt came into Heavenly.

'Molly,' her aunt said, 'I know you are busy today, but Sterling Bank rang this morning, and asked if, when you drop over their sandwiches, you could also drop over a selection of cakes or buns, as someone is leaving work there today. Do you think you will have time to do it? They need you there by twelve.'

Molly looked at the time.

'Yes, the sandwiches won't take long, and I can take over some scones, eclairs and caramel slices. I'm fine with it.'

'Thanks, pet,' said her aunt, as she put on her own apron and the two women got down to work.

★   ★   ★

By twelve Molly was entering Sterling Bank with a very large basket in her arms.

'Little Red Riding Hood, what have you got in that basket of yours?'

Molly turned, and saw Scott.

'Let me help you,' he said. He took the large basket from petite Molly, and they headed upstairs.

'Thanks,' Molly said. 'So who is leaving?' she asked.

'It's someone who works for me, actually, a very nice young girl, and a hard worker. She has decided to follow her boyfriend to Australia for the year. I advised against it, as not only is her career going very well here, but she is only going because she suspects he is cheating on her.'

'That's awful,' said Molly as they got into the lift.

'Yes, the poor girl told me about it the night of that summer barbecue. I spent an hour trying to talk her out of it, but she's stubborn, and insists on going. So all I can do now is wish her well.'

Molly thought back to the barbecue and realized that that must have been the girl that she had seen Scott with. So that hadn't been his girlfriend after all. It all made sense now.

'So, how is work with you?' he asked, sneaking a peek at all the cakes and sandwiches.

Molly filled him in on Ali's wedding, and before she knew it she was telling him her fears about messing the food up, or giving everyone food-poisoning. The more she got to know Scott the more she realized that, even though he still ate exactly the same boring sandwich every day, he was easy to talk to. He listened intently to her anxieties, before giving her a quick pat on the back.

'Molly, I eat your food every day and all you have given me has been a lot of pleasure and a bigger waistline. Believe in yourself: you are a great cook, and your friend is lucky to have you working for her.' Before Molly could reply the lift opened, and Scott was greeted by a secretary asking him to sign off on some document, so she took the basket from him and made her way alone into the large open-plan office. There she saw the girl from the barbecue, who was now being hugged and wished bon voyage by everyone. Molly put down her basket and started setting the cakes and treats out on paper plates. When she finished she headed back to the café, intending to collect the basket later.

After a busy day at work, and at least a hundred phone calls to Ali, Molly, Eve and Fran were cleaning up the kitchen and getting ready to go home, when Molly heard a knock on the door. She wiped her hands on her apron and opened it. Outside stood Scott Williams, with Heavenly's basket in his hand, except that instead of being empty, it was filled with tulips: pink, red, purple and white ones. Molly gasped.

'Before you say a word, Molly, I want to tell you something,' Scott said. 'For months you have been delivering my sandwich to me every day, and every day I've fancied you more and more. But I just didn't know what to do about it. I always presumed you had some equally successful chef boyfriend and I was just a boring banker to you. Well, I've decided I need a change. A change of sandwich and a change from being single. Molly, I know you are off to that wedding tomorrow, and are probably up to your eyeballs in work, but I just wanted you to know that.'

He handed her the basket. Molly looked at him, and thought of the compliments he always paid her cooking, and how he had invited her to the barbecue, and given her a lift home when she was upset over Luke. She realized that right here, under her nose, a nice guy had been interested in her for ages, and she had been too busy being upset about Luke, or chasing men at rock gigs to notice. She smiled.

'Well, Mr Williams, for starters you are right.' She noticed what great eyes he had. 'Your sandwich will have to change. Even if we just had Ballymaloe relish instead of mustard. Or maybe I could tempt you with some salami.'

'Salami I could do.' Scott smiled.

Molly's stomach was full of butterflies, and even though she was at a loss about what to say to Scott, she leant forward and gave him a quick hug.

'You know, I always did have a thing for Mr Benn,' she whispered, and Scott started laughing.

Inside the café Eve was just turning off the lights and handing her mum the keys when she stopped and saw Molly and Scott outside the big window.

'Finally!' she said. 'I knew he had it in him. You always said, Mum, that the way to a man's heart was through his stomach. And you were right!' And with that Heavenly closed for the day, but Molly didn't even seem to notice, she was walking up the road, chatting to Scott and starting to get to know him properly.

114

Sarah walked out of the Stone Studio. She was off to Kilkenny the next day and had been busy all day leaving notes for Clodagh and getting the gallery tidy for the usual busy weekend visitors. She was meeting her sister Mel after work to discuss the whole 'Hugh situation'. After changing into her runners and cut-off jeans Sarah was ready, and made her way to the pier. They both got an ice-cream in Teddy's and sat down on a bench overlooking the water.

'How do you feel?' asked Mel. Sarah stared at the boats bobbing on the water.

'I don't know, Mel. I mean, in one way I'm so sad not to see Hugh again, but then there is a part of me that knows it was the right thing to do. But I feel so cold and clinical for even reducing our relationship to such a statement as "the right thing to do". I do still wish I could have it all but that's not going to happen.'

Mel gave her sister a hug.

'It will all work out, Sarah, I promise. And I know I shouldn't say this but I'm glad you didn't go. I would have missed you so much, and so would John and Fiona.'

Sarah smiled and licked her ice-cream.

'Did you ring Maggie to say that now you are not going to Galway you can work full-time in the gallery again?'

'No, Mel, I didn't. I need some kind of change, and the one thing Hugh and then Ali's wedding invite has opened me up to is being an artist again, not just selling other people's work. So I'm going to start working part-time next week, and try to earn a living as a painter. Clodagh is delighted to get the extra hours and Maggie has big plans for exhibitions of my work. I'm still nervous, but I need something new, and now that I'm single and definitely not buying a house a new career is as good as any change.'

'That sounds fab, Sarah. My sister the famous artist! Great stuff. I had better buy some of your work now, while I can still afford it.'

The girls started walking down the pier.

'When Tom heard you were painting again he told me he wanted to buy a picture for his apartment,' Mel said. 'He is a philistine and knows nothing about art, totally unlike Hugh. But I do know that he thinks you are great, and am sure he would give you a good price.'

'Has he found someone to move in with him yet?' Sarah asked.

'No. He asked again if you wanted to, but I told him about Galway and all. But then, it was funny because last night, when he was over for dinner and I was telling the boys about you and Hugh breaking up, he actually seemed relieved that you were not going to Galway. John said he thinks Tom has always had a crush on you, but you being my sister made it a bit awkward for him. Of course I didn't tell John you used to fancy Tom as well. I know that was all years ago, but you never know, Sarah. Maybe something will happen. If it did, John and I would love it.'

Then Mel started telling Sarah all about Fiona's eating habits, but Sarah couldn't concentrate. Yes, she had only broken up with Hugh a day ago, but she couldn't help wondering if Tom really had cared about her moving to Galway.

115

The night before the wedding everyone had arranged to meet in Hennessy's, the pub near Ali's house. There was a big spread there, and Ali's dad was right in the middle of it all, welcoming everyone to Kilkenny. Ali had been busy all day, trying to get the house, marquee and herself all ready for tomorrow. It still all felt very surreal to her: surely it was impossible that tomorrow she would be a married woman! She had tried to talk to Robin all day, but with all their relations and friends ringing and arriving it had been difficult to exchange more than a few words. Robin was staying in a local hotel, and then tomorrow night they were both going to stay in the bridal suite of the nearest five-star hotel.

Ali was staying off drink tonight, but as she sipped on 7 Up, Robin was knocking back Guinness after Guinness, with seemingly everyone buying him pint after pint to help him celebrate his last night as a single man. It was only 7 p.m. and already Robin and the lads were singing and recalling old school days. Ali kept trying to remind him they still had some work to do that evening, but Robin was too busy drinking. Ali got a call from her mother saying her sisters were not fast enough with the table arrangement flowers, and that they were ruining the ribbon with their inexperience. Ali realized she had to go home to help, so she went outside to ring her mum, and said she would be home in five minutes. While out there she got a another call from her sister Jill saying that she had just checked the marquee and the party hire men had left the tables and chairs all stacked, and how was she supposed to lift them all into place herself? Ali put her phone down and felt a few tears roll down her face. She had underestimated how much work they had left to do. Just then Sarah and Molly arrived at the pub, but when they saw Ali looking so dishevelled and upset, they ran over.

'What's happened?' Sarah asked.

Ali explained, and before she could even finish the two girls were pushing her towards the car.

'We will come and help you, we can do the flowers. And Sarah, maybe you can grab a few guys to help with the marquee table and chairs,' Molly said.

'No, Molly, you have been working on the food all day, you deserve the night off,' said Ali.

'It is no problem, Ali, tomorrow is the biggest day of your life, so do not worry about it. You need to relax.'

Sarah ran into the pub, and went up to Robin to explain about the marquee, but he had people hugging and talking to him the whole time, and seemed to have had a good bit to drink, so instead Sarah looked round the bar, and suddenly saw Ali's friend, Laura.

'Hi Laura,' she asked, 'do you know many of these guys? I need some of them to help us with the marquee.'

Sarah explained about the flowers, tables and chairs, and Laura, understanding the urgency, agreed to help.

'You go with Ali,' she said. 'We'll meet you back at the house. I'll get some of the guys.'

Ali, Molly and Sarah all headed back to the house, while Laura scanned the bar for nice, burly, yet not-too-drunk men. She spotted Ben O'Connor, who she hadn't even realized had been invited. He waved and made his way over to her; he seemed nervous and tried to make small chat. He had a pint in his hand, but Laura could see it was almost full and he was sober, so getting her courage up she asked him if he'd help her.

'I don't want to upset Ali's dad by telling him the marquee is not ready, and I want him to enjoy his night, but we do need to find a few more guys.'

'No problem, Laura,' and with that Ben grabbed a few of the lads, and after he filled them all in, they put down their pints and headed for the farm and marquee.

When they got to the marquee Laura was surprised at how organized Ben was, he soon had all the guys lifting tables and chairs in military style, while Laura looked at the table plan and tried to work out which tables should go where. Laura and Ben worked well as a team and before long the room started to take shape. And despite Ali's twenty-year-old sister Jill swooning over Ben, thanking him profusely for helping the family, Ben seemed only to have eyes for Laura. Laura didn't know if she was imagining it, but Ben seemed to have grown up a lot since they briefly dated, so when he asked her if she wanted a lift back to the pub so they could get a drink, she accepted. She hadn't forgotten that he'd hurt her before, but tonight he was being a perfect gentleman.

Meanwhile, in Ali's family home it was like a sweatshop. Ali's mum had set up a production line, and now that her sisters had been fired from it, Ali, along with Sarah and Molly, was now cutting ribbons and trimming roses. She was trying to relax, but was disappointed that Robin was out having fun while she was stressed and trying to make countless table arrangements. As the girls sat at the large kitchen table they chatted and caught up. Molly filled them in on Scott, and even though she didn't know what would happen they were all very excited.

Even Ali's mum said that he sounded like 'a keeper'. Sarah told them all about Hugh, and even though she didn't mean to get upset, she couldn't help thinking how Ali was getting married and Molly had just met someone and she was back to being single and lonely again. But she held herself together, and instead changed the subject to her new career path, and they were all delighted, especially Ali. She said again that the moment Sarah had designed her invite she'd known that Sarah should go back to being an artist. The flower arrangements were looking great, and Ali took some photos for her wedding scrap-book. As they finished them off, Ali's mum opened a bottle of champagne and started telling all the girls about the day Ali was born, and how, even though they loved Robin, the family would miss having Ali all to themselves.

It ended up being a lovely evening, and as they carried the flowers into the marquee and set them on to the tables Ali looked around the farm, the family farm that she had grown up on, and loved. She thought that tonight was the last night she would just be someone's daughter. Tomorrow she and Robin would be a family of their own. It was a lot to take in, but when they got to the marquee, surrounded by mooing cows, Ali's mind went into wedding mode, and she and the girls started setting the table-numbers and place-names. The room really started to feel perfect, and as Ali tested the fairy lights she saw how the room would look the following night and started to get properly excited. Tomorrow was her wedding day!

116

Molly was wide awake by 7 a.m., and as Eve was due to arrive and help her at 9 a.m., she decided to get up and make her way to the marquee to make sure the kitchen was set up properly. As she dressed she received a good luck text from Scott. She smiled and thought already how different his attitude to her job was from Luke's. She was looking forward to being back in Dublin and seeing him again. She tied back her dark hair and said a quick prayer that her cooking and serving would all go OK today. And as she texted Scott back, she prayed that her love life would finally get some luck too, and that things with Scott would work out.

Sarah was also woken by a text, one from Tom, saying that as Mel and John were going away the following weekend he had agreed to mind Fiona in his house, and Mel had suggested that maybe Sarah might like to stay over, too, and they could look after their godchild together. Sarah laughed at how obvious her sister was: she and John must have planned this weekend away, just to try and get her and Tom together! But Sarah wasn't complaining, and she agreed to it straight away. She was glad to have something to look forward to after a week of upset and uncertainly. Tom texted back to say he looked forward to seeing her, and that he would make sure he got some grown-up food and drinks in, too, 'to celebrate your decision to stay in Dublin with us all'. As the day drew on, she hoped that maybe the weekend might lead to more than just looking after their godchild!

Ben felt a little groggy that morning, but knew he needed to check in with the office. The firm had a deal going through that day that he needed to check up on. His secretary had promised to go in on Saturday morning to make sure things went smoothly. As he rang her he almost laughed. I really am changing, he thought to himself. Here I am, checking in with the office, worrying about work, tired after spending a night organizing a wedding marquee – he really was starting to fill his father's boots. Ben ordered room service and gave his dad a quick call to check that he was feeling OK. His dad was recovering well, and Ben thought the time was right for him to move out of the family home and finally buy a place of his own. He had made an appointment with a real estate agent for when he got back from the wedding and was looking forward to seeing what he could afford.

He showered and checked his appearance, because he wanted to look well today for Laura. He had forgotten how attractive she was, and couldn't stop thinking of her big brown eyes and smile. He didn't know if he had imagined it, but he had felt last night that there had been a spark between them, and he didn't want to lose her again. He was through with playing the field, all he wanted was someone like Laura.

Ali was woken up by her whole family all peering in the door of her old bedroom.

'Oh, great, you are awake! Now we can do the presents!' said Jill, as Ali's mum and dad walked in too and sat down on her bed.

'How do you feel, pet?' asked her mum, giving her a big hug.

'Did you sleep OK?' asked her dad, who was wearing his old pyjamas and dressing gown. Just seeing them all there, her whole family, with their excited faces and gifts, made Ali start to cry.

'I don't want to leave this family,' she sobbed.

'Ali, you are not leaving us,' her mum said. 'We are gaining a gorgeous son-in-law, but you are not leaving us, pet. We all adore you, and today will be the happiest day of your life. Please don't be upset.' Ali wiped her eyes.

'The gifts will cheer you up,' said Jill. Ali sat up, and opened them. Kate and Jill had gotten her a large framed photo of the three of them sitting on their old donkey Ned. They were all dressed in eighties clothes and Ali laughed as she saw their old wellington boots, which Jill had always refused to take off, and even tried to wear to bed.

'It's so you won't forget all the fun we've down here, Ali. Don't forget that this is your home always,' Jill said. Ali hugged her sisters and promised to hang the large silver photo frame in her living room in Dublin.

Next her dad handed her a small jewellery box, Ali opened it, inside was a heart-shaped locket on a chain.

'I know Robin is after buying you that fabulous engagement ring and a wedding ring today, but you are my little girl and I can still treat you, too, and so I thought you might like a locket.'

'He picked it out all by himself,' added her mum. Ali put the locket on, and smiled, it was beautiful.

'I love you so much, Dad. I'm going to be so proud to have you walk me down that aisle today,' she whispered in his ear.

Finally her mum handed her a large rectangle-shaped package. Ali ripped open the paper and inside was a large hardback notebook. On it was written 'Ali's Memory Book'.

'What is this, Mum?' Ali asked.

'Well, when each of you was born I started a memory book for you, it contains everything: from how I felt when I was pregnant, to the story of the day you were born, to childhood anecdotes and old photos. I even wrote in what illnesses you had, so you would know for the future.'

Ali started reading the book and saw her mum had stuck in her hospital wrist band from the day she was born. It was so tiny.

'Oh my God, Mum, this is amazing,' Ali exclaimed.

'Can we have our memory books too, Mum?' asked Jill.

'No, you can't, you have to find men first, and get married, so it will be a while yet I think,' her mum said crossly.

Jill sulked off to get Ali some breakfast, while Ali was left reading her book, and enjoying being spoilt on her wedding day.

117

Ali was sitting in the hairdresser's with a glass of champagne in one hand and her phone in the other. All morning she had been receiving text messages wishing her luck. It was all so exciting. She had gotten her nails painted the day before and fake tan put on, so today it was all about her hair and make-up. Her hair was short, and she wanted to leave it down, so the hairdresser was just going to blow-dry it straight and fix in her veil for her. Her mum had been taking photos of her all morning, and now as her hair was being brushed she could hear the camera clicking.

'Mum, will you relax?' Ali said.

'Relax? You are my first born, my eldest daughter, and this is the biggest day of your life. I'll not relax, let me have my fun. You just take care with that champagne, we don't want you drunk before the church.'

Ali put down her glass and tried to read a magazine, but she was still distracted by her phone. It had been great getting the good-luck messages but there was one person she hadn't heard from – Robin. Last night he had sent some drunken message through, but Ali hadn't been able to decipher what he'd attempted to say. She knew they couldn't see each other today, it was bad luck to, but she had been disappointed that last night he hadn't been much use in the pub or back in the house, and now he wasn't even texting her. As she left the hairdresser's her Mum took a last photo, and the whole staff wished her luck. Her mum and sisters were not going to be finished for a few more minutes so Ali decided to head back to the house to relax. Just as she walked out, with her veil flying through the air, she ran right into Mark Searson. She froze. Mark and Ali had gone out for years: all through school, and even the first year of college. He had been her childhood sweetheart, and they had eventually broken up because his life was always going to be in Kilkenny, while Ali had wanted to settle in Dublin. Mark and Robin had been Ali's only two boyfriends.

'Ali, my God, you look great,' he said while giving her a kiss. 'I'd heard about your big day. Your dad is telling everyone how proud he is. Congrats.'

Ali was too shocked to say anything. One minute she had been feeling let down and disappointed by Robin and now here she was meeting her childhood sweetheart. Was it a sign from God?

'Wow, makes you wonder, doesn't it?' he said. 'All those years we talked about marriage?' He avoided meeting her eyes.

Ali literally had to lean against the wall to stop herself falling over.

Finally, he made eye-contact. 'I'm sorry for saying that, it is your big day. Good luck, Ali, your fella is a lucky man.' And with that he was gone.

Ali drove home in silence, ignoring her ringing phone, and went straight up the stairs to her bedroom, but just as she went to close her door her dad shouted up that Robin's brother, who was also his best man, had dropped something in for her and it was on her bed.

Ali saw a note and small box on the bed. She opened the note.

Ali, I can't believe it is our wedding day! I'm so sorry for getting drunk last night, and not being more help with the marquee and all. I tried to ring you late last night but your phone was off, I hope you slept well.

I know we can't see each other today, and I don't even think we are allowed phone calls! But I thought a note would be OK. I'm sorry about last night, but I want you to know, the day you said yes to marrying me on top of Table Mountain you made me the happiest guy in the world. I love you. I wanted to make sure you knew how much, and thought you might like to see your wedding ring, I got a little something added to it without you knowing. I love you, Ali, and can't wait to see you at the altar! Love Robin xox

Ali opened the felt-covered box, there was her wedding ring, exactly how she had picked it out, but inside it was now inscribed 'No One but You'.

A tear rolled down Ali's face. How could I have ever have doubted him? she thought. Then she got up and started getting ready. I'm going to be right on time today, I can't wait to marry the man of my dreams. Oh, get me to the church on time, she hummed to herself as she took out her dress and shoes.

118

Robin stood at the top of the church, with his brother and best man beside him. He scanned the crowd, it was a sea of faces, all looking at him with big and encouraging smiles. He could hear the sound of the church organ and see friends and family among the flowers, all dressed up, waiting for Ali to arrive. Robin had been waiting for this day since he had met Ali, and now as he stood in his tuxedo he realized how lucky he was.

Just then he heard a car arrive, and the church music change. The back door of the church opened and in walked Ali accompanied by her dad. Robin gasped: she looked like an angel, amazing. She walked up the aisle to the noise of cameras clicking and people wishing her good luck. When she finally got to the altar, Ali's dad handed her over to Robin. Robin gave her a big kiss.

'I love you,' he said, and with that the church ceremony began, and Ali and Robin became husband and wife. It was perfect.

119

Ali sat down with a glass of champagne in her hand. As her friends recounted how they felt when Ali walked up the aisle, Ali looked around. It had been a wonderful day. Really, the best of her life. The church had not only looked stunning, but the music, readings and blessing of the rings had gone to plan. Ali had felt blessed to have everyone she cared about and who cared for her all under one roof, helping her celebrate her marriage. After taking many pictures down at the river on the farm, they had made it into the marquee, which had been transformed that morning and filled with flowers, lights and music. And as everyone was welcomed with champagne Ali was told over and over how beautiful and glowing she looked. Robin had been as proud as punch and hadn't been able to stop squeezing her. Molly's food had been amazing, too, and Ali had never seen her dad ask for thirds before! Molly had really established herself as a professional and wonderful caterer. And even though Molly had had to keep avoiding the band, and especially the lead singer, Will, all night, she had seemed delighted by how her catering had gone. When the guests found out that Sarah had been the artist who designed the wedding invite, Ali had seen many of the girls ask for her number, with requests to do wedding, christening and birthday invites.

Ali looked down at her left hand, with its now gleaming gold wedding band. She still couldn't believe it. She was married and loving every minute of it. As she walked on to the dance floor to join Robin, she passed her two sisters – who had been asked to dance by the groomsmen – and her parents dancing and chatting, and she even saw Ben and Laura dancing, Ben hadn't left Laura's side all day!

Robin slipped his arms around Ali. He was so handsome, good and kind.

'How are you, wife?' he asked.

'I am blissfully happy, husband!'

Life is wonderful, Ali thought, as she looked around at all the people she loved and cared about. The day had brought change, and as she looked back over the last few months she thought of all the changes that she and her friends had made, and all the changes that still lay ahead of them, but she welcomed those changes, because that was what life was about, and she was ready for it.

Acknowledgements

To my editor, Francesca Liversidge. Thank you for giving me a chance and publishing my first book.

A big thank you to Lucie Jordan and all the team at Transworld, for their hard work, help and kindness.

To all at Gill Hess Ltd, Dublin, in particular Gill and Simon Hess, Declan Heaney and Helen Gleed O'Connor.

To my soulmate and gorgeous husband Mick. From a romantic proposal in Capetown to our becoming new parents, you have made me so happy. With your big, kind heart you are a great husband and father.

To my beautiful new baby daughter Holly – as I wrote each page of this book you were there. You are such a sweetheart and I love you.

To my wonderful family, the Conlon-McKennas! Thanks to my mum, Marita, for your encouragement, support, love and friendship. It started with a 'flip' and I never looked back! From a childhood filled with homemade puppet theatres, starting up our own local newspaper and countless hours of painting, writing and singing, is it any wonder I wanted to write?

To my dad, James. Bet you can't believe there is another writer in the family! Thanks for looking after us all so well.

To my two sisters, Laura and Fiona, and my brother, James.

You are my best friends and I would be lost without you all. You make me laugh every day, and I think we are all still enjoying the best childhood ever!

To my in-laws, the Heartys. You have all been so kind, welcoming and generous to me. Thank you to Tom, Breda, Liz, John, Geoff and little Rebecca.

I want to thank my friends, especially the Mount Anville girls, for all the years of friendship, fun and support.

To my friend Kim McGowan – from our summer adventure in Montauk to countless hours of laughing and chatting – you are such a great friend. Thank you for always being so kind, supportive, interested and caring.

Thanks to John Phelan for being such a kind and generous friend. From our days in the Blackrock Opera to Commerce exams at UCD, you are always there to help.

To my wonderful teacher Sister Joan Hutchinson who always made English class so interesting and literature so much fun. I hope this book will make you proud!